STAR WARS®

RED HARVEST

BY JOE SCHREIBER

Star Wars: Red Harvest
Star Wars: Death Troopers

No Doors, No Windows
Chasing the Dead
Eat the Dark

Books published by The Random House Publishing Group
are available at quantity discounts on bulk purchases for
premium, educational, fund-raising, and special sales use.
For details, please call 1-800-733-3000.

STAR WARS®
RED HARVEST

JOE SCHREIBER

DEL REY

BALLANTINE BOOKS • NEW YORK

Star Wars: Red Harvest is a work of fiction. Names, places, and incidents either are products of the author's imagination or are used fictitiously.

2012 Del Rey Mass Market Edition

Copyright © 2010 by Lucasfilm Ltd. & ® or ™ where indicated. All Rights Reserved. Used Under Authorization.

"Star Wars: Fate of the Jedi: The Saga Continues" copyright © 2011 by Lucasfilm Ltd. & ® or ™ where indicated. All Rights Reserved. Used Under Authorization.

Excerpt from *Star Wars: Scourge* by Jeff Grubb copyright © 2012 by Lucasfilm Ltd. & ® or ™ where indicated. All Rights Reserved. Used Under Authorization.

Excerpt from *Star Wars: Fate of the Jedi: Outcast* by Aaron Allston copyright © 2009 by Lucasfilm Ltd. & ® or ™ where indicated. All Rights Reserved. Used Under Authorization.

Published in the United States by Del Rey, an imprint of The Random House Publishing Group, a division of Random House, Inc., New York.

DEL REY is a registered trademark and the Del Rey colophon is a trademark of Random House, Inc.

Originally published in hardcover and in slightly different form in the United States by Del Rey, an imprint of The Random House Publishing Group, a division of Random House, Inc., in 2010.

"Star Wars: Fate of the Jedi: The Saga Continues" was originally published in *Star Wars: The Old Republic: Deceived* by Paul S. Kemp, published by Del Rey, an imprint of The Random House Publishing Group, a division of Random House, Inc., in 2011.

This book contains an excerpt from *Star Wars: Scourge* by Jeff Grubb. This excerpt has been set for this edition only and may not reflect the final content of the forthcoming edition.

ISBN 978-0-345-51859-0
eISBN 978-0-307-79603-5

Printed in the United States of America

www.starwars.com
www.delreybooks.com

9 8 7 6 5 4 3 2 1

Del Rey mass market edition: March 2012

To Christina, "I'm giving you a long look . . ."

REBELLION
0–5 YEARS AFTER
STAR WARS: A New Hope

Death Star
Shadow Games

0

STAR WARS: EPISODE IV
A NEW HOPE

Tales from the Mos Eisley Cantina
Tales from the Empire
Tales from the New Republic
Allegiance
Choices of One
Galaxies: The Ruins of Dantooine
Splinter of the Mind's Eye

3 *YEARS AFTER STAR WARS: A New Hope*

STAR WARS: EPISODE V
THE EMPIRE STRIKES BACK

Tales of the Bounty Hunters
Shadows of the Empire

4 *YEARS AFTER STAR WARS: A New Hope*

STAR WARS: EPISODE VI
RETURN OF THE JEDI

Tales from Jabba's Palace

The Bounty Hunter Wars
The Mandalorian Armor
Slave Ship
Hard Merchandise

The Truce at Bakura
Luke Skywalker and the Shadows of
Mindor

NEW REPUBLIC
5–25 YEARS AFTER
STAR WARS: A New Hope

X-Wing
Rogue Squadron
Wedge's Gamble
The Krytos Trap
The Bacta War
Wraith Squadron
Iron Fist
Solo Command

The Courtship of Princess Leia
A Forest Apart*
Tatooine Ghost

The Thrawn Trilogy
Heir to the Empire
Dark Force Rising
The Last Command

X-Wing: Isard's Revenge

The Jedi Academy Trilogy
Jedi Search
Dark Apprentice
Champions of the Force

I, Jedi
Children of the Jedi
Darksaber
Planet of Twilight
X-Wing: Starfighters of Adumar
The Crystal Star

The Black Fleet Crisis Trilogy
Before the Storm
Shield of Lies
Tyrant's Test

The New Rebellion

The Corellian Trilogy
Ambush at Corellia
Assault at Selonia
Showdown at Centerpoint

The Hand of Thrawn Duology
Specter of the Past
Vision of the Future

Fool's Bargain*
Survivor's Quest

*An eBook novella
**Forthcoming

THE STAR WARS NOVELS TIMELINE

 NEW JEDI ORDER
25–40 YEARS AFTER
STAR WARS: A New Hope

Boba Fett: A Practical Man*

The New Jedi Order
Vector Prime
Dark Tide I: Onslaught
Dark Tide II: Ruin
Agents of Chaos I: Hero's Trial
Agents of Chaos II: Jedi Eclipse
Balance Point
Recovery*
Edge of Victory I: Conquest
Edge of Victory II: Rebirth
Star by Star
Dark Journey
Enemy Lines I: Rebel Dream
Enemy Lines II: Rebel Stand
Traitor
Destiny's Way
Ylesia*
Force Heretic I: Remnant
Force Heretic II: Refugee
Force Heretic III: Reunion
The Final Prophecy
The Unifying Force

35 | *YEARS AFTER STAR WARS: A New Hope*

The Dark Nest Trilogy
The Joiner King
The Unseen Queen
The Swarm War

 LEGACY
40+ YEARS AFTER
STAR WARS: A New Hope

Legacy of the Force
Betrayal
Bloodlines
Tempest
Exile
Sacrifice
Inferno
Fury
Revelation
Invincible

Crosscurrent
Riptide

Millennium Falcon

43 | *YEARS AFTER STAR WARS: A New Hope*

Fate of the Jedi
Outcast
Omen
Abyss
Backlash
Allies
Vortex
Conviction
Ascension
Apocalypse**

*An eBook novella
**Forthcoming

Dramatis Personae

Dail'Liss; librarian (Neti male)
Darth Scabrous; Sith Lord (human male)
Dranok; bounty hunter (human male)
Hartwig; Sith student (human male)
Jura Ostrogoth; Sith student (human male)
Kindra; Sith student (human female)
Maggs; Sith student (human male)
Hestizo Trace; Jedi Agricultural Corps worker
  (human female)
Mnah Ra'at; Sith student (human male)
Pergus Frode; mechanic (human male)
Rance Lussk; Sith student (human male)
Rojo Trace; Jedi Knight (human male)
Tulkh; bounty hunter (Whiphid male)
Wim Nickter; Sith student (human male)
Xat Hracken; Sith Combat Master (human male)

A long time ago in a galaxy far, far away. . . .

STAR WARS

RED HARVEST

1/Ring

▄▄▄ ▄ ▄▄▄▄ ▄ ▄▄▄

3645 BBY

WIM NICKTER STOOD JUST OUTSIDE THE CIRCLE, AWAITING first blood.

The cold morning air of Odacer-Faustin tasted like ozone, numbing his tongue and lips, making his heart pound harder in his chest until it actually shook the heavy fabric of his wind-resistant tunic. He had climbed the seventy-seven steps to the top of the temple with the other students, muscles aching, sweat from his exertions still drying in the wind. The lightsaber training session was over. Now the duels would begin.

In the three standard years since he'd arrived at the academy, Nickter had come to anticipate these duels with a special kind of excitement. A tall, rangy seventeen-year-old with a thatch of jet-black hair, he gazed into the circle with hungry blue-gray eyes that matched the un-forgiving landscape almost perfectly.

Nickter looked down. From the top of the temple, the Sith academy resembled nothing so much as a partially demolished wheel, its spokes radiating crookedly out from the central hub of the tower. Its ancient chambers, enclosed walkways, tunnels, and temples, and the great library that served as its haunted heart had all long ago begun to crumble and deteriorate from decades of accumulated snow and ice and the constantly shifting tectonic eccentricities of the planetary crust. The result was a sprawling ruin of forgotten spaces—some of them palatial—groaning under tons of age-tortured Sith architecture.

It was here that they'd come, Nickter and several hundred others, to learn everything they needed to know about the dark side of the Force.

Directly across from him, Lord Shak'Weth, the Sith Blademaster, took three steps forward into the open space, turning to regard the students from beneath the hood of his cloak. For a moment, the wind had fallen still; all was quiet except for the scrape of his boots across the flat, uneven surface. The Blademaster's stony countenance betrayed no hint of expression. The thin, lipless slit of his mouth never moved. No comment was made, nor was any needed. This was the moment when the first challenge would be made, and Nickter—along with all his peers—had heard the rumors.

This was the day that Lussk was going to issue his challenge.

Rance Lussk was the academy's top student—a Sith acolyte of such fierce promise and potential that few, if any, dared approach him, let alone face him in a duel. These days he spent most of his time in private training sessions with Shak'Weth and the other Masters at the academy. Some said that he'd even sat in meditation with Lord Scabrous himself, up in the tower . . . although Nickter had his private doubts about this last bit. He hadn't met a student yet who actually claimed to have been inside the tower.

Even so, he waited, holding his breath.

The group had fallen absolutely silent.

A moment later Lussk stepped forward.

He was an agile, muscular figure in a robe and tunic, with a long face and flaming red hair that he'd grown long, pulled back and kept braided so tightly that it pulled on the corners of his pale green eyes, giving them a slightly slanted look. But his most outstanding feature was the self-contained silence that hovered around him like a lethal cloud. To approach him closely was to experience a climate of dull dread; the one or two times Nickter had accidentally bumped into Lussk in the halls of the academy, he'd actually felt the temperature drop along with the oxygen content. Lussk emanated menace; he breathed it out like carbon dioxide.

Nickter felt his whole body fall still, save his pounding heart, as Lussk turned slowly to regard his fellow acolytes with an indifferent, almost reptilian stare. As far as opponents went, there were only a few worthy of his time. Lussk's gaze passed over Jura Ostrogoth, Scopique, Nace, and Ra'at, some of the most skilled duelists in the group. If challenged, Nickter wondered, would any of them accept? The humiliation of backing down was nothing compared with the potential catastrophe of losing to Lussk in the circle; in his hands even a training blade, with its durasteel shaft and millions of microscopic toxin-filled barbs, could deal out disastrous injury.

Lussk stopped, and Nickter realized that the red-haired acolyte was staring at him.

Lussk's words hung in the air.

"I challenge Nickter."

At first, Nickter was certain that he'd misheard. Then the reality sank in and he felt his innards drop, as if the ground itself had abruptly vaporized beneath his feet. Time seemed to have stopped. He was aware of Shak'Weth and all the apprentices turning around to look in his direction, waiting for him to step forward or back down. As a purely practical matter, Lussk's selection made no sense—although he could hold his own in practice, Nickter was clearly the other student's inferior, providing no opportunity to hone his skills or even offer the others a good performance.

Still the challenge hovered in the air between them, unanswered.

"Well, Nickter?" the Blademaster asked. "What do you say?"

Nickter lowered his head, feeling a slow familiar warmth crawl into his cheeks and neck. He was aware that a formal reply wasn't necessary. Simply bowing his head and stepping back would be answer enough, and a moment later the whispers would begin as what little prestige he'd manage to garner here in the last two years began to evaporate around him. It was an unwinnable dilemma, of course, but at least this way he would walk away intact. Several of Lussk's previous opponents hadn't been so lucky—the last three had left the academy after losing to him. One had taken his own life. It was as if losing to Lussk had . . . done something to them, inflicted some profound inner wound from which there was no recovery.

The answer was obvious. Nickter would just step backward and bow out.

And so he was as shocked as any of them when he heard himself say, "I accept."

The murmur of surprise rippled audibly through the other apprentices. Even Shak'Weth cocked one thorny eyebrow.

Nickter blinked, unable to believe what he'd just said. He hadn't meant to speak at all. The words had bubbled out of him involuntarily. Looking up at Lussk, seeing the slightest hint of a smile curling at the corners of that small, unremarkable mouth, Nickter realized that, of everyone here, only Lussk was unsurprised by his response.

And for the first time, Nickter saw what was happening.

This wasn't about dueling at all.

It was about something else entirely.

"Well, then," Lussk said, beckoning with his free hand. "Come on."

Before he knew it, Nickter felt himself being sucked forward into the ring, one foot and then the other, dragging the rest of his body along with it. His heart raced as his body registered that this was actually happening. *No,* his mind protested, *I'm not doing this, I don't want this,* but that didn't matter because all he could see now was Lussk's smile broadening enough to show a faint yellow glint of canines behind the lips. Nickter knew what was going on, and what was worse, Lussk *knew* that he knew. Lussk's eyes were braziers of pure, sadistic pleasure, and their intensity transformed his otherwise plain face, distorting it somehow, making it appear horrible.

They were face-to-face now, close enough that Nickter could feel that terrible coldness spilling out of Lussk's pores, and Lussk raised his training blade, its shaft hissing up through the air as he placed himself in standard ready position.

Don't, Nickter wanted to say, his eyes silently pleading, but instead he saw his own blade go up. It was too late. Whatever was being done to him—whatever Lussk was *doing* to him—

Lussk's blade swung down hard and fast. Nickter reacted instantly, with instinctive speed and agility ingrained from countless practice sessions. Metal struck metal with a clang that shook the air, reverberating through the circle around them and making it hum like a high-voltage circuit. Something snapped to life inside Nickter, and when Lussk came at him again he was ready, deflecting Lussk's next thrust with a sharp, unhesitating parry and snapping back with a move that suddenly created an opening between them. From what sounded like far away, Nickter heard the crowd let out a slight, appreciative mutter. He'd already outlasted their most pessimistic expectations.

Lussk charged forward again, and Nickter sprang to deflect the thrust, less skillfully now. That fleeting sense of competence was already gone, stripped away, replaced by a dizzying loss of perspective. How had he gotten so close, so quickly? Lussk was moving too fast, and Nickter's blade seemed to have come to life all on its own in his hand, jerking and slashing to hold Lussk off, but Lussk's cold smile told the whole story. *I own you, maggot,* it said, the strength of the other cadet's will booming through Nickter's skull, *and you will do as you're told.*

No. Nickter's jaw clenched, summoning what remained of his resolve. He understood now that his only hope lay in freeing himself, wresting his will away from Lussk's authority. What the other acolyte was practicing on him now was obviously some advanced Force mind control technique learned from one of the Sith Lords at the academy, perhaps at the knee of Scabrous himself. Had the rumors of his secret tutelage been true after all? Whatever the case, for reasons known only to Lussk, he'd decided to try it out this morning on Nickter, and Nickter had nothing to counter with.

With an audible grunt of effort, Nickter surged forward again, blade at the ready, only to be met by a bemused smirk of contempt, as if Lussk expected nothing else. In a series of moves, Lussk sequenced seamlessly from a brutal and precise Makashi attack to the more acrobatic Form IV, flipping up from a standing position, spinning midair, and landing behind Nickter before he'd even had a chance to react. Too late, Nickter heard the blade hiss off to his right, whipping across his elbow, and he let out a sharp, agonized cry as his hand went numb, fingers springing open to release his blade.

Helpless, disarmed, he felt the cold tip of Lussk's dura-steel come to rest against the back of his neck, biting into the skin just below the base of his skull. There was that awful numb sensation that Nickter knew all too well, the second before the nerve ending registered an overload of pain.

At least it was over.

Now, Lussk's voice throbbed inside his head. It was low and toneless, an irresistible command. *Push yourself backward into my blade.*

Nickter resisted, straining forward, muscles drawing taut in his neck—but it was useless. He couldn't hold back. The pain swelled, doubled back on itself, grew infinitely worse, shrieking through him, and some grim, instinctive part of him knew that he was seconds away from severing his own spinal cord, shorting out his brain, and extinguishing all remaining thought in that final instant of consciousness. He sucked air through his teeth and looked out, as if from some great distance, at the faces of the others outside the circle, staring him down. Their eyes were bright and eager, awaiting the inevitable coup de grâce.

Curse you, Nickter thought, *curse every stinking one of you, I hope you all have to endure this torture or worse, I hope you each suffer like I am suffering now, I hope—*

With a gasp, Nickter lurched forward, suddenly free, away from the blade, reaching up to place one hand over the painful but ultimately superficial wound it had left just above the bony knob of his vertebral prominence. He could barely manage to keep his hand upright. The battle—both physical and mental—had reduced his body to a blurry hologram of its former self, muscles trembling, wrung to rags, skin and hair drenched in fresh sweat. His head felt like it was going to explode. He couldn't catch his breath. Turning around to face Lussk on legs that seemed as though they might betray him and buckle at any moment, he caught a glimpse of the other acolyte's impenetrable green eyes.

You only lived because I let you, those eyes said, and Nickter understood that in the end, Lussk's act of mercy had sentenced him to the greater humiliation of unwarranted survival.

He looked away, turned, and made his way through the crowd. No one spoke or made a sound as he followed the stony steps downward from the top of the temple to the snow-strafed walkway below.

2/Crack

BY NOON, NEWS OF NICKTER'S DEFEAT HAD TRAVELED through the entire academy. None of the other students had seen what had happened to him afterward, but Jura Ostrogoth assumed that Nickter had gone to the infirmary to be treated for his physical wounds . . . or back to the dorms to lick his less tangible ones.

"Either way," Jura told Kindra, the two of them ducking past the crooked slab of stone that marked one of the five entranceways to the academy's library, "it doesn't matter now, does it? He was barely scraping by anyway."

Kindra nodded but didn't say anything. They were on their way to the dining hall for their midday meal. After a brief reprieve this morning, it was snowing again, harder now—thin, sand-dry pellets seething over the ground in front of them, creeping up over the walkways and drifting up against the academy's outer walls. Jura, who'd grown up on Chazwa in the Orus sector, was well adjusted to such weather and walked with his robe open at the throat, hardly noticing the wind gusting through its fabric. He'd seen other acolytes from warmer climates trying to affect the same air of brazen indifference through chattering teeth and blue lips, but the cold truly didn't bother him, never had.

"What about Lussk?" Kindra asked.

Jura cast a sidelong glance at her. "What about him?"

"Did anybody see where he went?"

"Who knows?" He wasn't quite able to disguise the annoyance in his voice. "Lussk comes and goes as he pleases. Days go by without anyone seeing him. From what I've heard . . ."

He let the words trail off, looking up at the tower that rose from the very center of the academy, an immense black cylinder jutting against the gray sky. Every so often, black vapor would billow up from the top, staining the sky, raining down thick and gritty bits of ash, and the smell was bad enough to make his eyes and nose water. Unlike the cold, Jura had never gotten used to smoke and ash.

"What have you heard?" Kindra asked.

He shook his head. "Just rumors."

"I've heard them, too." She was staring at him pointedly. "And not just about Lussk."

"What are you talking about?"

"Nothing," she said, and walked past him into the dining hall.

His midday meal in front of him—a stringy lump of mubasa hock and canned montra fruit—Jura Ostrogoth pondered the dining hall around him with a watchful eye. He'd been around long enough to know that violence begat violence, that news of what had happened to Nickter could easily inflame some other apprentice's desire to move upward in the academy's pecking order—and Jura was just high enough up to be a target.

He ate alone, as did most of the students, with his back to the wall as much as possible. There wasn't much talk, just the steady clink of utensils and trays. When you were here, you powered through the meal as quickly as possible and got back to your training sessions, or study, meditation, and Force drills. Time spent socializing was time wasted—it showed weakness, a lack of discipline and vigilance that was practically an invitation to your enemies.

"Jura."

He paused and looked around. Hartwig was standing there with Scopique by his side. Their trays were full, but neither one of them looked like he was planning on sitting down there.

"What is it?"

"You hear about Nickter?"

"What, at the temple?" Jura shrugged. "That's old news."

Hartwig shook his head. "He disappeared."

"Shocker." Jura shrugged, turning back to his food. He was peripherally aware of the other apprentices nearby inclining their heads ever so slightly forward to eavesdrop on the conversation, and wondered if there might be more worth hearing. "He's probably off someplace feeling sorry for himself."

"No, I mean, he literally *disappeared*," Hartwig said. "The med tech, Arljack, told Scopique all about it. One minute he was at the infirmary getting treated for that cut on his arm. Arl went to check on one of the other patients and when he came back, Nickter was gone."

"So he just walked out."

Hartwig leaned forward, lowering his voice. "He's the fourth one this year."

"What's that supposed to mean?"

"You know what they're saying."

Jura sighed, realizing where the conversation was going. "You've been talking to Ra'at too much."

"Maybe so," Scopique said, speaking up for the first time, "but maybe in this case, Ra'at knows what he's talking about."

Jura turned all the way around and glared at him.

Scopique was a Zabrak, and his tribal tattoos and the array of vestigial horns sprouting up from his scalp had always been a source of deep pride. In conversation, he tended to keep his head tilted slightly forward for dramatic effect, and with the light behind him, so that the shadows of the horns cut down over the geometry of his face like daggers. For a moment the two faced each other in tense silence.

"We've all heard the same thing," Jura said, keeping his voice even. "Thinning the herd, the experiments . . . What's your point?"

Scopique leaned in close. "Lord Scabrous."

"What about him?"

"If he *is* abducting students for his own purposes," Scopique said, "then someone needs to find out who might be next."

Jura let out a dry little laugh, but it didn't come out as dismissive or scornful as he'd hoped. "And how do you plan on getting that information?"

"I'm not," the Zabrak told him, and pointed at him. "You are."

"Me?"

"You're perfect for the job. Everyone knows you have the survival instincts of a hungry dianoga. You'll find a way."

Jura pushed back his chair and stood up in one fluid motion. Swinging one hand forward, he reached up and snapped his fingers tight around the Zabrak's throat, clamping down on the windpipe hard enough that he felt the cartilage pop. It happened so fast that, despite the strength and weight discrepancy, Scopique was caught off guard—but only momentarily. When he spoke again, his voice was calm, almost casual, and quiet enough that only Jura could hear him.

"There's a saying on my home planet, Ostrogoth. Only a fool turns his back on an unpaid debt. You think about that." Scopique nodded slightly at Jura's arm. "Now, because you do still have some value to me, I'll allow you to remove your hand from my throat voluntarily and save face in front of our peers. But the next time I see you, you *will* tell me what you've found out about the disappearances." The Zabrak smiled thinly. "Or else the rest of the academy will soon see a side of you that I don't think you want them to see—a very unflattering side. Do we understand each other?"

Jura's jaw tightened; he was too angry to trust his voice for a reply. Instead he managed a curt nod.

"Good," Scopique said. A second later the Zabrak turned and walked away. When he and Hartwig stepped out the door, Jura Ostrogoth carried his untouched meal to the waste receptacle and dumped it in, tray and all.

He'd lost his appetite.

Outside the dining hall, back out in the cold, Jura stalked through the snow, fists clenched and trembling at his sides. After he'd gone a few meters from the doorway, where he was sure no one could see, he stepped into a narrow alcove and stared at the stone wall. Fury boiled in his chest.

Or else the rest of the academy will soon see a side of you that I don't think you want them to see, Scopique's voice mocked in his head. *Do we understand each other?*

Jura's thoughts flashed back four standard years to the day he'd first arrived at the academy, a scared and ignorant kid from the other side of the galaxy. He'd spent his first couple of days keeping a low profile, avoiding everyone, hoping to get his bearings before anybody had a chance to push him around, but that wasn't how things worked around here. On the third morning, he'd been in the dorm, making up his bunk, when a fist swung out and smashed him hard between the shoulder blades, knocking him to the floor, where he lay gasping for air.

When Jura managed to roll over and look up, he saw a gigantic Sith apprentice named Mannock T'sank looming over him. T'sank was stronger and older than Jura, and the smirk on his face was one of nearly homicidal glee.

"You look good lying there on the floor, newbie," T'sank leered at him. "You know what you'd look even better doing? Licking my boots." He'd held out one of his filthy leather dung-kickers, waving the toe right under Jura's nose, close enough that Jura could smell the tauntaun droppings—T'sank had been sentenced to cleaning the paddocks for some minor offense. "Go ahead, newbie. Give them a good tongue-polish."

Even then, Jura had known this was a test; how he responded would determine the way he was treated forever after in the Academy's court of public opinion. Grimly, with the air of someone planning his own funeral, he had stood up and told T'sank exactly what he could do with his boot.

The result had been even worse than he'd expected. T'sank punched him in the face so hard that Jura blacked out, and when he woke up his entire head was a gonging carillon of pain. He couldn't move. There was a dirty rag stuffed in his mouth, crammed so far back that he almost choked on it. Looking down, he saw that he was naked and tied to the bunk by his feet and ankles while T'sank stood over him, grinning with malevolence that bordered on madness. When Jura tried to inhale, he started gagging and panic took hold of him; he lost all control and burst into frightened tears, while T'sank howled with laughter.

And then, abruptly, the laughter had stopped. His last memory of T'sank was the thin, surprised yelp that the sadistic apprentice had let out right before he'd gone flying backward out the door. When Jura had craned his head and looked up through tear-blurred eyes, he'd seen Scopique standing there. The Zabrak had made no immediate move to untie him. Instead he'd been holding what Jura realized was some type of holocam, pointing it at him while the lens autofocused.

"Smile," Scopique had said from behind the cam, walking around the bunk, still recording Jura where he lay struggling to regain control of baser bodily functions. "Hold on, let me get your good side."

When he was satisfied with the footage, he'd put the recorder away, yanked the rag out of Jura's mouth, and untied him.

"Get up," he told Jura. "Come on." He glanced back out the half-open doorway, where T'sank had landed, half conscious and crumpled. "I gave him a good shot to the head, but it won't keep him down forever."

Jura struggled to his feet, wiped the blood and snot from his nose, and hurriedly struggled back into his robes. "Thanks," he mumbled.

Scopique waved Jura's gratitude off as if it disgusted him, then ejected the holocartridge from the cam and slipped it into his pocket, giving it a protective little pat. "For safekeeping," he said, and Jura got the message. None of what happened had been about kindness or mercy. Jura was in his pocket now, and however long he stayed here, the Zabrak wasn't going to let him forget it.

"And newbie?" Scopique had said, on his way out the door. "Welcome to the academy."

Welcome to the academy.

Jerked back into the present moment by the blazing flames of his own anger, Jura blinked away the image of the cartridge in the Zabrak's pocket. Standing here in the shadows between buildings, the urge to lash out was something he could no longer master. He raised both hands and unleashed a burst of dark side energy into the wall itself. Electric heat leapt through his wrists and palms, slamming into the rock, cracking it down the middle.

He closed his eyes and exhaled, momentarily relieved. He knew he should have saved his anger, held on to it and used it in one of the combat drills, but he couldn't help himself.

Opening his eyes again, he looked at the cracked wall. It had been strong, but now it was damaged, its value weakened in some fundamental way by what had been inflicted on it.

I am that wall.

Turning away, he stepped back out of the shadows, his mind already trying to work out how he was going to get Scopique's information for him.

3/Deep-Down Trauma Hounds

NICKTER AWOKE IN THE CAGE.

He had no memory of how he'd gotten here, or how long he'd been inside. The last thing he remembered was sitting in the infirmary, waiting for Arljack to come back and check the wound on the back of his neck. And in fact, for one disoriented moment, he thought he was still there. *It's cold in here,* he'd started to say. *Hey, Arl, you mind turning up the heat a little bit?*

But this was not the infirmary.

He tried to sit up and slammed his head against the metal bars above him hard enough to make him let out an angry moan of pain. Just exactly what was going on here? The cage was small, forcing him to remain hunched forward, either on his hands and knees or in a slouch-shouldered sitting position. The top part of his tunic had been ripped away, leaving him naked from the waist up. His back hurt, *really* hurt, from the base of his skull all the way down to the bottom of his spine—a low, steady throb that made his molars ache.

As if to mock his immediate claustrophobic situation, the room outside the cage was very large, and very dark. From inside, Nickter could see almost all of it. It was a circular space, perhaps fifty meters across, illuminated by an irregular assemblage of flashing monitor equipment, candles, and torchlight. Laboratory equipment crowded every available surface and corner. Pipes and wires were draped from tables and desks, connecting odd piles of disjointed equipment, condensers, flasks, beakers, and burners. The walls were glass, and although he couldn't see anything out there but darkness, Nickter had the vague feeling that he was very high up.

Sudden realization blindsided him.

He was at the top of the tower.

"You're awake," a voice said.

Nickter jerked upright at the sound of the voice and very nearly screamed.

Standing outside the cage, staring down at him, was a tall, broad-shouldered, black-robed figure that blended almost imperceptibly into the shadows. Nickter already knew exactly who it was, even before the flickering torchlight of the room revealed the man's face—a long, bony sculpture of bone and half-lidded eyes, the famous curvature of the peaked upper lip, how it always seemed to be smiling slightly at some secret thought. A fresh spasm of apprehension leapt through him, raising hackles across his back. The eyes were the worst part, he thought: how almost silver they were, how they seemed to glitter with a feverish accumulation of ambition and indifference.

"Lord Scabrous," he said, or tried to say. His mouth felt parched, and his lungs couldn't seem to get enough air. "What am I doing here?"

The Sith Lord didn't answer. But the eyes kept staring down at him . . . past him, somehow, as if there were something else inside the cage with him.

He could smell himself, the stale cheap grease of panic and perspiration seeping through his skin. The pain in his back had intensified from a throb to a sharp stabbing agony that shot down his ribs and up into his neck. It was getting worse by the second, like the sting of sweat in an open wound. Whatever injury had been inflicted upon him, it was deep, and whole packs of nerve receptors—those obedient trauma hounds—were circling back and forth, busily delivering the bad news.

Groping around behind him, Nickter felt something cold and smooth and hard sticking out of his skin just above the base of his spine. He looked around and saw what Scabrous had been looking at—it was some kind of tube, implanted directly into a vertebra. The sticky ring of exposed flesh around the wound site felt raw and hot, swollen, and it burned when he touched it. Sliding his hand upward, he felt another tube above it, and another, coming out of his back, all the way up to his neck. There were at least six of them protruding out of him, as big around as his finger. He realized that he could feel them pulsating inside his spinal canal—that was the source of the gnawing pain.

"What . . . what is this?" he asked, aware of how different his voice sounded already, high-pitched and wobbly. "What did you do to me?"

Scabrous still didn't answer. He wasn't even looking at Nickter anymore. He had walked around behind the cage now, where the tubes ran between the wire bars into what looked like some kind of mechanized pump with a wide flask mounted on top.

Rattling around inside the cage, Nickter stared at it. The flask was full of murky reddish yellow liquid. Next to the pump sat a small black pyramid covered in lines of engraved text—what he realized, through his pain and fear, had to be a Sith Holocron. They'd learned about them at the academy, but he'd never actually seen one before.

And then he saw other things, dozens of them, in glass bottles lined up across the wide platform next to the pump.

Flowers.

All black.

All different.

All dead.

Nickter squirmed in the cage. None of this made any sense, and the irrationality only intensified his mounting terror. He was sweating profusely now—it was *dripping* off him in big, oozing droplets. The urge to beg, to grovel, to bargain for his life, or at least for an end to the pain, was almost irresistible. The only thing that stopped him was the suspicion, based on everything he'd heard about Scabrous, that the Sith Lord wouldn't even listen. Scabrous stood behind the cage, alternating his attention between the flowers and the Holocron. Finally he selected a flower, opened the glass chamber on top of the pump, and dropped it inside.

"What is that?" Nickter asked. "What are you doing?"

Scabrous glanced at him, as if hearing him for the first time. When he finally spoke, his voice was low and resonant, deeper than Nickter remembered. There was an awful intimacy to it, as though the Sith Lord were whispering directly in his ear.

"You were humiliated today at the temple, Wim Nickter—humiliated *badly*. You have shown yourself to be weak and easily defeated."

"It was Lussk!" Nickter burst out. "He used the Force on me, he—"

Scabrous lifted his hand. "There is still one way in which you may yet prove useful. That is the offer I make to you, one of redemption."

Then he pressed a button on the pump.

Staring at it, Nickter saw the black flower swirling in the reddish yellow fluid, its petals shredding as it dissolved. The pump let out a faint whining noise, like half a dozen odd vacuum parts called into dubious service. At first he felt nothing except for the odd vibration of the tubes in his back.

Then the pain he'd been enduring up till now became abruptly, horribly worse. It slammed through his body, gouging through every millimeter of his nerve endings, turning them white-hot.

Nickter arched forward and screamed. The pain owned him: he surrendered to it utterly. It became a vast, all-encompassing neutron star, and as it sucked him forward he saw Scabrous watching him through the cage.

The last thing Nickter saw before he blacked out was Scabrous turning away from him, swinging his arm across the long counter above the pump, sending the flowers and their vessels crashing to floor.

4/Dranok

PERGUS FRODE DIDN'T MIND HIS MAINTENANCE DUTIES AT
the academy's landing pad. It meant he got the first look
at the new arrivals, often a pretty sorry lot, and he was
privy to some sensitive information even before some of
the Sith Masters found out about it. Not a bad gig for a
pilot-turned-grease-monkey whose last job had been
wiping down engines at the Kuat Drive Yards.

Tonight, for instance—when the Corellian cruiser
banked and began descending into the snow-strewn
landing lights—Frode knew exactly who it was. He
would have known even if Darth Scabrous's HK droid
hadn't been standing right next to him, whirring softly
to itself in anticipation. Frode didn't mind droids—most
of the time he actually preferred them to organic
life-forms, especially on Odacer-Faustin.

"Statement: I shall alert Lord Scabrous, sir," the HK
said, "that his guests have arrived."

"Sure, good," Frode said, watching as the cruiser extended its landing gear, feeling the decks absorb its
settling tonnage. A moment later the main hatchway
whooshed open, and the landing ramp dropped down
with an unceremonious *clank*.

Coming forward to meet it, Frode watched as the two
bounty hunters stepped down—*swaggered* down was

more like it. The first, a tall, stocky, bald man with a permanent sneer in green-tinted goggles, stopped at the bottom of the ramp and looked around disdainfully as if he wasn't at all sure he even wanted to stay. He was carrying a metal case under one arm, linked to his wrist with a thin chain.

"What do you think, Skarl?" the bald man asked. "Cold enough for you?"

The flight-suited Nelvaanian standing next to him wrinkled his snout and gave a brief snarl, revealing a row of sharp, inward-pointing upper teeth. Then he and the man both turned and glared at Frode, who had already taken a step back.

"Where's Scabrous?" the man demanded, lifting the metal case. "We brought his package. He's supposed to meet us here."

"I will take you to Lord Scabrous, sir," the HK said, gesturing back in the direction of the academy's main grounds. "He is my master, and I have been dispatched to escort you to the Tower. You and your"—the droid glanced uncertainly at the Nelvaanian—"copilot?"

"Skarl's my partner," the man said. "My name's Dranok. Anything that's worth having in this galaxy, you can get through us." He made no move to follow the HK. "Speaking of which, your boss better have the rest of the credits he owes me for this little beauty. It wasn't exactly easy to procure."

The HK responded promptly. "Answer: Payment has been arranged in full, sir. Rest assured that you will receive it shortly."

Dranok nodded, the surly expression never quite leaving his lips as he glanced around the snowy terrain surrounding the landing pad. "What a pit." Glancing at Frode, he jerked one thumb back in the direction of the ship. "Keep her hot, Ace. We're not staying on this rock one second longer than we have to. And refuel her while you're at it—think you can handle that?"

"Sure," Frode said, "no problem." He'd already decided he didn't care for the man or his partner, but he was careful not to let it show in his voice. "It'll be ready when you get back."

Ignoring him, the bounty hunter turned and followed the droid with the Nelvaanian easily keeping pace to his right, paws crunching in the snow.

By the time they reached the tower, Dranok had already decided how he was going to handle this.

Right up to the moment they'd landed, he hadn't been entirely sure about his course of action. It was nothing personal: he and Skarl had always worked together well enough. The Nelvaanian was a superior tracker, and always good in a fight. Plus he was loyal, a trait that Dranok obviously didn't share. But money-wise, things hadn't been going so well lately—their last few jobs weren't paying as much as he'd hoped, and Dranok was tired of splitting everything down the middle.

So it was settled, then. Once Scabrous paid the balance of what he owed them—

"Statement: It's through here, sir," the HK said, gesturing up at the tower. "Right this way."

Dranok paused in his tracks and looked up. He'd seen some weird architecture in his time, but the Sith Lord's tower was unsettling in a different way. It was imposing, yes, and much taller than it had looked from the air, but there was another quality to it, an indefinable sense of *wrongness,* as if it had been built at some unnatural angle so that it seemed to curl down on top of him like an immense black claw. He'd once overheard talk in some spaceport about the Sith, how they'd learned to manipulate spatial geometry itself, creating buildings that were, in themselves, detached from physical reality.

The guy telling the story had claimed you could get lost inside a Sith labyrinth and never escape. Dranok had dismissed it as a lot of drunken superstition, but looking at the tower now, he wasn't sure. He didn't like standing in front of it, and liked even less the idea of going inside.

But that was where the payment was.

And that settled it.

"All right." He turned to Skarl. "You better wait out here, just in case something goes wrong."

The Nelvaanian looked at him and gave an uneasy growl. *This isn't how we normally do things,* that growl said. *This isn't standard operating procedure.*

"Hey," Dranok said, with all the brusque, hail-fellow-well-met heartiness that he could muster, "trust me, will ya? We're both safer if you're out here watching the door. I'll settle up with Scabrous and bring the money out."

And before Skarl had a chance to argue, he followed the droid inside.

Even though they were out of the wind, Dranok felt the temperature drop sharply. It was dark enough that his first few steps were guided mainly by the pale blue lightspill from the HK's dorsal processor array. A second or two later, his eyes began to adjust and he could make out the wide, circular space around them, supported by pillars and massive stone arches that made up the tower's lowest level. The air smelled wet and dirty, and there was an unpleasantly musty human component to it that reminded him of the bathhouses on some of the Inner Rim planets he'd visited.

"Statement: Follow me," the HK's voice said from up ahead, gesturing to a waiting turbolift. Dranok ducked inside, and as the door sealed shut behind him, he realized that the droid had not followed.

He was alone.

The turbolift shot upward fast enough to leave his

stomach behind. Dranok felt the first prickle of unease down the small of his back. The lift was still rising. Was it taking him all the way to the top?

Finally it halted, and the doors opened.

"Lord Scabrous?" Dranok called out, loud enough to make himself heard. "Your droid sent me up." He realized that he was holding the metal case in front of him like a shield. "I brought your package."

Silence. It was a big circular room—to his eyes, it looked like a laboratory furnished by somebody with a serious fetish for the arcane. Dranok had heard that some of these Sith Lords could be decidedly peculiar, mixing technology with the ancient ways of their people, preserving the old ways whenever possible. This proved it.

Tall arching windows made up the surrounding walls, with sconces, candles, and torches protruding above them, along with pulsing panels and banks of lights. Machinery hummed with a low, irregular drone that made the air itself seem to vibrate in Dranok's nostrils and the pit of his throat. He made his way past the piles and tables of scientific equipment, not particularly liking the way the torches made his shadow leap and twitch across the bare stone floor behind him, as if there was someone following on his heels. A smell hung in the air, thick and familiar but as yet indefinable—chemicals? No, it was sweeter than that, almost cloying, like a cooking smell.

He walked over to the window and glanced down through the falling snow at the academy below. From here it looked like a ruin, abandoned and forgotten. The occasional faint glimmers of light that burned in the windows of one of the buildings—some kind of dorm, he assumed—only made it look more hollow somehow, a place that had fallen into the possession of ghosts.

You're getting jumpy, he scolded himself. *Cut it out.*

He turned and walked back toward a stack of machinery half buried in shadow. Something crunched under his boot, and he paused to look at it.

Flowers.

Squatting, the bounty hunter set the metal case aside— it was still cuffed to his wrist—and reached into his pocket for a glow rod. He switched it on, shining it down in front of him. The crunching had come from broken glass, test tubes or vessels that Dranok guessed had held the different species, before they'd all been dumped or thrown unceremoniously across the floor.

He opened the metal case and looked at his own flower, the alleged Murakami orchid itself, comparing it with all of those scattered over the cobblestones. The black-market spice dealer who'd sold it to him had guaranteed that it was a genuine article, the rarest in the galaxy, stolen from a secret Republic bio-lab on Endor. The dealer had even provided him documented proof, complex chemical and gas spectroscopy equations that Dranok had pretended to understand.

But now, looking at these other flowers on the floor— rejects all—Dranok found at least two that looked exactly like it.

His breath caught in his throat.

He'd been duped, and now—

"Dranok."

The bounty hunter froze at the sound of his own name, the voice turning his breath to dry ice in his lungs. Up ahead, standing between him and the exit, a tall, dark-cloaked figure gazed back at him from the other side of a long stone table. Dranok realized that he was looking into the face of a man with long, refined features, the aquiline nose, raked brow, and prominent cheekbones stretched out until they were almost a caricature of arrogance. Thick gray hair, a strange silvery blue color, swept back away from his forehead. The figure extended one long-fingered hand, gesturing him forward, and at the same moment Dranok saw the man's eyes flicker and pulse as if reflecting the burst of some far-off explosion.

"Lord Scabrous."

"Did you bring the orchid?"

"I—"

"Where is it?"

A bluff, then—the bounty hunter realized that it was his only way out. He had bluffed his way out of tight spots before. This would be no different.

"This is it," he said with manufactured brusqueness, holding up the open case to show its contents. "The Murakami orchid, as you requested."

When Darth Scabrous didn't move to take it—in fact, he didn't seem to move at all—Dranok unlocked the chain from his wrist, set the case down in front of the Sith Lord, and stepped back. Still, Scabrous made no indication of coming around to examine the flower. His eyes remained locked on Dranok.

"Did you come alone?"

"My associate is waiting outside," Dranok said. "Just in case."

"Your associate."

"That's right."

"And you have brought no one else with you?"

Dranok scowled a little. "Who else would I have brought?"

Scabrous apparently didn't judge the question worthy of reply. The bounty hunter frowned, genuinely flummoxed now, his confusion only tightening the clenched fist of anxiety in his guts. "Enough questions," he shot back, hoping the tone of impatience might help mask the fear. "I delivered the orchid as we agreed. Now where's my money?"

Scabrous still didn't make any move to respond. The moment stretched, and in the ensuing silence Dranok realized that he smelled something else gathering around him, growing more potent, stronger than the reek of dead flowers: an aroma of roasting meat that had slowly begun to fill the air. Despite the tension, he felt his mouth beginning to water. It had been a while since he'd eaten. His stomach gave a noisy growl.

"You have failed me," Scabrous said.

"What?"

"That is not the Murakami orchid."

"How can you tell? You haven't even looked at it!"

Scabrous lifted his head slowly. His entire body appeared to stiffen, to grow taller somehow—an illusion, certainly, but Dranok still felt himself taking a step back, like an unruly child being taken to task, spreading his hands out in supplication. "Now, wait a second—"

"Sit down."

Dranok felt his knees buckle involuntarily, and he dropped down hard on the stone bench that he hadn't realized was there.

"Despite your failure, your payment awaits you." Scabrous gestured behind him, to an arched doorway that Dranok hadn't noticed before, and the HK droid stepped out pushing a cart with a huge silver tray on top. The droid wheeled the cart to the table and set down a plate and utensils in front of Dranok, along with a cup and a pitcher. "Help yourself."

Dranok shook his head. Whatever was underneath the lid of the silver tray, he wanted no part of it. And he realized now, with the merciless clarity of hindsight, how everything he'd done—taking the job, trusting the shady fence who had sold him the orchid, coming back up here alone—had all been links in some colossally ill-advised chain of disaster leading up to this penultimate moment of reckoning. Yet he could not stop his hand from stretching forward toward the platter.

And reaching out, he lifted the lid.

He stared at what lay underneath, sudden horror piling up inside his throat like a clogged siphon. It took less than a second to realize that the shaggy thing in front of him was the severed, stewed head of his partner, Skarl. The Nelvaanian's mouth had been pried open wide enough to accommodate the ripe red jaquira fruit that had been thrust between its jaws. Dead, boiled eyes gaped up at him with what almost looked like accusation.

"What's wrong?" Scabrous's voice intoned, from what sounded like very far away. "You fully intended to betray him, did you not? I simply saved you the trouble." And then, leaning forward: "A traitor and an incompetent. One wonders how either one of you managed to survive this long."

Dranok tried to stand up and discovered that he couldn't lift his weight from the bench. Suddenly every part of him seemed to weigh a ton.

"Let me go."

"Every traitor makes a meal of his allies." Scabrous held up a knife and fork in front of the bounty hunter's face. "This is your last meal, Dranok, and you must eat it, every morsel. That is the offer I present to you. If you can do that, I will allow you to walk out of here alive."

Dranok recoiled, struggling harder to pull himself free. But the only part of his body that he could move was his right hand, the one that Scabrous was allowing him to lift in the direction of the dining utensils. Jaw clenched, he grasped the knife from the Sith Lord's hand—and then thrust it forward, as hard as he could.

The knife didn't even get close to its intended target. Scabrous flicked his own hand in the bounty hunter's direction, a simple, almost offhand gesture, an act of disinterested dismissal, and Dranok felt his throat pinch shut, his windpipe siphoning down to a pinhole. A sharp and immediate weight seemed to have clamped down over his lungs. Tears of panic flooded his eyes, and his heart started pounding as he thrashed frantically in the seat, blackness already closing in around the edges of his vision. All at once everything seemed to be happening from a great distance away.

As Scabrous released him, allowing him to slump down from the seat to the floor, the last thing Dranok heard was the sound of some kind of creature shuffling and breathing and making a noise that sounded oddly like laughter.

5/Pain Pipe

"MASTER, I AM READY TO BEGIN AGAIN."

Seventeen-year-old Mnah Ra'at stood in the center of the academy's combat simulator, the one the students called the pain pipe, wiping the blood from his split and swollen lip. He felt no pain now, only a burning desire to attack and avenge what had been done to him. The fact that the damage had been inflicted by an automatic system as part of his training didn't matter at all to Ra'at. He was angry, and his anger made him strong.

Up above, Sith Combat Master Xat Hracken sat back inside the control booth, one hand resting on the wraparound suite of controls. Though he was human, Hracken was built more like an Aqualish, bald, bulky, and broad across the shoulders, his wide, olive-skinned face pinched into a perpetual scowl like stapled bundles of oiled suede. The hour was late, and he and Ra'at were the only ones in the simulator. Hracken, like Blademaster Shak'Weth, had been teaching here at the academy for decades, and he had seen students like Ra'at come and go—acolytes who seemed to require little or no sleep, who insisted on continuing their training late into the night, sometimes into the morning—and he'd seen how it caught up with them in the end. After a moment's consideration, he tapped the intercom.

"That's enough for tonight," Hracken said.

"No." Ra'at glowered up at him with red and baleful eyes. "I want to go again."

Hracken rose from behind the control deck and stepped forward so that the apprentice could see him through the transparisteel window. "You defy me?"

"No, Master." Ra'at's tone was only slightly mollified— a symbolic obeisance to the Master's authority. "I only wish to train under the same regimen as Rance Lussk."

Hracken nodded to himself. He'd expected as much. From the moment he'd arrived here, Lussk had set the pace for the academy's most driven pupils, all of whom wanted to fight, train, and study as intensely as he did. What none of them seemed to understand was that there could only be one Lussk, and those who challenged him found themselves sharing the fate of Nickter, among others.

Still, Master Hracken had to admit that he found Ra'at's ambition intriguing. Ra'at was easily the smallest in his class, wispy-haired and fine-featured, and two years of training hadn't added more than a few ounces of muscle to his spindly frame. But he had deep steel in him, a kind of gritty, semi-psychotic rage, and a will to power that drove him to do whatever was necessary to get ahead. He also had some very peculiar ideas. It was Ra'at, after all, who had started the rumors that Darth Scabrous himself was abducting students and taking them up to the tower in an effort to find one powerful enough to succeed him. He'd argued the case so successfully that some of the students—and even a few of the Masters—wondered if he might be right.

Now Hracken wondered if he had finally grasped Ra'at's ultimate goal.

He touched the intercom again. "All right, then, once more."

Without so much as a nod of acknowledgment, Ra'at dropped back into fighting stance, shoulders squared, jaw set. It was as if he'd known all along that the Master would acquiesce.

All right then, Hracken thought, *let's see how good you really are.*

He tapped in a sequence of commands and watched the simulator come to life below him. An automated series of heavy swing-arms arced out from either side, each one of them two meters wide, closing in so that Ra'at had to jump to avoid being crushed. He dived between them easily before going into a tuck-and-roll, successfully dodging the third obstacle, a spring-loaded picador pike, five meters long, that thrust itself unexpectedly downward from the ceiling. Hracken nodded again. It had been the pike that had caught Ra'at last time. Now he was faster.

Are you fast enough, though? That's the question, isn't it? How about when you can't see?

Picking up a pair of thermal lenses from the counter beside him, Hracken adjusted them over his eyes, then reached over and switched off the lights. Darkness swallowed the room, vast and total. Hracken flicked on the goggles. His vision helioscoped into a hundred brilliant variations of fluorescent green before resolving itself into focus, and he leaned forward with keen interest.

Down below, the now-blind Ra'at stopped in his tracks, processing what had just happened, and in that second the wall behind him burst open in a whistling array of heavy rubber whips, slashing into the air. Ra'at jerked forward, but it was too late—the whips drove him to his knees. Hracken saw the apprentice's face clench, his lips drawn back in pain.

It's over, he thought, and reached to switch the lights back on.

But it wasn't.

Ra'at was on his feet again instantly, jumping clear of the whips. Hracken immediately realized that the apprentice was no longer hampered by vision, or lack thereof: now he was relying entirely upon the Force. When the swing-arm came down again, Ra'at reached up, grabbed it, and actually held on—a move that the Sith Master hadn't seen before, even from Lussk—riding it all the way up to the ceiling. At the apex of its arc, he let go, twisting and launching himself headlong through open space to catch hold of the spring-loaded rod as it came spiking out of the wall.

It was a move of unprecedented grace and absolute precision. Ra'at spun himself around the rod once, twice, three times, building speed, and fired himself directly at the window of the control booth.

Master Hracken jerked backward. Ra'at slammed into the transparisteel with both hands, actually clinging there for a split second, long enough for Hracken to see the student's face staring straight in at him.

Then he dropped.

Hracken whipped off the goggles and turned on the lights. Light roared across the room, filling every corner. He saw Ra'at standing down below, his face flushed, shining with sweat, shoulders rising and falling with the effort of catching his breath. Despite his obvious exhaustion, the apprentice's face was almost incandescent with leftover adrenaline. When he saw Hracken coming down the stairs, his eyes filled with expectation, awaiting the Sith Master's judgment.

"Interesting," Hracken said. "Tomorrow we'll see if you can do it again."

Ra'at blinked at him. "Master?"

Hracken looked around. "What is it?"

"Lussk . . . in combat simulation, has *he* ever . . . ?"

The Sith Master waited for Ra'at to finish the sentence, but in the end the apprentice simply nodded and looked away.

"Tomorrow," he said.

* * *

Walking back to the dorm with his cloak drawn up over his shoulders and his wounds throbbing in the frigid night air, Ra'at stopped and glanced back at the simulation bunker. He was aware of what the other students and Masters said about him—how he was too small, too weak, in thrall to his own paranoid delusions—and he didn't care. Tonight he'd shown Hracken what he was capable of. Soon the rest would see.

He stepped over a high snowdrift that had formed outside the library, making his way around the eastern wall of the building until he found himself in the shadow of the tower. It was snowing steadily, but Ra'at could still make out the tracks leading up to the tower's main entryway, two sets of prints along with the familiar tracks of the HK droid.

Ra'at felt the requisite twinge of jealousy. The tracks in the snow meant that Lord Scabrous had brought visitors here, very recently. The Sith Lord had invited them into his sanctum, and they had stepped inside. Ra'at, who had never been inside the tower and could only imagine its secrets, wondered who the visitors had been. Lussk? Nickter? One of the Masters?

Slipping off his glove, Ra'at placed one bare hand directly on the closed hatchway, imagining for a moment that he could feel the power pulsating out from inside, power that he would do anything to possess.

Someday, he thought, *I'll go through there myself.*

Until then, he would keep practicing.

6/Hot Ships

IT WAS AFTER MIDNIGHT IN THE ACADEMY'S MAIN HANGAR.
Finishing up the last of his maintenance chores, Pergus
Frode found himself glaring at the Corellian cruiser still
taking up space in the corner of the landing pad. He'd
refueled the craft and kept its engines hot, as its pilot had
demanded, but that had been several hours ago and
there'd been no word from the bounty hunters. Now it
was late and he wanted nothing more than to shut things
down, go back to his quarters, and collapse into his bunk.

With a sigh, he went back to the hangar's control
booth and sealed the hatch behind him. At least it was
warm in here, a haven away from the wind. When he'd
first taken over the job almost ten standard years earlier,
Frode had retrofitted the booth to meet his needs, in-
stalling a personal thermal convection unit for hot meals
along with a datapad for his favorite holobooks and
holomags. As a hired hand, he had no Force powers and
no particular allegiance to the Sith per se; he'd only encountered Darth Scabrous on a handful of occasions.
But the last and only time that he'd ignored orders to
stay up and wait, he'd spent a week in lockup icing a
broken jaw.

Settling back with a reheated cup of Javarican espresso
and a well-worn holo of *Hot Ships,* Frode saw some-

thing flicker past the booth. He sat up and wiped a hole in the steamed-up glass, peering out. The HK was standing there, its photoreceptors focused in on him.

Frode stood up and opened the hatch. "Hey."

The HK turned and looked back at him. "Query: What is it, sir?"

"How much longer are those guys going to be in the tower?" Frode pointed at the cruiser. "I mean, their ship's just sitting there, eating our fuel."

"Response: I suppose you ought to shut it down."

"But that guy Dranok said—"

"Statement: He won't be coming back, sir. He, or his partner."

Frode blinked. "What, you mean, like, ever?"

"Response: That is my understanding, sir, yes."

Pushing back his mission cap to scratch his head, Frode turned his attention speculatively back to the bounty hunter's vessel. "You know," he remarked casually, "a ship like that's gotta carry a pretty sophisticated flight computer."

"Statement: I'm sure I wouldn't know anything about that, sir. The equipment of such vessels is not part of my programming, and—"

"You don't think Lord Scabrous would mind if I yanked her out, do you?"

The HK regarded him blankly.

"You know, set it aside. Scrap-market value on that thing's not too shabby."

"Statement: I'm sure you could help yourself," the droid said, with bottomless indifference, already turning away to go about its business.

Settling his cap back on his head, Frode nodded and got his tools, whistling a little under his breath as he did so.

Maybe, he thought, tonight would turn out well after all.

7 / Marfa

HESTIZO TRACE ROLLED OVER, DREW IN A DEEP, RESIGNED breath, and lifted her head from the pillow. The small, nondescript sleeping chamber where she'd awakened had already begun to fill with soft artificial light. Although she was all alone here, she could feel the orchid waiting for her down below, some two hundred meters away but close enough to hear its voice quite clearly in her mind.

Hestizo! Emergency!

She sat up, pushing off her covers. *What is it? What's wrong?*

My incubation chamber! Come quickly!

Realizing now what the voice must be referring to, she relaxed back down. *Oh.*

"*Oh?*" Alarm flashed through the flower's tone. *This is serious!*

I'll be down in a second.

Hurry, please!

Okay, she told it, *all right. Hold on to your petals. I'll be down there in a minute.*

The orchid retreated in her mind, only marginally placated, as if still awaiting a formal apology. Honestly, Zo didn't mind its presence in her thoughts; the bond that they shared was, after all, part of her identity, a Jedi in the Agricultural Corps, one of the talented handful whose psychic green thumb kept her here in the nurseries and labs of the Marfa facility.

Marfa was a hothouse, its varying atmospheres, temperatures, and moisture levels all carefully maintained to foster the widest variety of interstellar fauna in this part of the Core Worlds. But it was the Force sensitivity of Zo and her fellow Jedi that drove the different species to their fullest potential. At twenty-five, Zo understood that there was innate value, even a kind of nobility in such things, nurturing every form of botanical life and encouraging every facet of its development and exploration.

Rousing herself fully from the last lingering vestiges of sleep, she slipped into her robe and headed up the corridor to the refresher. The faint sense of unease followed her, an unwelcome remnant of some other unremembered dream. She dressed for the day, choosing her lab frock and hood from a rack of identical uniforms, attributing the tinge of restlessness to that same nameless malaise that sometimes waited for her upon awakening here on Marfa.

Opting out of breakfast, she followed the concourse up to Beta Level Seven. Marfa's planetary status was constantly shifting with the position of solar activity and galactic cloud patterns, but B-7 was currently the busiest and most vibrant of the various cultivation and growth bays honeycombing Marfa's surface. Usually most of her fellow Jedi could be found there in the mornings, starting their day with de facto meetings to update one another on progress and research, and share their immediate plans for the future.

The turbolift doors opened on an eye-watering expanse of green, and Zo stopped there as she always did, letting the great familiar cloud of humid warmth wash over her. The smells of countless different plants competed for her attention—sap, fruit, and flower mingling in a mind-boggling banquet of fragrances.

Tilting her head back, she looked up on 150 standard meters of high-ceilinged vines and dangling root systems. All around were narrow, self-sustaining forests of succulents and subspecies and high trellises overrun with loops and whorls of growth so varied in color and size that only through sheer day-after-day familiarity was she able to process it all.

She could already feel them.

Her mind tuned instantly to the internal hum of hundreds of different vegetative life forces, each vibrating according to its own particular emotion, some low and oscillating, others pulsing high and bright to match the explosions of flowers that sprang from their stems. Many of the plants were local enough that she recognized their greetings in her mind, as she passed by. Zo walked among them, allowing their rustling enthusiasm of leaves and stalks to distract her from the nagging tug of unease that had followed her up from below.

"Good morning, Hestizo." Wall Bennis was the first actual voice she'd heard this morning. A tall, soft-spoken man with calm brown eyes, the Jedi ag-lab director was waiting for her behind the thick red stalks of a malpaso tree with an extra cup of caf. "Sleep well?"

"Until the orchid woke me."

Bennis handed her the cup. "Any idea what's going on?"

"I've got a pretty good guess."

"You do?"

"Mm-hm."

"That's good, then." He went distractedly back to his own work and then seemed to remember something. "Oh, and Zo? When you get a minute, would you mind taking a look at the pulsifarian moss colonies on B-Two?

There seems to be some kind of secondary parasite growing in the soil."

"You always save the glamorous stuff for me."

"You're the only one who can understand it."

"The moss or the parasite?"

"Both, I think."

"I'll take a look." She carried the caf across B-7 until she'd reached the private incubation chamber in the far corner of the room. Deactivating the air lock, she stepped inside, resealing the door behind her.

Finally, the orchid burst out. *What took you so long?*

You're not the only plant on this level. She took her time checking the temperature and moisture readouts on the wall unit, making incremental adjustments to both, and then walked over to the only plant in the chamber, a small orchid with black petals and a thin green stalk, its fronds seeming almost to quiver with impatience. For a moment she stood sipping caf and looking at it.

I was cold during the night. Exceedingly unpleasant.

Actually, I turned the temperature down in your incubation chamber, she told it. *Almost a full two degrees, on purpose.*

Why?

I've been telling you for ages that you're a lot heartier than you thought. Now you know it's true. Fact is, you could probably survive a twenty-degree temperature drop, maybe more, and you would have been just fine.

That's cruel to test without warning!

If I'd told you, Zo replied, *then you would have gotten yourself all worked up over nothing.*

The orchid withdrew into sulky silence. As flora went, it was one of the most Force-sensitive species in the galaxy. The problem was that it knew it. Zo put up with it anyway, and most of the time she was happy to dedicate herself to studying its abilities and providing for its needs. Every so often, though, it needed to be reminded why it had endured for thousands of years: it was far more durable than it gave itself credit for.

Zo? the orchid said now.

What is it?

Something's wrong.

What now?

Outside . . . something's happening.

Zo reopened the incubator's hatchway and stepped back out. Standing motionless in front of the chamber, she realized several things simultaneously.

First, that the initial sense of wrongness she'd been experiencing up until now had nothing to do with her work here on Marfa. Contrary to what she'd initially supposed, the feeling was emanating from an outside source, an interloper, something that clearly didn't belong here. It hadn't been a dream; it was an alarm.

And second, despite the silence, she wasn't alone.

Zo? the orchid's voice asked. *What is it?*

Give me a second. She listened to the entire greenhouse with her ears instead of her mind. She heard no audible voices, but that was to be expected. Her fellow Jedi often worked for hours among their individual species without speaking a word. Much of their daily routine was accomplished in absolute silence.

Pausing halfway down a long aisle overgrown with leafy stalks, Zo looked up. Far overhead, she found what she was looking for, an 800-year-old panopticon willow, a perfect specimen of organic surveillance, draping its limbs in a dense canopy of emerald-dripping lace. Each bud was tipped with a tiny golden eye.

Zo placed one palm flat against the shaggy trunk, allowing its root strength to pulse through her, aware at the same time that the tree was embracing her as an equal. She felt her ground-level perspective surging up through its branches, spreading out along colonies of sharply focused eyes. Her vision shifted, wobbled, and became clear again. She was now gazing down at herself and the entire floor from far above, from the willow's point of view. The tree's branches shifted and Zo felt a slight shimmer of cognitive dissonance as her perspective aligned itself and she saw the familiar robed figure of Wall Bennis leaning face-first against the sinuous, downy-tufted trunk of a Malpassian squid pine.

But Bennis wasn't leaning.

He was slouched forward, motionless, his torso hanging at an unnatural angle, arms dangling at his sides, impaled by the spear that had been slammed through his back into the trunk of the tree. A long dagger-shaped bloodstain ran from between his shoulder blades down his back, soaking through his belt. The cup of caf he'd been holding lay on the floor between his feet.

Zo realized that she could see Bennis's face. It hung ashen and slack, a dangling meat-mask from which all life had fled. His blood spilled down the spear's rough-hewn shaft, and Zo watched, with the willow's unblinking acuity, as a droplet formed at the end, grew heavy, and fell into the already congealing pool on the floor by his feet.

Plip.

Something rustled behind her in the leaves.

Spinning around, her consciousness dropping back from the willow's branches into her own optic and auditory nerves, Zo realized too late that she'd let her guard down. On the other side of the tree, somewhere just inside the thick green canopy, the rustling grew louder, closer. A branch snapped. Twigs crackled, trampled underfoot. Zo felt the presence of this new thing, whatever it was, making its way directly toward her, no longer bothering to be quiet or stealthy.

Fear took hold of her, vacuuming the air from her

lungs. The buzz of plant emotion had fallen quiet—even the orchid was still—and the entire research level felt far larger and more desolate than it had just moments before. Glancing around, hearing only the faint click of her own throat, she suddenly wanted more than anything to run, but she was no longer sure in which direction to go. The noises she'd heard on the other side of the tree now seemed, impossibly, to be closing in from all sides. She felt helpless, isolated, alone, except for the buzzing weightless swarm of her own terror.

A shape burst out of the green, into full view, two meters tall. The bulky, fur-shrouded torso stood well above her. The long, squinting face was inhuman: cheekbones and brow jutted forward; a pair of stained tusks pushed upward from the lower jaw; the eyes that glinted from beneath its forehead were shining and intent. It was a Whiphid, Zo realized—the biggest she'd ever seen. Somewhere in his chest, he gave a thick grunting sound that might have expressed anything from appreciation to disinterest.

Zo turned and fled. She had taken three steps when an arm the size of a load-bearing girder slammed sideways against her skull, spraying bright fragments of pain through the right side of her head. Her vision shattered into a wide field of star-rattled blindness.

When the blindness cleared she was on the floor, neck-deep in pain, looking up at the Whiphid, the underside of one horned foot plunging down to smother her face. She could smell him now, his pungent and claustrophobic-inducing stench like mildew and death. This time it occurred to her that the death she smelled might be her own.

Pressure engulfed her skull, squeezing agonizingly, as the mottled flesh of his foot covered her nose and mouth. A vacuum of fetid-smelling blackness sealed tight. Muffled, from far away, she heard his voice for the first time.

"The orchid."

Zo squirmed and felt the weight lift ever so slightly to allow her to answer. "What?"

"The Murakami orchid." The voice from within the broad, tusked mouth was low and hoarse, more of a growl. "Where is it?"

"Why?"

The eyes narrowed. "Don't waste my time, Jedi, or you'll end up a corpse like your friend." He leaned down until she could actually *feel* the fetid stench of his breath seething through the slits of his nostrils. "Where. Is. It?"

"It's . . . in the primary incubation cultivator." Zo sat up just enough to nod to the left and felt a bright sliver of spun glass shoot through her brachial plexus where the Whiphid had pressed his weight. "Over there, behind you. But you can't just—"

"Show me." Grabbing her arm, he dragged her behind him. Zo caught a glimpse of the longbow and the quiver of arrows strapped across the muscled hump of his back, the tangles of its gray-golden mane swinging back and forth. Small bones, some decidedly humanoid, mandibles and phalanges, were tied and braided into the ends of its hair where they clicked against one another. Whiphids, if she remembered her taxonomy right, were born predators—they lived to hunt and kill. Those venturing from their homeworld found good work as mercenaries and bounty hunters, or worse.

The Whiphid swung her forward by the neck and slammed her against the door of the incubator. "Open it."

"You just have to push the air lock."

Shoving her aside, he kept his right hand around her neck while his left hand gripped the latch and disabled the lock. The door opened and he pulled her in, keeping her at arm's length while groping around the incubator. Zo tried to tilt her head upward to take the pressure off her throat, but he was holding her almost half a meter off the floor . . . she couldn't touch, even with her tiptoes. From the far corner she heard an explosion of electronic components bursting apart. Something heavy toppled over and crashed to the ground. When the Whiphid's hand came back, his fingers were wrapped around the orchid's stalk, the flower already beginning to wilt in his grasp.

"What's wrong with it?" the Whiphid asked.

"It's special," Zo managed. "It can't survive out of the incubator, it needs—"

"What?" he demanded, relaxing his grip just enough that she could finally slide down and touch the floor.

She forced the word, hating herself for it: "—me."

"What?"

"If it's out of the incubator, I can't be more than a meter away from it. I need to be close. Or else it loses its powers."

Zo looked out of the incubator, back in the direction from which she'd come. Her gaze flashed across the lab floor to the body of Wall Bennis. No longer pinned to the tree, his corpse lay in a crumpled heap, one palm open as if grasping for some final, unavailable lifeline that had failed to appear. The spear that had impaled him against the tree had been yanked free.

Zo had just enough time to wonder when the Whiphid had pulled it out when she saw the butt end of it flying downward toward her face, slamming her in the right temple and plunging her deep into a wide and starless night.

8/Polyskin

THROUGHOUT ITS HISTORY, THE ROCKY DESERT WORLD OF Geonosis had suffered its share of catastrophes and mass extinctions, including the rogue comet strike on its largest moon that had very nearly wiped out the planet's entire population. Taking into account the resulting debris field, the flash floods, and the random solar radiation storms, it wasn't difficult to see why the ancient Geonosians, what remained of them, had moved underground.

Not much had changed since then.

Standing here amid the caverns and rock spires of whatever remained, Rojo Trace realized that the Republic officer in front of him had finished talking, or had at least paused for breath. The officer's name was Lieutenant Norch, and despite the fact that he was staring Trace directly in the eye and almost shouting to be heard above the wind, he still managed to sound both officious and insincere in his delivery. In other words, a perfect product of the bureaucracy to which he'd sworn allegiance.

"Furthermore," Norch continued, "on behalf of the Republic's military and security divisions, we appreciate the Order's timely response." The lieutenant gestured at the huge polyskin tent spread out in front of them, half a kilometer of rippling silver micropore, flapping and

popping in the wind like the sail of a ship going nowhere. "Given the nature of our discovery here, I'm sure
you understand the urgency of our request."

Trace nodded, wincing a little at the grit that blew
into his face. He was a dark-haired man of unremarkable build and complexion, tall and steady and vaguely
handsome in a way that didn't draw attention to the
unshaven jawline, the green eyes, and the faintly smiling
lips. Yet for every moment that he stood motionless outside the tent—perhaps listening, perhaps not—a sense of
intensity seemed to gather around him, a sense of acute
psychological awareness of its own rarefied state.

"We got the initial report of it last night," Norch said,
raising his voice even louder over the baked-dry wind.
"Independent long-range hauler on its way through the
Outer Rim picked up on an unfamiliar heat signature.
They thought it was a distress signal. But when they
landed they saw this."

And with a gesture no doubt intended to be dramatic,
he turned to the tent and flung back the flap, allowing
Trace inside.

Trace ducked under the polyskin, glad to be out of
the wind, and stopped, looking down. The crater was
still smoking, but he could see the wreckage piled up
inside, perhaps one hundred meters down, where it had
punched a hole and permanently altered the landscape.
Peering down into it, he was aware of the lieutenant
watching him intently with a sense of barely reserved
judgment, until he was no longer able to contain himself.

"Well?" Norch asked. "What do you make of it?"

"It's a Sith warship, obviously. The five engine pods,
the boxy design . . ."

The lieutenant shook his head. "With all due respect,
you mistake my meaning. We're *aware* that it's a Sith
warship. We saw our share of them in the sacking of

Coruscant." And then, puffing inside his uniform: "The question is what caused it to crash here on Geonosis, and whether its arrival here ought to be considered an act of deliberate aggression."

"Why would you assume that?" Trace asked.

Norch narrowed his eyes as if reassessing the Jedi Knight's trustworthiness. "The Republic has been evaluating this planet as a possible defense stronghold in the Arkanis sector—that's strictly confidential, of course."

"And?"

"And when I contacted the Jedi Council, they informed me that you were in possession of certain telemetric abilities that might clarify our enemy's underlying intent."

"That's true."

"Well, in any case." Now Norch was giving him the Full Scowl—out of impatience or the simple exertion of shouting out over the flapping tent, Trace couldn't be sure. At last the lieutenant cleared his throat and found some speck out on the horizon to stare at. "It was my personal understanding that upon arriving here, you would use your particular, ah . . . abilities to assist us in our investigation."

"And it was *my* understanding," Trace said, "that I would be given complete authority here to perform my investigation, without any outside interference." He was still looking down into the great smoking hole, at the warship and the colossal planetary bullet wound that its impact had created. It was even deeper than he'd initially suspected, and he could already hear the subtle, lethal whisper of escaping pressure.

"What exactly do you want from me?"

Trace looked up at him. "Get your men and clear out."

"From the tent?"

"From the planet."

One eyebrow arched up, a trick the lieutenant had been saving until now: "I beg your pardon?"

"It's not safe."

"We've already reinforced the ground around the site for a kilometer in every direction—"

"I'm not talking about the ground." Trace allowed his voice to become slightly sharper. "Do you hear that hissing sound? The warship struck a subterranean gas deposit, a big one by the sound of it, and the underground gases here on Geonosis are notoriously unstable. If it sublimates while your men are around, you won't *have* men anymore."

"Listen here. I'm in charge, and—"

"Then you'd do well to listen to what *this* man says," a new voice cut in.

Trace turned to see a female Republic officer, perhaps in her early thirties, dark-haired, and attractive, smiling at him. From Norch's salute, she clearly outranked him, but she didn't even acknowledge the response.

"Rojo Trace? I'm Captain Tekla Ansgar. Welcome." Her pale blue eyes glimmered at him, sharp and confident. "It's a pleasure to meet you. I certainly hope you won't judge your experience here on the basis of one unpleasant conversation."

"Frankly," Trace said, "my own experience here couldn't matter less. I'm here to do a job."

"Oh, I'm sure there's more to it than that." She stepped toward him, casually brushing his arm with her own. "I have to confess, I've always admired the Jedi Order, but I've never had the opportunity to get to know a Jedi Knight personally."

"I'm afraid that's not going to happen today," Trace said.

She frowned a little. "But—"

Before she could continue, Trace moved past her, turned, and jumped straight into the crater.

* * *

The plunge took the better part of thirty seconds, but to Trace it seemed both instantaneous and, in an unreal way, much longer. Shearing downward through the chasm, he summoned the Force, generating a cushion of resistance beneath him until he felt his free fall slackening, the crater walls slowing down, individual molecules meshing to buffet his descent. Now, with a little bit of concentration, he could see every crack and divot in the rock as it passed.

By the time he noticed the rest of the warship lodged at the bottom of the pit, he'd decreased his rate of descent to the point where he could reach out and catch hold of the broken fuselage. Cold durasteel slapped his hands. Swinging his legs around, Trace dropped through a ragged gash in the hull, boots thumping off a narrow band of twisted metal that had once been part of a catwalk.

He took a breath and looked around.

Even from here, the warship was a predictably ugly thing, inelegant and utilitarian, the work of a culture that saw nothing of beauty in the galaxy. The impact of the crash had actually improved its aesthetics, giving it some makeshift degree of originality. Standing here, he could feel the hulking weight of the craft tipping unsteadily around him, the wreckage still settling, rocking into place. Sharp edges rasped and scraped against the deep sedimentary layers, carving random glyphs into the soft sandstone. Beneath it all, omnipresent and lethal, was the stealthy *whoosh* of escaping gas. He didn't have much time.

Edging his way deeper into the vessel—bulkheads shifting even as he passed through—Trace paused, expanding his senses to draw in any indication of any remaining life aboard.

There was nothing.

Up above in the tent, the military officer had told him that the initial bioscan had come back negative . . . though he feared that a handful of Sith survivors might somehow be jamming the reading, preparing an ambush.

Trace could have told him already that was not going to happen. But he'd come this far, and simple curiosity drew him onward. Dropping farther, taking his time, he clamored through the main flight deck and groped in the dark until his fingers brushed against something smooth, damp, and still faintly warm. There was a soft organic pulpiness to it. Without needing to look, he knew he'd come across the first corpse.

Slowly his eyes began to adjust. The remains of the Sith flight crew lay smashed and bleeding, burned, skin bubbling over exposed bone and melted into the fabric of their uniforms. Fire and impact had fused several of the bodies into a single twisted mass of faces and broken limbs embedded into the seats where they'd died.

He could smell the gas now, its sulfuric rotten-egg fumes trickling into his lungs, and knew time was short. He closed his eyes again but didn't remove his hand from the mass of dripping flesh and bone. Proximity was important; physical contact was even better. Beneath the inner geometry of his own thoughts, he began to hear the curses of the crew as the ship's navigational system failed, felt their dawning horror as they realized the engine pods were going to bury them deep below the planet's crust. In the end, the impending inevitability of death had reduced them to something as brainless and scurrying as Mustafar lava fleas, their faith in the dark side, their sworn oath to the Sith Lords with their incantations and ancient sigils, stripped away in a final spasm of animal panic.

And then silence.

Always silence.

Trace exhaled, reminded now of other terms he'd

heard used to describe the Republic's role in crash sites like this. The officers might call them investigators, but the enlisted men on the ground had other names. Names like *corpse counters* and *dirt tourists*.

The nicknames meant little to him. That was the job; everything else was a distraction, including female officers who wanted to get to know him personally. He was aware of his reputation for being cold and impersonal: it didn't bother him in the least.

He withdrew his hand, preparing his ascent to the surface—

And sucked in a quick breath between his teeth. The bright lancet of sudden overwhelming fear that he'd just experienced had nothing to do with the warship or the remains of its crew.

Something else was happening, somewhere far distant.

Something far worse.

He saw his sister's face.

There could be no doubt about it. It was Zo and she was screaming in a frenzy of pain and helplessness. And although Trace couldn't see her attacker clearly, he realized from the erratic sunbursts of her thoughts that she had no defense against the thing that loomed above her, dragging her out of the Jedi Agricultural Corps facility, toward—what?

He stopped, frozen, his current locale utterly forgotten, blindsided by a storm of disjointed images: the shaft of a spear, dripping with blood; a flash of green; a whiff of something rancid and feral. His nostrils burned with the stench of a place that had been bottled up too long, a place of death and solitude and agonized last breaths. He could feel her confusion and apprehension pumping through his own circulatory system, as if they shared the same heart. For a moment he could feel the presence of her abductor.

Listen to me, Trace told him. *I don't know who you are, but I am in possession of a very special set of skills. If you bring my sister back right now, unharmed, then I'll let you go. But if you don't, I promise you, I will track you down. I will find you. And I will make you pay.*

Of course there was no response.

From beneath him came a stuttering, squealing lurch, then a deafening crash as the fuselage of the crashed Sith warship swayed under his feet and abruptly gave way in a waterfall of sparks. There was a sudden *whoosh* and a plume of flame as a gas pocket blasted open from the wall.

The explosion rocked the crater to its depths. Snapping around, Trace felt huge slabs of scorched rock scaling loose, tumbling down toward him. On reflex, he threw up a solid bubble of air, pressing it outward to ensure enough breathable oxygen—too little and he'd suffocate inside here, a bug in a jar.

The bubble did its job. Debris hammered down on top of it, shale bouncing and skittering across the dome. Trace scarcely noticed. He cast his thoughts back toward Zo, back to the place in himself where he'd seen and felt the final compulsive timpani of her distress, straining for any hint of where she might be, where her captor was taking her.

But there was nothing there now, only dead air as deep and final as that which followed the crash of the warship where he now stood.

And awful silence.

Rising upward with the bubble, Trace made for the surface of the crater, the light from above growing brighter, broadening to illuminate the deep frown etched onto his face.

9/Mirocaw

Zo awoke staring into the empty sockets of a skull.

Not human—it was a misshapen thing, one eyehole appreciably larger than the other, and a third gaping just above it, its gap-toothed grin seeming to welcome her into some murderous new realm where proportions were a joke and nothing made sense. There was a dusky blue sapphire, probably fake, embedded in the thing's one remaining incisor. The skull's current owner had strung several lengths of thick cable through its facial sinuses so that it dangled like a grotesque bead on a string, and when Zo sat up and tried to move away from it, the fullness of the chamber where she'd awakened came into view.

She was inside a kind of trophy room.

The cable ran from one side of the room to the other. Rows of similar skulls hung on either end, dozens of them, grouped together in clusters while others were set apart in twos and threes to create a kind of ghastly abacus. Beneath it, an irregular array of vats and stained crucibles bubbled steadily over heating elements. In them, Zo saw more bones and shanks of raw-knobbed limbs protruding upward, some sheathed in yellow fat and sinew while others seemed to have boiled down to the marrow. Moss and mildew covered the ceiling, years of lichen and mold, colonies of life competing for airborne fat molecules coming off the pots. The smell of scalded viscera hung permanently in the air.

Swallowing, trying not to gag, Zo squirmed again and felt something slick and oily brush against the backs of her arms. Turning around, she saw that the entire wall behind her was lined with skins and hides, each one crawling with layers of tiny blind beetles industriously gnawing away. She watched, helpless, as they burrowed in and out of the hanging flank, hauling off chunks of grayish flesh.

"Boski scarabs," a voice behind her said.

Zo snapped back around and saw the Whiphid standing in the doorway. His gaze was intense, corrosive, as if he could already see through her skin to the skeleton she would inevitably leave behind—bones he might boil out of her if she weren't worth waiting for the natural decay process to do it first.

Zo moved her head slightly and winced at the pain in the base of her neck. She remembered those last few moments at the Marfa facility—the butt end of the Whiphid's spear, a glassy rocket of agony, the blurry slither of the corridor as it warped past the lens of her ever-dimming consciousness.

And just before she'd blacked out, the hatchway.

Zo looked past the Whiphid, regarding her surroundings through this new, unwelcome perspective. The whine of turbines under the floorboards, the persistent shiver of the bulkhead—though the room was without any sort of viewport, offering no sight of their greater surroundings, she realized they had to be in flight.

"Is this your ship?"

The Whiphid nodded once. "The *Mirocaw*."

"Where are we going?"

This time, he didn't answer, lumbering instead over to the nearest of the pots. She watched as he lifted the lid and dipped in with an oxidized pair of tongs, hoisting a grubby clump of something that she realized was a type of shank. Bits of gristle and musculature, part of a leg, dangled from its lower edges. With an unimpressed grunt, the Whiphid dropped the part back into the pot and slapped the lid back down, then turned to walk out again.

"Wait," she said hoarsely.

The bounty hunter didn't stop.

The hatch slid shut.

A moment after he left, Zo found the orchid.

It was still inside the half-crushed specimen flask, strapped almost haphazardly between a cargo drop panel and a swing bin above the vats of limbs and skulls. Her captor had used the same greasy cable he'd strung through the skulls to tie the containment vessel into place. From where she stood below it, she saw that the orchid had flourished even while she'd lain here unconscious. Simple physical proximity seemed enough to keep it alive, despite the fact that for a good bit of the time she'd been out cold.

Zo looked at it.

Hello?

Nothing.

It's me. Can you hear me?

The initial process of communication was never easy. At first it had felt almost unnatural. Yet with practice, through countless mornings spent sitting alone with the orchid, she'd soon reached a level of mastery that eased the transitory awkwardness into a smoother and more organic leap.

Are you there?

Within its glass vessel, the plant finally twitched, brightening slightly in recognition of her presence. Zo watched its dust-colored stem inclining toward her like a beckoning finger. At the same time she felt its life essence stirring within her, filling an almost physical void directly behind her breastbone and between her lungs, a place she thought of almost colloquially as her soul. She heard the first coarse whispers of its voice, gender-neutral, incoherent at first and then becoming clearer, like a foreigner adapting to the nuances of an entirely new language.

Zo? What happened? Are we well?

Zo gave a rueful smile, felt the lump on the back of her head. *I wouldn't exactly say that.*

The orchid was silent a moment. Then: *I sense that things . . . have changed.*

"You can say that again," she murmured aloud.

Repeat?

We've been abducted, Zo told it. *Taken.*

Another silence. Then: *Yes, that is true. By this creature . . . Tulkh.*

Her eyes darted back up to it. *That's his name?*

The Whiphid? Yes. He's a . . . Hunting for the correct phrase: *What is it, this word . . . ? One who takes people for money?*

A bounty hunter, Zo said, and felt the orchid nodding in agreement.

Yes. Solitary, a bloodthirsty species, and aggressive.

Zo waited, processing the comment. The orchid had a gift for understatement, and she couldn't help but wonder about the criteria for this assessment.

And a flower collector to boot, she told it.

If the orchid had an opinion on this, it didn't voice it.

What does he want? she asked.

The orchid stayed silent. Staring at it, Zo began to realize how her fully wakened presence had already affected the trophy room's biosphere. The naturally occurring moss on the ship's ceiling had started spreading at a noticeably accelerated pace, sprawling to swallow up the exposed bolts and seams in the interior walls. There was some kind of switch plate just above her head with a sign written in another language—the Whiphid's mother tongue, she assumed—but it was already so moss-covered that she couldn't make out the letters. Scraps of green rot within the skulls had begun extending their first tendrils up as well, reaching outward through eye sockets and trepanned holes. Simply by being here, she'd jump-started the growth of the *Mirocaw*'s incidental flora.

Do you at least know where he's taking us?

Again, no immediate reply from the orchid. Zo wondered if she'd reached the outer limits of the flower's knowledge.

Then she felt the spacecraft jerk hard to one side, the nearly subsonic whine of the turbine pitch-shifting into afterburner mode, and realized she was about to get the answer for herself.

What's going on? Are we crashing? she asked.

Going down, the orchid said.

Where?

Silence again, then:

The worst place in the galaxy.

10/Strapping on Ghosts

THE IMPACT KNOCKED HER SIDEWAYS AGAINST THE WALL of skins, and Zo recoiled, found her equilibrium, and brushed off the scuttling, hard-shell beetles that clung to her skin before they could sink their hungry little mouthparts into her. The things fell to the deck, scuttled blindly for an instant, and then vanished between the cracks, as if the Whiphid's ship were just another corpse for their investigation.

Below her feet, the engines had fallen silent. In the stillness, she sensed the *Mirocaw* resigning itself to gravity, redistributing the vicissitudes of torque through its thousand tiny joists and connectors with a deep and exhausted sigh.

Zo still couldn't tell if they'd crashed, or if it had just been a rough landing. She waited, scarcely breathing, as the thrusters cooled, ticking and ultimately falling silent. From outside, she could hear the wind. The sound brought with it a kind of alien desolation that seeped in from somewhere outside the durasteel-reinforced hull. She felt the skin on her back tightening with a shiver. It felt as if they'd landed in some windowless crawl space in the bottom of the galaxy, a place inexplicably devoid of entrances and exits. Her gaze flicked back to the orchid, hoping for an explanation, a means of understanding what she felt.

Something's gone wrong out there, she thought. *Can you feel it?*

Across the room, the vacuum-sealed gasp caught her by surprise. The Whiphid was standing in the open hatchway again, clutching his spear in one hand and a bunched-up bundle of furs and hides in the other. He tossed the furs at her feet.

"Put those on."

Zo didn't budge. "What are we doing here?"

"Get the plant."

"Are you going to answer me?"

He turned and stalked out again, this time leaving the hatch open behind him, an unspoken demand to follow. Was there some other component to his brusqueness besides just impatience? Was the bounty hunter as uneasy as she felt?

Zo looked down at the pile of furs and pelts. They had been stitched into crude mittens, boots, a hat, and what looked like a kind of cloak. Squatting, she pulled the boots over her feet and found that, despite their bulkiness, they fit well enough when she lashed them tight around her ankles. They were recent kills, she realized—she could still feel the residue of the lives that had worn them as skin. It was like strapping on restless layers of ghosts.

Picking up the cloak, she slung it around her shoulders and reached up to the sealed transparent lab packet containing the orchid, slipping it free from the cable that pinned it down. The orchid seemed to shiver and flattened its petals against the wall of the chamber closest to her hand as if drawn to the warmth. It was murmuring to itself, not out loud but in her mind, in one of a thousand languages that she didn't understand, an obscure tongue of hums and hisses.

She stepped out into a long, narrow corridor lit by irregular panels of interior lights and followed it forward, through another open hatch. Here the walkway narrowed even further, the ceiling lowering until she thought she'd somehow gone the wrong way.

Hunching her shoulders to negotiate a turn, Zo realized how truly cold it was. An abrupt blast of arctic air slashed across her face and forearms and she turned, openmouthed and startled, tasting the first iron-flecked coldness in the back of her throat. White flakes swirled up the landing ramp, and in the sickish pale green glow of the landing lights she got her first look at where they'd settled.

They weren't sitting on any kind of pad—if it was out there, they'd missed it completely. The landscape outside the ship presented little more than a broad snow-seething steppe of white on white. The wind brought a thin film of tears to her eyes, and Zo wiped them clear. In the distance, across the void, she could just make out the jagged peaks cutting upward like a black spinal column. There was something both erratic and oddly deliberate in the outline of those mountains.

An instant later she realized what it was.

They weren't mountains at all.

She tried to swallow and felt no moisture in her throat. The freezing dry air had sucked it away, eliminated it entirely. In her arms, tucked against her, the orchid had started to make the same repetitive clicking sound over and over again, as if it were stuck on a thought, a compulsive stammering noise that she didn't like at all.

The tip of a spear touched the back of her neck, just above the rough hem of the collar.

"Move," Tulkh's voice said from behind her.

Zo's feet wouldn't budge. They seemed to have been riveted in place.

"Wait," she said, not turning around. "Those black shapes out there in the distance, they're—"

"I know what they are."

"Which planet is this?" she asked thinly. "Ziost?"

The spear tip slipped a little against her skin, but it didn't hurt. She was far too lost in what lay in front of them to feel the pain.

"We shouldn't have come," she said. "There's a toxicity level that I can't account for. It's—"

"Move."

"Do you have a droid you could send out to sample the atmosphere, just to make sure—"

The spear tip pushed harder.

Insisting.

Hurting now.

Zo started down the landing ramp.

Fresh kills or not, she was immediately grateful for the boots and skins, the heavy fur pelt piled around her shoulders and around her neck. The snow wasn't deep—in many places its crust was firm enough that they actually walked on top of it—but the wind was surgical, a precision instrument with needles for teeth, and it found even the tiniest exposed places on her skin, attacking them. In minutes her face was a numb mask, her cheeks heavy and lifeless.

She fixed her stare on the black crooked spine of peaks on the horizon. They were closer now, and any initial resemblance to mountains had long since vanished. The ruins and escarpments had a crudely mechanized appearance, and the resulting sprawl looked as if the massive skeleton of some ancient machine—city-sized, planet-sized—had been half buried here, abandoned while it was still alive enough to dig itself out.

In the midst of it, like some pivot upon which it all turned: a great black tower.

It rose up crookedly, a sloping monolithic pile constructed of sleek black rock, the grave marker of some long-dead deity. Even from here, its height dwarfed the half-ruined complex below: a good pilot could have parked a long-range freighter atop its flat roof. Red lights swarmed and shimmered inside its upper levels, their erratic patterns flooding the cloud of snowfall in a deep arterial glow. It was like watching a digitized read-out of a brain going insane and dying.

The crunch of Tulkh's footsteps faltered and slowed to a halt, and Zo lowered her gaze to what lay immediately before them. Twenty meters ahead, the ground dipped and a kind of crude gateway rose up, webbed with clots of ice. She was aware of a silence here, the wind shearing abruptly away, leaving them in a pocket of utter quiet. Zo took a breath and held it, then finally spoke aloud the words that had been haunting her since she'd first emerged from the bounty hunter's ship.

"This is a Sith academy."

The Whiphid marched on, the unspoken silence of his confirmation hitting her even harder than she had anticipated.

"What planet is this?"

He ignored her.

"Why are we here?"

He skulked past her to the gate. Despite his size and imposing stature, there was a hesitation to his approach, as if he didn't know quite what to expect beyond this point.

"It's the orchid, isn't it?"

Tulkh turned back to her, spear in hand. She saw knots of ice dangling from his hair. His eyes were lost in shadow.

"You were right to be afraid," she said. "Whatever's inside there is worse than you can possibly imagine. I'm only trying to warn you," she went on. "You know I'm a Jedi. I can feel—"

Something happened then, some truncation of motion, as if time itself had been tricked, cheated out of its rightful due. Before she knew it, an icicle of pain, a single radial spike, jagged upward into the underside of her chin, and when Zo opened her eyes she saw Tulkh standing directly in front of her, the sharp part of the spear thrust upward into her flesh, biting in, drawing blood. He had moved faster than she'd ever imagined, faster even than her enhanced powers of perception could quite register.

Zo pulled back, freeing herself. "What do the Sith want with the Murakami orchid?"

Tulkh blinked at her once, slowly, the blink of a creature that preferred to spend its time alone.

"You can tell me now," she said, "or you can kill me. But I'm letting you know, I'm not going another step without knowing what's waiting for me in there." She thought about everything she'd heard of the academies, hives of darkness so black and toxic that they blazed with their own special kind of evil, unimaginable to those who'd never witnessed it firsthand. Even those darkest of places seemed clean compared with the rancid feeling of contamination wafting out from in front of these peculiar half-ravaged structures, their slabs and the black tower overhead. "But you already know the orchid can't live without me."

For a long time, Tulkh didn't answer—so long, in fact, that Zo wondered if he planned on ignoring her entirely.

A moment later, though, he spoke.

"Have you heard of Darth Scabrous?"

Zo felt something clenching deep in her chest. It was familiar, this tightness, like an emotional echo of some long-forgotten childhood fear. She remembered feeling it the moment the ship landed. And now it had a name.

Darth Scabrous.

She felt her gaze sucked inexorably back toward the tower.

"He wants the plant," Tulkh said. "I'm bringing it to him. That's the job I was hired to do."

"I see."

"No," Tulkh said, "you don't." He shook his head. "But you will."

Zo tried to speak, but all that came out was a croak.

Tulkh stared at her from the other end of the spear, the inarticulate ultimatum communicating more than words ever could.

A moment later she stepped through the gateway.

11/Mind Eraser, No Chaser

"Rojo Trace, welcome to Marfa. I'm Niles Emmert. We were told you were coming."

The silver-haired agricultural-lab attendant stood with his hand extended. Trace paused just long enough to give it a perfunctory squeeze, his eyes already scanning the area, taking in everything at once as they walked across the landing bay. The ship he'd commandeered was a generic midsized star skiff, big enough for a crew of eight, small enough to escape scrutiny, retrofitted with ion engines and a Class One hyperdrive for long-range travel. He traveled alone.

"I want to see the research level."

"Of course." Emmert nodded. "The incubation chamber is on B-Seven. That's where your sister took care of the orchid."

The lift was waiting. Ten minutes later Emmert guided him between the rows of plants and vegetation, heading for the chamber's air lock. The panel hung open, and Trace looked in at the broken electronics equipment inside, squatting down to place both hands directly on the dirty, scratched surface of the chamber floor.

"As far as we can tell," Emmert said, "Hestizo was—"

Trace cut him off with a gesture, not bothering to glance up. A flurry of activity surged through him: he heard Zo's voice, and saw the face of her attacker—it was a Whiphid, he realized, the biggest one he'd ever seen—yanking her and the orchid out of the chamber. Trace felt his sister's surprise blurring into pain as the blunt end of the Whiphid's spear slammed her in the head. He felt the blinding impact as she jerked back, slumping unconscious to the floor, the flower tumbling from her grasp. The Whiphid bent down, hoisting her over his shoulder and grabbing the orchid at the same time before he turned and lumbered away.

"He came for the flower," Trace said.

Emmert nodded. "The Murakami orchid is renowned for its Force abilities. It possesses power, but it requires a keeper, someone with an equally high midi-chlorian count, to keep it fully alive."

"Was there anyone else in this part of the facility at the time?"

"Just Wall Bennis, the lab director."

"Is he still—"

"Unconscious," Emmert replied, "in the bacta tank. Our physicians estimate he'll be awake in a day or so."

"We can't wait that long," Trace said. "What about surveillance in the loading and landing facility?"

"Our sensors recorded the arrival and departure of an unlicensed ship early this morning." Emmert glanced away, abashed. "It must have come in under some kind of cloaking device and managed to evade our detection . . . but we went back to the morning's footage and found this."

He reached into the pocket of his lab smock and pulled out a datapad, thumbing it awake. Trace looked at the screen. It showed a shot of the main hangar below, centering on an oblong vessel that looked as if it had been grafted together from scrap. Despite its ungainly shape, or perhaps because of it, the ship had a canting, rough-hewn meanness, a crude bulk that defied anyone to get too close, for fear of whatever might have been waiting inside. There was a series of partially worn numbers and letters on the side of the hull.

"Can you enhance this image?" Trace said.

Emmert pressed another button, magnifying the picture until Trace could read the name on the side: MIROCAW.

"We haven't been able to fully identify the call letters yet."

"That's because they've been scraped off just enough to make them illegible. It's an old smuggler's trick." Trace frowned a little. "You said it got through using some kind of cloaking device?"

Emmert nodded. "Yes, but . . ."

"What's that?" Trace pointed at the screen, at a series of pale bluish green discolorations along the *Mirocaw*'s portside. The marks had an oddly phosphorescent glossiness, almost as if that portion of the ship's outer plating had been streaked with a layer of iridescent oil.

"Carbon scoring?"

"No." The Jedi Knight shook his head. "That's Thulian vapor residue—it's a galactic anomaly, a mixture of post-industrial airborne pollution and crystal fog. You only find it in about three places outside the Mid Rim."

Emmert gave him a blank look.

"Have my ship ready," Trace said. "I'm leaving in five minutes."

Within the hour he'd confirmed his suspicion—the nearest Thulian cloud formations in existence cast a permanent shadow over Kwenn, a dreary post-industrial outpost along the outermost borders of Hutt space.

By day's end, Trace had landed there. The Kwenn Space Station was a polluted sprawl of docking bays, warehouses and repair facilities, cantinas, and unlicensed gambling parlors. Without drawing undue attention,

Trace walked through a dozen different establishments, talking to the pilots, fugitives, mechanics, and fringe dwellers that made up the station's population. He bought rounds of drinks, fighting his own impatience, and listened to long, seemingly pointless monologues from barflies who hadn't enjoyed such an attentive audience in years. In the end, it was a one-armed Bothan smuggler named Gree who told him what he'd needed to know—the former whereabouts of the *Mirocaw*'s owner, a Whiphid bounty hunter who went by the name Tulkh.

"Haven't seen him around in a while," Gree said, after Trace had bought him a series of drinks, including a local favorite called a Mind Eraser, and crossed his one remaining palm with a stack of credits. "Word is that he picked up a pretty sweet gig, nobody knows what."

Trace met the smuggler's gaze, holding it fast, feeling the Force flow through him into the Bothan's mind, completing the task that the liquor had already begun. "Did he say anything about a flower?"

"A . . ." Gree's face went smooth, all reluctance draining away from his voice so that the words came easily. "Yeah, that's right—he was going after a flower. Tulkh wasn't much of a talker, but we got liquored up one night and he started telling me about it."

"Who hired him?"

"A Sith Lord named Darth Scabrous."

Trace felt a sudden coldness pass through him. "Located where?"

"I don't know . . . a Sith academy . . . ?" Gree grimaced a little, struggling with the memory. "I want to say . . . Odacer-Faustin?" He blinked. "Hey, you think I could get another drink?"

But Trace was already gone.

12/Ingredient

STEPPING OUT OF THE TURBOLIFT, ZO FELT HER HOPE dwindling away.

Escape was no longer an option, if it ever had been. The Whiphid had led her through the ruins of the academy, passing a few Sith students and Masters who had stared openly at them, their faces darkened with anger and determination. If the orchid registered any of this, it said nothing.

It was midafternoon when they reached the tower.

An HK droid had met them at the entryway. It confirmed Tulkh's identity with a retinal scan that left the Whiphid blinking and wiping his eyes in annoyance, and escorted them through. The turbolift had sucked them upward and dispensed them here.

Into this room.

For a moment Zo could only stare at it. A laboratory like nothing she'd ever encountered in years of research sprawled out to fill the space in front of her. She could hear small things shifting and moving in the corners. It seemed, in some horrible way, to be an insidious dark analogue of the plant lab on Marfa, its instruments designed not to foster life but to inflict and sustain dosages of pain on whatever might still be alive here. There was something rustling in a cage in the shadows, making little smacking noises with its mouth.

"Do you have it?"

With an involuntary breath of surprise, Zo turned and looked back. In the center of the lab, a tall man in a dark robe stood watching them, his face a chiseled amalgam of shadow and bone, the cheek structure cruelly sharp, the hollows of his eyes like the sockets of a skull. Zo felt a thin wire of fear probe downward through her chest and into the pit of her stomach, where it dangled, twitching in the darkness. She thought of the name that Tulkh had mentioned on their way here: *Darth Scabrous*.

The Sith Lord was staring at her, his expression inscrutable, although the raw intensity in his stare was unmistakable. It was as if he was looking at something that he wanted simultaneously to possess and to destroy.

Without a word, the Whiphid took the orchid from Zo's hand. He walked over to where the Sith Lord stood and held the flower out to him.

"This is it."

Darth Scabrous took the flower, giving it only the most cursory of glances before returning his attention to Zo. There was a glimmer in his eyes that hadn't been there before.

Tulkh stood waiting. "My money," he said.

If the Sith Lord heard him, he showed no sign. He was still staring at Zo.

"Her name's Hestizo Trace," the Whiphid said. "She's the orchid's keeper. It needs her to—"

"Survive," Scabrous said. "I know. That's how I knew you were bringing me the genuine article." He reached up and touched her face, his gloved hand cold against her cheek, like leather wrapped around an iron rod. "It was the one piece of information that I withheld about the orchid."

"Then our business here is finished," Tulkh said.

The Sith Lord nodded. "My droid will pay you on the way out."

The Whiphid nodded and walked away.

"No," Zo called out after him, watching him go, *"wait!"* She felt a steel band of panic tighten around her chest, pressing painfully inward, crowding out her breath. She heard his footfalls growing quieter down the long stone corridor, then the faint hydraulic *whoosh* as the lift doors opened and shut again.

Then he was gone.

The Sith Lord was still looking at her. A new silence spread out, seeming to fill the lab with a stinging mist of cold, dry air. Zo was aware of the orchid making anxious noises inside her mind, a soft, irregular click of nervous energy awakening to what might happen next. Although she knew she was the only one who could hear the sounds, she still felt an irrational impulse to hush it.

"You are a Jedi," Scabrous said.

"I am." She braced herself for his contempt, even rage, but the Sith Lord simply nodded as if he'd expected nothing less than her appearance here—had, in fact, anticipated it. He reached out with one hand, not quite touching her, and she felt a certain heaviness underneath her left breast, as if his palm were pushing directly against the muscle of her heart.

Then he lowered his hand, and the pressure disappeared. He picked up the flower and carried it across the laboratory to the place where Zo had heard the soft lip-smacking noises.

What she saw inside made her stomach do a slow, nauseated barrel roll. The teenage boy in the cage was staring up at her with bright, unblinking shoe-button eyes that bespoke nothing less than utter madness. On closer examination Zo saw a vine-like tangle of plastic tubes sprouting directly out from the young man's back, where they seemed to have been implanted into his spine and the base of his skull. Thick yellowish red fluid crept sluggishly back and forth through the tubing. Zo followed the lines across the floor to where they connected to an electronic pump with a large glass cylinder on top. A ghastly kind of circuit had been created here, she realized, a hybrid between human and machine.

Scabrous made an adjustment to the pump. The fluid in the tubes moved faster. The boy went rigid and then began pounding his face against the cage, over and over, with a terrible kind of rhythmic intensity. The cage clanged with the crash of impact until the boy's face began to ooze blood, trickling scarlet from his nostrils and lips and the corners of his eyes. Still the boy did not stop. He was beating himself senseless, Zo realized, trying to knock himself unconscious or perhaps simply to kill himself, ending whatever torment was yet to come.

"Stop!" Zo stared back at Scabrous. "What *is* this?"

"Watch and see."

"What are you doing to him?"

Scabrous didn't answer. A moment later he opened the top of the cylinder of reddish yellow fluid and dropped the orchid inside.

Jura Ostrogoth witnessed the whole thing.

He'd slipped inside the tower when the Whiphid had stepped out, not giving himself time to deliberate. Experience had taught him that such opportunities ought not to be wasted. And so he had gone.

Ever since Nickter's disappearance the previous day, the academy's rumor mill had been humming along at lightspeed about Darth Scabrous and what might be going on up in his lab. Earlier this morning, Jura had overheard Pergus Frode, a technician at the academy's hangar, telling one of the other Masters that Scabrous had had visitors—two bounty hunters—who hadn't returned to their ship last night. And now Kindra had told Jura that she'd seen two more offworlders, a Whiphid and a girl, heading into the tower. They were carrying something with them, Kindra said. Nobody knew what.

It was only a matter of time until someone came out.

After lightsaber training, Jura had gone off by himself and crouched down underneath the snow-encrusted stones of a half-collapsed ruin facing the tower's main entrance. The cold hadn't bothered him in the least. It had given him time to think, to clear his head. He had already decided that he wasn't going to spend his life worrying about being exposed by Scopique. If he was going to escape from underneath Scopique's thumb, he needed to change the game. Of course he couldn't counterattack now—having just cornered him, Scopique would be expecting retribution—but once Jura found out what was happening inside the tower, he decided, he would arrange a private meeting with the Zabrak. He would tell Scopique everything, confide in him. Gain his trust. And when Scopique was off guard, gloating, Jura would . . . what?

Kill him?

Maybe.

Or perhaps just humiliate him, the way that Scopique had humiliated Jura.

In any case, things were about to be *very* different.

How different, Jura could never have guessed twenty minutes earlier, as he had slipped out of the turbolift and made his way across the open laboratory at the top of the tower. Candles and torches dotted the room with flickering, intermittent light. He'd been worried that he might be heard—the lift was hardly silent—but even before the doors opened, he'd heard someone screaming and a metallic crashing noise. The sound bounced off the windows and stone ceiling, blocking out everything else.

Jura slunk through pools of shadow, making his way

between the clusters of equipment until he could make out the unmistakable shape of Lord Scabrous and some-one else, a girl, standing next to what looked like a caged animal: the source of the crashing and the screaming.

Jura stopped again, narrowed his eyes, looked more closely.

The caged animal was Nickter.

Nickter was thrashing in his little prison, shrieking and writhing and blubbering out noises that sounded only slightly like words. There was blood running down his face, sticking and clinging to his cheeks, as if he'd been sitting under a melting red candle. He was half naked, his exposed torso gleaming with sweat.

But the worst were the tubes.

They ran directly out of his back, long, pipelike con-duits from his spine leading to a machine with a large transparent cylinder mounted on top. Scabrous was doing something to the machine, holding up some object that Jura couldn't identify, putting it inside the cylinder. The fluid inside it began roiling, changed color, became sud-denly, remarkably incandescent, pulsing through the tubes into Nickter's vertebrae.

The screaming stopped.

Jura watched Nickter collapse to the floor of the cage, motionless and silent, mouth half open, eyelids sagging. Now the only sound was the high, steady drone of a heart monitor in flatline. Jura let out the breath that he'd been holding in his lungs for the last ten seconds.

He didn't need to get any closer to see that Wim Nick-ter was dead.

Zo stared at the dead Sith student in the cage. His eyes were still open, glassy and lifeless. His mouth sagged, a bloody spit bubble clinging to the corner. A waxy pallor had already begun to spread over his cheeks, turning his skin a pale shade of gray.

In her mind, the orchid was still screaming.

She couldn't move, couldn't think. Nothing in her experience at the Marfa facility or before had prepared her for this. In the past forty-eight standard hours, the routines of her daily existence had become a blood-soaked travesty of reality.

Her eyes flashed up to the glass cylinder where Scabrous had dropped the flower. It wasn't there anymore—the fluid seemed to have absorbed it, dissolving it in chunks—but she could still hear it, wherever it had gone, whatever had happened to it, crying out, begging her to do something, to help it, to stop the pain.

Burning, Zo, it's burning, it's BURNING—

Scabrous was watching the cylinder.

In the cage, the dead boy sat up.

13/Dragon Teeth

▬▬▭▭▬▭▬

JURA NEVER SAW THE DOOR BLOW OFF THE CAGE.

It happened so quickly that the only thing his mind registered was the wire mesh flying across the lab, slamming into a vented power-cell housing that protruded down from the ceiling. Metal struck metal with a flat, declarative clang that reminded him somehow of the sound of training blades clashing at the top of the temple. It was a noise that said: *Things have been put into motion, and whatever happens next, there will be no going back.*

From his hiding place, Jura stared, crouched in the shadows as if welded to the spot. He saw Scabrous and the girl staring at the cage, neither one of them moving.

The thing that crawled out of the cage wasn't Wim Nickter.

It was draped in Nickter's skin, yes, and it wore some version of Nickter's face, but the eyes were ovals of smeared glass behind which pupils darted back and forth in the torchlight, like tiny black insects trapped inside a dirty bottle. It cranked its head to the right, and the yellow grin that wrinkled its lips back was unlike anything Jura had ever seen. Watching it, he felt himself melting inside, a breathless terror invading him, stripping away strength, reducing him to a shuddering pool of nerves. The intuitive voice of the Force was shouting at him now, *Wrong, wrong, wrong,* but he couldn't seem to move.

The Sith Lord gazed upon his creation. A terrible, prescient smile crept across his face.

"Nickter," he said. "Come to me."

The thing shuffled another step forward, and Scabrous held out one hand, beckoning it forth like an animal.

"Yes. That's right."

All at once Nickter sprang forward with an entirely different kind of urgency, the tubes ripping out of its back, flailing free, leaving a row of raw-looking open wounds down its spine. Reddish yellow stuff splashed and spewed from the open tubes, spraying out into the air. From his hiding place, Jura saw the Sith Lord rear backward, his arms in front of his face, as the thing that had once been Wim Nickter landed on top of him and without hesitation sank its teeth into Scabrous's face.

Scabrous swung one arm upward, and the thing flew back across the lab, its body reduced to a momentary blur, flailing into a tall rack of unused flasks and beakers not far from where Jura was still crouched. The rack exploded in a deafening cacophony of shattered glass, the thing tumbling over the floor, and Jura saw it push itself upright, its cheeks and forehead glittering with broken shards like dragon teeth. Astringent smells of alcohol and ammonia and carbolic acid filled the air.

Jura saw the girl stand up and run for the turbolift. She never looked back, not even as the doors sealed shut behind her.

A roar of fury shook the chamber around him, loud enough that Jura felt it reverberating in the hollow of his chest. On the opposite side of the lab, Scabrous rose up. The right half of his face hung down in a pale bloody flap. Above it, his eyes coruscated with anger so ferocious that it looked like something entirely different, something dangerously close to madness.

The Sith Lord flung out his right hand, palm raised, in the direction of Nickter's corpse. The corpse jerked back again, tumbling like a thing on wires, and this time Jura Ostrogoth realized that he was the one crouched directly in its path.

The realization came too late to save him. Nickter's corpse collided with him, knocking him off his feet and pounding the air out of his lungs, hurling both of them backward into one of the wide curved viewports that formed the tower's wall. Jura's final impression—that the entire world was bursting apart around him in a brittle, deafening explosion—was not altogether wrong.

Then he fell.

14/Dropouts

"Lussk."

Rance Lussk stopped walking, paused a moment, and turned around. He had been on his way to the academy's library for an afternoon of solitary meditation and study when the voice piped up behind him.

It was Ra'at.

The smaller, wiry-framed apprentice stood with both hands behind his back, gazing at him defiantly through the veil of falling snow. He looked radically different from the last time Lussk had seen him—something changed in his posture, his bearing, the way he held his shoulders. Even his voice was bolder, more direct and confrontational. His eyes were polished stones, filled with a new and willful sense of determination.

"What do you want?"

"You weren't at lightsaber practice this morning."

Lussk didn't even bother to shrug, communicating his indifference solely through lack of expression. Everyone at the academy knew that he only attended training sessions when he felt like it, when he wanted to test himself or prove a point to one of the Masters. He took a step closer to Ra'at. They were alone here behind the library's immense sprawl, the academy's Masters and students otherwise engaged in training or the rigors of midday study. Above them, the tower stood, its shadow banded across the walkway like premature twilight, and it occurred to Lussk that this, too, might have been deliberate on Ra'at's part. Perhaps he had hoped Lord Scabrous might happen to be looking down.

"Well, what is it?"

Ra'at brought his hands out from behind his back, revealing what Lussk had already guessed would be there: a pair of training lightsabers glinting in the gray afternoon light.

"Does Blademaster Shak'Weth know that you ran off with two of his toys?" Lussk asked.

Ra'at didn't smile; the intensity of his expression never wavered. "I challenge you."

Cocking an incredulous eyebrow, Lussk asked, "Now?"

"*Now.*"

For an instant, certainly no longer, Lussk almost considered it. Then he shook his head. "You don't want to do that."

"What are you afraid of?"

"From you?" Lussk blinked lackadaisically. "Boredom, for a start."

"Then I'll be sure not to bore you," Ra'at said, and tossed one of the blades in Lussk's direction. Lussk caught it on reflex but lowered it to his side.

"I'm busy right now," he said. "If you're determined to humiliate yourself, you'll have to do it publicly in front of the—"

Masters, had been the last word of that sentence, but Lussk didn't get a chance to say it before Ra'at jumped at him, his feet hardly seeming to touch the ground. As opening salvos went, it was brutal but effective, a move whose grace would have been easier to admire if it hadn't ended with Ra'at's blade thwacking him across the chest, raising a hot streak of pain just below his collarbone.

Lussk spun back, blade up, aware now that he was in

this whether he wanted to be or not. And with Ra'at, he realized, it wouldn't be as simple as flattening him—an example would need to be made, or else every student would be out here trying him. More than anything, Lussk felt a kind of exasperation. Hadn't Nickter been enough of a lesson? Was Ra'at suicidal, or simply insane?

He dived forward with his own blade, tensed for impact, but Ra'at wasn't where he'd been just a second before, seeming almost to have vanished in a cloud of snow. Lussk looked up. The other apprentice was somersaulting directly over him, spiraling down, and Lussk's instincts flung him out of the way a split second before Ra'at landed.

"Your Ataru has improved," Lussk grunted. "You've been practicing." Pivoting hard, he brought his own blade around where he predicted Ra'at would be, and this time he was right. When Ra'at looked up, he found himself facing the tip of Lussk's blade. One stroke would finish the duel; two would kill him.

But there was another option.

"Now," Lussk said, meeting the other apprentice's stare and letting the Force flow through him like an electric current. "Drop your blade."

Ra'at held his mouth taut until the tendon stood out in his jaw. His arm quivered, but he didn't release the blade.

"Drop your blade," Lussk repeated.

Still Ra'at didn't move. Lussk felt real anger taking hold of him, the kind of rage he rarely experienced. Without hesitation he thrust his own blade at his opponent. If Ra'at was so determined to die like this, out here behind the library, then Lussk would oblige him.

As he swung forward, he heard a window shatter overhead.

Looking up, he saw something explode out of the top of the tower, momentarily arrayed in a glinting halo of broken glass. At first Lussk thought it was some kind of alien species—it had too many arms and legs—and then he realized he was actually seeing two people, one wrapped around the other.

The drop from the tower had to be a hundred meters or more. They fell together, twisting in midair, plummeting downward, slamming into the rocky, snow-covered walkway with a sickening, meaty crunch.

Despite his reputation for toughness, Lussk had to look away. Gravity had made a meal of the corpses, contorting them into unfamiliar shapes. Broken bones punctured the flesh. One of them—a shirtless, blood-smeared sack of leaking viscera—lay at such an angle that Lussk could see its right eye protruding from the socket.

Then it sat up.

Lussk gaped at it, paralyzed by a dozy wave of perfect awe. *That's impossible,* he thought. *Nobody survives a fall like that. Nobody—*

His thought, whatever was left of it, broke off cleanly. The blood-smeared one was looking straight at him with its one good eye, a savage, inhuman smirk swimming over what remained of its face. Besides knocking the eye out, the fall had done something to its spine and shoulders, wrenched them around sideways, jamming the clavicles outward, shoving the bone of his arm up through the skin. It looked like a suit of flesh-colored clothes that had been recklessly draped on its hanger.

Yet it was still moving.

Its broken arms grabbed the other corpse, scooping it up in one flopping, eager gesture, and raked it toward its mouth, and that was when Lussk realized that behind the broken bones and layers of blood, he was looking at the mangled bodies of Wim Nickter and Jura Ostrogoth.

The thing that had been Nickter bobbed its head and buried its teeth in the pulpy remains of Ostrogoth's face. Almost immediately Lussk could hear the noises, a series of greedy, slobbering grunts. Ostrogoth—what was left of him—made no move to resist.

"What is *that*?" Ra'at's voice was murmuring behind him. "*What is that thing?*"

Lussk shook his head, stepping back. He had no idea what he'd just seen—this would all take time to process, to decide how he was going to fight it or use it to his own advantage—but for the moment, he'd take it on its own terms.

"You figure it out." Tossing his blade aside, Lussk turned on Ra'at and grabbed the smaller apprentice by the tunic with both hands, yanking him forward hard enough to snap Ra'at's teeth together like castanets. Ra'at's shock had left him vulnerable, an easy target. Ra'at's own blade slipped from his hand, clanking off rocks before it stuck in the new-fallen snow.

"Wait, what are you doing?" Ra'at asked. "You can't—"

Lussk spun him around and shoved him backward, as hard as possible, in the direction of the slobbering, eating thing that was crouched over Jura Ostrogoth. Ra'at squealed, arms pinwheeling as if something in the air could hold him up. Almost immediately his feet tangled beneath him and he stumbled, staggered, slid, and finally fell, landing first on his knees, then on his back.

The Nickter-thing lifted its head. Fresh blood drizzled from its jaw, dripping off its lips. Its one functional eye shivered like a raw egg in a cup. It thrust Jura's corpse aside and devoted its full attention to Ra'at with the appetite of a creature being offered live meat.

"No," Ra'at was saying, scrambling upward, or trying to. "No, *no*—"

Lussk turned away, legs already tensed to run. The last thing he heard, the moment before he bolted into the library, was Ra'at's scream.

15/Triage

▬▬▬:▬▬▬:▬▬

I<small>T TOOK</small> S<small>CABROUS LESS THAN THIRTY SECONDS TO FLUSH</small> the wound on his face with saline, start an IV on himself, and activate the auto-diagnosis cuff. Everything was exactly where he'd left it. He worked steadily, without the slightest hesitation, the swift and practiced smoothness of his movements betraying none of the anger that sat in his chest like a scalding red lump of coal.

There was a faint electronic beep from his right wrist, denoting the thirty-second mark. He checked the cuff's glowing blue readout and saw that it was still calibrating the initial blood sample.

Meanwhile, the girl—the Jedi scum—was already gone.

Scabrous hadn't seen her leave, but he'd known, of course, that she would try to flee the second she got the chance. That was a given. No matter—the orchid had done its job, and there would be plenty of time to catch up with the Jedi later. She would serve her purpose well enough when the time came.

At the moment he had more pressing matters to attend to. He continued working, holding his emotions carefully in check. Critical thinking was what had gotten him this far with the project; his mind was an engine of clinical detachment and he had an absolute unwavering commitment to do whatever was necessary to make the experiment a success. The emotions that fueled that engine—ambition, boundless rage, a natural depraved indifference toward anything except himself—lay carefully insulated in the dark vessels of his heart, where they would not be permitted to distract him from his goal.

And yet, all the same, he hated her.

Hated her with the brutal, grinding hate of the entire Sith war machine; hated her with the blazing intensity of ten thousand dying suns—this Jedi, whose orchid was the linchpin upon which everything would revolve, and whose very presence here would allow him to see the project through to fruition.

And it was *good* to know that hate was there, where he could access it whenever he wanted, like a fine wine to be decanted and sipped sparingly. It would be good to find her and to—

Well, to finish things.

Hestizo Trace would die screaming.

And he would live forever.

Beep! The one-minute mark. Scabrous flicked his eyes down to the auto-analysis unit. The blue numbers pulsed red. He frowned, just a little. Initial contamination levels were higher than expected: peaks and waves that the system was already rediagnosing, in order to isolate the specific antigen and lay the groundwork for the next step.

He couldn't afford to wait any longer. The hemodialysis pump was portable by design, a flat shoulder pack that held six liters of fresh blood and a vacuum tube system. Sliding the straps over his shoulders, Scabrous attached the pump to the IV in his right arm and started the first infusion. A steady feeling of warmth crept up through his arm, filling his chest, loosening the tension, allowing him to breathe more deeply. He set the counters. At the current rate, the blood supply would last him six hours—assuming things didn't change dramatically in the meantime.

Scabrous bypassed the turbolift, crossing directly toward the shattered window, casting his gaze out at the broken, snow-stricken terrain spreading out into the horizon. A feeling of confidence stirred within him, bringing with it a renewed sense of purpose. This was his academy, his planet—nobody knew it as well as he did. There was nowhere that the Jedi could hide that he could not find her.

Without a moment's hesitation, he sprang forward and jumped out the broken viewport. He cleared it easily, plunging out into the night, knifing downward through the air, using the Force to guide his descent a hundred meters down. At the base of the tower, he hit the ground running. His mind was humming now, his body inhaling doses of fresh blood, sucking it down like pure oxygen, feeding muscle and brain.

Activating his comlink, he brought it to his ear and waited for the voice on the other end to respond.

"Query: Yes, my Lord?" the HK droid asked.

"Activate all outer perimeter barriers in all quadrants," Scabrous told it. "Target is Hestizo Trace, the Jedi. Scan the lab for DNA and pheromone sample." He paused, but only for a second, the wind blasting over him. "Use whatever means necessary. But I want her alive."

16/Convocation

HESTIZO?

Zo was still running when the orchid's voice rang through her head. It was enough of a surprise that she faltered, almost halting in her tracks.

She hadn't stopped moving since she'd left the tower's turbolift. Whether that was ten minutes ago or half an hour, she didn't know. Time had become wildly subjective, a crazed and illogical sprawl, much like the landscape of the academy itself. Sprinting down between the gray, partially collapsed buildings and ruined temples, she'd focused on putting as much distance as possible between herself and the tower, but every time she looked back, the tower seemed to be in a different place.

Her head was swimming. She tried not to think about what had happened up there, but those thoughts kept seeping through her defenses like a cut that wouldn't stop bleeding. She saw the face of the boy—was it a boy?—as he'd crawled out of the cage and jumped at Scabrous, the way he'd smelled, the noise that he'd made. He'd been like an animal, but far worse.

Hestizo, the orchid's voice cut in, *stop. Stay. Crouch.*

Zo looked around. She was standing in front of an enormous statue of some ancient Sith Lord that had fallen over on its side, so that the right half of its features had been worn smooth, abraded by decades of wind and snow. Sinking to her knees, she heard other voices—several of them—talking among themselves from the far side of the monument.

She peered over.

A group of students was making their way down a walkway, twenty meters in front of her. An older man, a Master, she presumed, strode in front of them. His long gray hair was pulled back from his face in a single silver braid, accentuating the angular, hawk-like structure of his nose and forehead. The late-afternoon light threw his shadow straight ahead across the crisp, freshly fallen snow, the black outline of his robe making it look as though he had wings.

How many? the orchid murmured in her mind. *How many, Hestizo?*

She counted twelve, eighteen, twenty-four, and then looked again, across a hillock of rock and ice, where a second, much larger group of students had gathered with two or three other Masters in attendance, the group too large to count. Apparently some kind of outdoor assembly or group meditation was in progress. For a moment Zo just watched. Despite the fact that they walked together, some of them even talking among themselves in low voices, she had never seen a group of individuals so utterly detached from one another. When they exchanged glances, she saw only coldness in their eyes, as if they were sizing one another up, trying to find some advantage over the others.

"Attention." The Master's voice was flinty and sharp, one hand upheld. "Silence."

The students down on the other side of the walkway fell silent, many of them drawing in closer to listen.

"For those of you who just arrived, I will explain this only once." The words were strident, rising up effortlessly over the windy terrain. "Although in truth, I shouldn't have to explain it at all. Your own Force sensitivity ought to be sufficient for you to realize that we're dealing with an unforeseen development at the academy—a chain of events that, at this point, is still unclear." He squared his shoulders and faced the group. "Most of you have already detected a disturbance in the normal daily routine. At this point, we suspect that the academy has been targeted by some form of sabotage, and that it may have spread outward from the tower."

Despite herself, Zo found herself listening, and as she did, she realized that the group of students had grown. Now there appeared to be several hundred of them, perhaps the majority of the entire student body, all looking up in the Master's direction.

"As a precaution, we are suspending all lessons and drills until further notice. Evening meal will be served as usual. Otherwise you are to return to your dorms for private study and await further instructions. One of the Masters will be in contact when our course of action changes."

Zo realized as she listened that she could hear a slight but unmistakable tremor of concern in the Master's tone. He was doing everything he could to cover it up, and perhaps the students were fooled, but to her mind he might as well have been wearing a placard: I'M DOING MY BEST TO SPIN A SITUATION THAT I HAVE ABSOLUTELY NO ABILITY TO COMPREHEND, LET ALONE CONTROL, AND—

Hestizo! The orchid's voice was urgent, alarmed. *Get down, now!*

She turned her head to the right, and realized that one of the students at the edge of the group was staring straight at her.

The student's name was Ranlaw. Like the rest of his classmates, he'd been feeling increasingly jumpy this entire afternoon, and he didn't know precisely why—it had affected his sparring performance earlier, and he was still angry about the black eye it had cost him. But something had gone wrong here at the academy. The Force was telling him to watch his back, and the Masters' calling them to convocation only affirmed it.

When he saw the girl looking at him from behind the statue, he'd stopped walking and gazed back at her, sensing that she had something to do with it.

She's a Jedi.

That realization was all it took. Ranlaw felt a bright spark of violence leap up in his chest. Whatever purpose the Jedi girl had for spying on them, he'd drag her to the Masters himself, and they could beat it out of her.

The rest of the group was listening to Master Traan, no one noticing that Ranlaw had been looking the other way. That was fine with Ranlaw, who fully intended to get all the glory of this discovery. In a single leap he sprang up over the fallen statue, tackling the girl and throwing her to the ground, pinning her by her wrists. She was easy prey—almost too easy.

"What's your business here, Jedi?"

She glared up at him, breathless and furious. "Let me go."

"Right." Taking one hand off her wrist, he grabbed her hair and jerked her upright. "Let's see what the Masters have to say about you." Ranlaw rose to his feet, dragging her with him, and took in a breath to call down to the others.

He was still in the process of inhaling when a clawed hand clamped down over his lips, silencing him. Ranlaw tried to squirm free, and the back of a wooden spear slammed across the top of his skull with a sharp crack, dropping him sideways.

Zo saw the Sith student tumble forward, his grip falling slack, releasing her hair as he fell. In the place where he'd been hunched over, she saw a great three-fingered hand gripping her shoulder and forcing her back down out of sight, and she realized that she was looking at Tulkh. His shoulders were arched enough that she could see the quiver of arrows strapped to his back.

Spinning the spear easily around, the Whiphid raised the business end again, swung it around, and thrust its point directly in Zo's face, close enough that she could feel it pressing against her cheek. All of this was accomplished in absolute silence.

"What are you doing?"

Tulkh didn't budge. His expression was stone. "There's something I need to show you."

"I don't—"

"*Move.*"

THE LIBRARY WAS SILENT.

To her knowledge, Kindra was the only student in the academy who came here on any kind of a regular basis. Without exception, it was the largest and oldest structure on Odacer-Faustin, predating the tower itself, which also meant that it was in the worst condition. Centuries of hostile weather and shifting planetary tectonics had savaged its stacks, closing off entire chambers, stairways, and corridors under tons of snow and ice. From within, it resembled nothing so much as a grand monument that had suffered a head-on collision with something even bigger than itself, crumpling it badly at both ends and the middle.

She sat in the southwest wing, at one of the long stone tables under the cracked cathedral ceiling, staring at the most recent sections of Sith scrolls that she'd uncovered. The inscriptions were archaic, and she'd been working most of the afternoon on translating them. The process was slow but gratifying—yielding ancient secrets that she knew would only help her advance faster through the ranks of her fellow students. There were rumors that Darth Scabrous himself had come here, that he had found something, a relic of almost immeasurable power, hidden in one of the secluded rooms. Whether that was true—an object like a Sith Holocron wasn't outside the realm of possibility—Kindra had already found enough to make her research here worthwhile.

She paused, her index finger marking a spot halfway through a long intaglio of etchings, and cocked her head slightly.

Something was wrong.

It wasn't as obvious as a noise or even a vibration; more like an intuitive sensation of disquiet that settled into her stomach and emanated out through her chest, as if millions of tiny cilia had extended from within her, shivering with unease.

She stood up, the scrolls forgotten.

"Who's there?"

Her voice rang out in the emptiness, hollow and fading into silence. There was no reply, and a moment later she realized that she hadn't truly expected one. It wasn't that kind of feeling; it was more abstract, like a suddenly remembered nightmare whose full contents she couldn't quite summon up.

What is that? What's happening?

She drew a shaky breath, not comprehending this inexplicable mutiny of her nervous system. Studying to be a Sith warrior was about engendering fear in others, not oneself—yet her palms had begun to sweat and her heart was beating twice as hard as it normally did. All at once she wanted to be out of here, in less confined quarters. She looked back at the tall staircase leading upward to the gallery and the concourse beyond it, the one that would lead her out.

She stuffed her notes into her bag, grabbed her cloak, and turned to go.

From above her, the broken ceiling let out a long creaking noise, and when she looked up she saw one of the cracks splitting wider.

"Who is it?" she said, louder. "Who's there?"

Now the chasms had spread open enough that she could see something stretching out inside them, uncoiling in the ceiling's depths to expose a series of long, clutching branches. They forked downward, snake-like, showering bits of grit and rock as they insinuated farther through open space. A moment later, Kindra saw the great wooden face of the librarian, a Neti, staring down at her.

"Dail'Liss." She swallowed, managing to find her voice. "What do you want?"

"Something unsettling you, Kindra?" His voice was thick and raspy. "Some uncertainty of the mind, yes?"

"No."

The librarian didn't respond, just continued to slither his branches downward until the great bulk of his trunk dangled upside down in front of her, the warty, centuries-old eyes narrowing with myopic consideration. Dail'Liss had been the curator of the library for as long as anyone could remember, perhaps going back a thousand years or more. Although his elaborate root system was permanently embedded somewhere deep in the foundation, a seemingly endless network of branches and limbs allowed him to slide unimpeded through its walls and hollows. Ironically, it was this constant writhing and squirming that undermined the infrastructure of the building itself. Rumor was that it would only be a matter of time before the Neti brought the library down on top of him, sealing himself forever amid his own precious holdings—a fitting enough end, when Kindra thought about it.

"Feel it, too, I do," he said at last. "Yes, yes." Except that his strange accent made the words come out like *jess, jess.*

"I didn't say—"

A branch grazed down past her face, fussing over the pile of scrolls, straightening and brushing off the ones that she'd left out. "Didn't have to say anything. Written all over your face, yes?"

"I don't know what you're talking about."

"Talking about the Sickness, out there in the wind."

That brought her up short. "What?"

"In the wind," the Neti repeated. "Disease. Taste it. Feel it. Don't you?"

Kindra didn't want to linger here—a long, cryptic conversation with a tree was the last thing she was interested in at the moment—but she realized the Neti had perfectly encapsulated her own feeling of unease.

There *was* a sickness in the wind, some type of disease, and she could feel it. Under such circumstances, the direct approach seemed best.

"Do you know what it is?" she asked.

"Ought not to venture out," the Neti said, his branches clutching at the scrolls, beginning to roll them up with slow, deliberate movements. "Safer here, *jess*?"

"If there's trouble, I can handle it."

"Not this kind, no, don't think so."

"Look." Kindra shook her head, increasingly irritated by the librarian's evasiveness. "Either you have answers for me or you don't. Either way I'm not going to stay in here and hide."

"Best course of action, I would say."

She pointed at the scrolls. "Leave those out for me. I'll be back for them later. Understand?"

"I think it is you, Kindra, who does not understand."

She shook her head. "Whatever."

The Neti didn't argue, didn't say a word, only gazed upon her with his sorrowful wooden stare as she mounted the steps and headed out.

18/Just Another Day in Paradise

RA'AT OPENED HIS EYES SLOWLY, AS IF AFRAID OF WHAT HE might find. He didn't know how long he'd been sprawled out here unconscious at the bottom of the rock pile under the tower, but it was almost dark now, so several hours might have passed. A fine layer of snow had accumulated in the folds of his clothes.

He was so cold that he almost couldn't feel it anymore, although the pain might have had something to do with that. His right arm throbbed terribly, just below the shoulder. Touching it, running his hand under the torn sleeve, he drew back with a hiss. Live wires of raw tendon seared and shivered just beneath the skin.

He probed again, more gingerly. The gash was deep, almost to the bone. He tried to lift his arm and discovered that it was virtually useless. The left one worked better, but his entire right side ached so badly when he moved that it wouldn't do him much good in a fight. Almost as bad, he had a sick disequilibrium in his stomach, like a heavy sandbag swinging back and forth at the end of a rope: due to a concussion, maybe. He wondered how hard he'd smacked his head when he'd fallen.

In an attempt to get reoriented, he cast his mind back to what had happened. The details of the attack rose reluctantly into his memory, like debris bobbing up from an underwater explosion, and after a moment he recalled it in detail, the thing that had fallen from the tower: the thing that had once been Wim Nickter. The other corpse, Jura Ostrogoth, was nowhere to be found. Ra'at wondered now with a sickish curiosity if maybe the Nickter-thing might have eaten it.

Whatever the case, he had never fought anything like Nickter's corpse, its eye dead and flat but gleaming with fierce hunger, mouth open so wide that it had actually started splitting at the corners. In extremis, Ra'at's logical mind had bypassed the whole question of credibility. Disbelief wouldn't help him here; it would only slow him down, so he'd taken it at face value. Apparently, dead bodies were coming back to life, and this one wanted to eat him.

He remembered how the Nickter-thing had shrieked when it had first lunged at him, how he had reacted automatically, springing out of the way, using the same accentuated Force skills he'd been developing in Hracken's pain bunker. Up in the air, he'd grabbed hold of the overhanging rock slab of the structure behind him and swung himself on top of it, only then daring to look down.

Using the resourcefulness that he'd been taught as part of his training, Ra'at had grabbed the biggest chunk of loose stone that he could lift—it must have weighed as much as he did—and flung it over the edge. It was a direct hit, knocking the Nickter-thing back down to the ground, where it immediately shoved the stone away and started to climb again. If anything, it was clamoring up faster, driven forward by unmistakable appetite. Already Ra'at realized he couldn't stay up here indefinitely—he needed a better plan. Glancing around behind him, he'd spotted an even larger pile of rocks, the remains of a second level that had collapsed long before.

He'd worked quickly but carefully, piling the slabs up, scraping his fingers and knuckles along the way, until he had a tall, precarious stack that was staying upright only because he was holding on to it. Summoning the Force, Ra'at had focused it on the pile and removed his hands. The rocks teetered but did not fall. Looking around, he saw the Nickter-thing dragging itself up onto the overhang, its eye locked hungrily on Ra'at.

"Come on, then," Ra'at said, taking a single step away.

Nickter charged, and Ra'at let the stones fall, slamming down on the corpse's leg, just below the knee, pinning it there. The thing jerked and spasmed and screamed at him until Ra'at picked up another rock—using his hands again—and swung it down hard on Nickter's neck. There was a surprisingly loud and deeply satisfying crunch as its cervical spine shattered, and the thing went limp.

Taking no chances, Ra'at hoisted the rock a second time, intending to beat the thing's skull in with it, and that was when it jerked back to life, lashing out at him, hissing and screeching, coming within centimeters of biting his wrist. Jerking backward, Ra'at had lost his footing and plummeted backward off the overhang.

After that, everything had gone black.

Now, rubbing the back of his head, he wondered if the thing might still be up on top of the overhang, crouched in the dark, waiting for him. He had no intention of finding out. What he needed now, more than anything else, was a trip to the infirmary where he could get the cut on his arm cleaned and treated, and get his concussion checked out. A fleeting thought—

What if it's too late?

—shot through his mind, and Ra'at shoved it aside, determined now more than ever to keep his wits about him. He knew a little bit about medicine, knew that the odds of herniating one's brain from a simple closed head injury were very long. Anyway, he certainly hadn't spent years here training and working to die from something like this.

Clutching his arm, he began walking around the outer rim of the library's west wall. The pain wasn't as bad now as it had been just a few minutes earlier. Either his endorphins were kicking in, numbing the wound, or he was just getting used to it.

He walked past the library, occasionally glancing up at the tower, where the lights were on at the very top.

A scratching sound came from somewhere off to his right, and he stopped and held his breath.

"Whoever's there, come out where I can see you."

The figure stepped out, a dark-haired girl in an academy uniform—it was Kindra, he saw, one of the female students, maybe a year or two older than he was.

"Ra'at?" She frowned. "What happened to you?"

"I'm fine."

She took a step toward him. "You're covered in blood."

"It's not as bad as it looks."

"That cut on your arm—"

"Stay back."

"Whatever you say." Kindra's expression sharpened from bewilderment to active suspicion, but she didn't say anything, instead glancing right and left, head tilted, as if listening to the rest of the area. Ra'at found himself listening more actively, too. Within the last few moments, the darkness had thickened around them, taking on additional depth and dimension, and the thin haze of light that escaped from inside the cracks in the library's walls was hardly a sufficient remedy.

Ra'at's nauseated belly gave a queasy, volcanic shift, and this time it was followed by a moment of imbalance so sudden that he almost fell over. He had no idea whether Kindra noticed it or not, but he realized now that he could use her—at least until they got to the infirmary—as a kind of insurance policy. She wouldn't fight to defend him, but together they might stand a better chance against whatever was out there. He would just have to be careful not to reveal how weak he truly was, and that meant coming up with a cover story to explain his injury.

"I was . . . working out with Master Hracken," he said. "I guess things got a little out of control. I got my bell rung, that's all."

Kindra raised one eyebrow but still didn't respond. "Where is everybody?"

"Around." He shrugged, trying to act casual. "I don't know."

"You sure you're—"

"I'm fine," he repeated, "but Hracken told me that I should go to the infirmary and get checked out. You headed that way?"

She shook her head, seeming preoccupied. "I'm going back to the dorm." Craning her neck, she looked all the way up to the top of the tower, until Ra'at wondered if she might actually have seen the two bodies come spilling outward earlier, and was putting the pieces together about what had really happened to his arm and his head. But in the end, all she said was, "Something's wrong."

"Meaning what?"

"I've got a bad feeling."

It was an odd remark, he thought, uncharacteristically revealing, and not the sort of thing she'd ever shared with him before. They'd never really had any reason to talk. Immediately Ra'at suspected that she was trying to gain his trust, to make him let his guard down.

"About what?"

"I don't know—this night, everything. You feel it?"

"Nope." He shook his head, feigning an indifference

that he didn't even remotely feel. "Just another day in paradise, as far as I'm concerned."

She didn't smile, didn't even seem to hear him. When the wind blew the hair back from her face, Ra'at saw that the corners of her mouth were pinched in a grimace.

"What's wrong?"

"Whatever it is"—she still didn't look at him—"it's coming."

19/Header

ON THE OTHER SIDE OF THE ACADEMY, FRESH SNOW HAD begun drifting up outside the dormitory where Scopique had recently returned from his afternoon workout. The Zabrak had just finished his shower—it was his routine to wash up at this time of the day, when he had a rare moment of privacy—and was stepping out of the foggy stall with a towel wrapped around his waist, when he noticed a trail of blood across the floor.

He stopped and looked down at it. The blood hadn't been there a moment before, when he'd gotten into the shower. The splatters were fresh and bright, streaking across the floor in the direction of the bunks.

Scopique felt his defense mechanisms tensing, going into a state of vigilant readiness, his natural aggression already ramping up to the next level. Easing his way silently the rest of the way out of the shower, he dressed quickly in his uniform and followed the blood trail to the right. He could smell something now, the rancid odor of meat that had started to decay. It seemed to be growing worse with every second.

That was when he saw the body lying on his bunk.

It was dressed in a tattered academy uniform, its limbs and back contorted at unnatural angles so that the head lolled sideways from the obviously broken neck. Staring at it, Scopique murmured a whispered childhood curse in his native language. The possibility that this might be a trick, some kind of poorly conceived prank, never crossed his mind. Someone had beaten a Sith academy student to death and abandoned the corpse here on his bunk—as a warning or threat, he didn't know which.

He edged closer, hoping he might be able to recognize the victim from what remained of its face. There wasn't much left to identify. The skull was badly crushed, half the face swollen and purple, the other half grotesquely pancaked so that one corner of the mouth peeled upward in a hideous parody of a smile.

Scopique took another step, leaning forward, reaching down to turn the head over.

The corpse swung itself up and lunged at him.

It was Jura Ostrogoth.

Scopique sprang back, instincts taking over as the thing charged at him in a ragged, flopping blur. He flew across the dorm floor, then Force-leapt straight up, grabbing the ventilation fixture that hung five meters above the beds, legs dangling, using the vent's beveled surface for purchase while he scanned the room below for any kind of weapon.

Below, the corpse snarled and lunged at him, every leap taking it closer to where Scopique hung on. Thick ropy spit swung from the half-pulverized jaw. From above, the Zabrak thought he could actually see colonies of maggots squirming in the thing's lacerated scalp. No doubt about it: death had come for Jura Ostrogoth, but it hadn't finished the job.

The Zabrak stared down at the corpse, heart pounding, killing instincts fully engaged. On some level, from that first moment when he'd made the tape of Jura on his bunk, he'd known there would be an hour of reckoning between them. Now that the moment had arrived, couched in terms that he never could have expected,

Scopique was filled with a wild, adrenalized bloodlust and he felt himself grinning a crazy grin. Was he actually *enjoying* this?

Yeah, he thought. *Yeah, I guess I am.*

Drawing on the Force, gathering it inside as he'd been taught during hundreds of hours of training, he jerked the vent fixture from its housing. It came loose with a hollow metallic *pop,* bolts rattling free, opening a rectangle of cold space that fed into an open air shaft above. Still dangling from the open shaft, Scopique turned the vent fixture over in his free hand, evaluating its immediate utility as a weapon. It was thin and aerodynamic, with sharp edges—it would serve the purpose well enough.

He looked down at the thing that had been Jura.

"Whatever you are," Scopique muttered, "say good-bye to your head."

Swinging himself around, he flung the vent housing as hard as he could at Jura's corpse.

The makeshift discus whistled down through the air and found its target perfectly, shearing Jura's head from its shoulders and sending it tumbling forward across the floor. Thick, half-clotted blood spurted from the stump of the corpse's neck. The decapitated body took another shambling step, tilted sideways, and fell to its knees, then down on its belly.

Still dangling from the open vent—he was taking no chances—Scopique stared down at the thing in frank fascination. Nothing he'd learned at the academy even came close to what he was looking at right now. When he told the others—

Thumping noises from below: the headless monstrosity was still moving. In fact, it was leaning forward, groping around the floor until it found its severed head, sitting back up again and holding the head face-forward in front of its chest, tilting it up in Scopique's direction, so that those runny black eyes were staring straight up at Scopique, mouth working up and down as if it were chewing on something.

The mouth opened, and it screamed.

Scopique saw the decapitated corpse of Jura Ostrogoth haul back and fling its own head straight at him, its mouth still wide open. Without thinking, the Zabrak swung his free hand in front of his face and felt teeth clamp into the tender flesh of his forearm, ripping through the skin and muscle, right down to the bone. The pain was unbelievable, chemical somehow, as if the incisors were coated in some kind of fast-acting acid. Agony shot up through Scopique's arm to his clavicle, and he let go of the vent and fell, the head still affixed to his arm, and hit the floor hard. Blurrily, he looked down at the head. It was making little gurgling sounds now, its jaw tightening and releasing, the eyes still gleaming.

"Get off me!" Scopique shouted, trying to shake his arm free but unable to muster much strength. Was the arm broken? *"Get off!"* He grabbed a hank of the thing's hair and pulled as hard as he could, but it still wouldn't release. *"Get off my arm!"*

For several horrible seconds, he tried slamming it against the floor, pounding it as hard as he could, but nothing seemed to affect it. It was locked on tight, the burning liquid pain continuing to drip through the wound in his forearm.

Scopique stood up. The floor felt crooked under his feet. Staggering toward the bed, he underestimated the distance and crashed to the floor a second time, this time landing on his face. Blackness was crowding up through his vision, eclipsing the light, and he realized now that the pain in his arm had basically stopped, overwhelmed by a cool numbness that had begun spreading through his entire body.

Scopique fell utterly still.

All sound faded.

The numb feeling deepened, bringing with it a kind of near euphoria that swept through his consciousness in one solid black wave.

This isn't so bad was his final, fleeting thought. *This isn't so bad at all.*

Sometime in the next thirty minutes, a group of students came back to the dorms to find the room in disarray. They didn't see what was left of Scopique—he had crawled under the bed—but they did find Jura Ostrogoth's severed head.

And by the time they heard the noises coming from behind them, under the bunk, it was far too late.

20/Lockdown

IN THE DINING HALL AN HOUR LATER, 120 OF THE ACADE-
my's acolytes—more than half of the student body—
were finishing their evening meal when the mag-bolts in
the doors clanked shut behind them, sealing them in.

Whether it was one of the Masters who initiated this
sequence or some other factor was never made clear. A
fifth-year apprentice named Rucker was the first to discover that they'd actually been locked in. Preoccupied
by thoughts of the next day's early combat training, he'd
just shoved harder on the hatchway, assuming it was
stuck or broken again, but it still didn't give. Rucker
cast a furtive glance over his shoulder to see if he was
being messed with, but that did not appear to be the
case. None of the others was even looking at him.

By the time he'd started trying to use the Force to get
it open, several of the other students *were* standing behind him, growing audibly impatient with Rucker, waiting to get out. Even those who hadn't left the tables were
watching, waiting to see how this mini drama would
resolve itself.

None of them was looking back in the direction of the
kitchen—until the screaming started.

When he heard it, Rucker stopped fighting the blocked
hatch and turned to see what appeared to be a group of

six or seven Sith students swarming out of the food preparation area, launching themselves at the apprentices still seated over their meals. There was something seriously wrong with the tilt of their faces—he saw that right away—that made them look almost as if their features had been ripped off and stitched sideways on their heads. Their eyes were black and dead, their oily skin putty-colored and lifeless, except for their mouths, which were twisted back in grinning scimitars of unmistakable hunger.

And they were screaming together, as one.

At this point, Rucker—who had approximately thirty seconds left of life as he knew it—saw the things overtaking the room completely in a series of brief, high-contrast impressions. It was like watching some kind of parasite latch onto its prey. Their already-wide mouths somehow spread out even wider still, clamping down on the faces and necks and chests of the first rows of victims, taking them down with phenomenal strength and speed. Trays flew. Bright helices of blood spurted and looped in the air. A great bundle of steaming intestine splattered on the floor to Rucker's right with the ripe coppery smell of meat fresher than anything that had ever been served here before.

All around him, Rucker saw the other apprentices fighting back. They were using Force techniques, chokes and pushes and jumps, but the corpses tore through them indiscriminately. The only thing that seemed to have any effect was crushing the creatures, or pinning them under something so heavy that they couldn't get free. When one of the things seized him around the throat, Rucker raised one hand and tried to lift the table in front of him, flipping it over, but the thing on his neck was too strong, too hungry. Rucker's knees buckled, his legs caved in, and he dropped to the floor, smelling the fetor of the thing's breath even as its teeth gouged through his flesh.

His vision flickered and grew intensely sharp, as if, in the final seconds, his senses had grown more acute, desperate to take in all that they could before oblivion descended. Across the dining hall, he caught a glimpse of one of the apprentices standing on a table with both arms outstretched. Two of the living corpses went flailing backward, slamming into the opposite wall thirty meters away. The attacking apprentice—he had long, flaming red hair and penetrating green eyes—stood perfectly still, waiting for the things to come back. Nothing about what was happening seemed to perturb him in the least. In fact, Rucker realized, he could actually catch a hint of what the other student was thinking as he looked at the bodies, and—

The power, the power—

—and the other student *wanted* to be like them.

Rucker let out a silent groan. Blood was trickling down into his vision now, blackness closing in fast, but just before it covered him up completely, he could finally make out the identity of the redheaded apprentice standing on the table.

It was Lussk.

Rucker saw now that he was about to get his wish.

"Come on then!" Lussk was laughing, jeering as the things charged at him. He'd stopped fighting them off and instead had allowed them full access to his wrists, which Rucker saw he'd slashed open with a dinner knife. Blood poured from his arms. *"Come on and take me!"*

His voice became a scream.

21/Headstone City

TRACE LANDED AT NIGHTFALL.

The main hangar of the academy was empty.

Disengaging the ship's main hatch, he jumped down from the cockpit and forced himself to stop and wait on the landing pad, his senses—both physical and telemetric—tuned for any immediate threat. The challenge, of course, was that this entire planet was a threat. Besides the blizzard raging overhead, the Sith academy was a black hive of dark side energy; Trace could feel it buzzing around him like a huge swarm of venomous insects. The psychic contamination was so thick, so total, that for a moment he felt a blur of vertigo attacking his balance, tilting it dangerously off kilter.

She's here.

He knew it, even though he hadn't received any further bursts of distress from her along the way. Zo's kidnapper had brought her here; Trace felt her presence, recognized it somewhere amid the snowy ruin of the academy itself.

He moved quickly across the hangar, measuring every ambient sound as a possible threat. Since there had been no way of disguising his arrival—his ship wasn't equipped with a cloaking device—he'd decided to head straight into the thick of things, anticipating a hostile reception that he'd likely have to fight his way out of.

He ran past a control booth and stopped there—the hatchway hung open, dangling sideways, as if it had been partially ripped off its housing. The chair lay on its side in front of the main flight-control console, a data-pad, and a pile of old holomags with titles like *Hot Ships* and *Kuat Classics*. Reaching inside, Trace rested two fingertips on the chair.

A vivid splash of violence erupted in his mind's eye—a man screaming, jerking backward, while a pair of pale hands groped through, clutching his shirt and trying to pull him out. Trace felt the man's trapped panic, his horror, as he tried to keep whatever it was away from him . . . that part of the image was just a crazed, blood-soaked blur, defined more by its frantic strength than any kind of shape or form. An instant later the image faded.

What else had happened here?

He left the control area and strode the rest of the way through the hangar. It was becoming fully dark as he stepped outside and stared at the ruins stretched out around him, fading into the horizon. He'd glimpsed the academy during his descent, but it looked bigger from the ground, kilometers across, all of it, he thought, honeycombed with subterranean passageways and countless hiding places. Lights flickered, dotting the twilight with motion, or the illusion of motion. People were moving out there, he sensed them—Sith students and Masters.

That didn't matter. He would find her.

A sudden gust of wind slammed him in the face, carrying with it a rich and fetid stench of decay. Trace narrowed his eyes, assaying the winding networks of broken walkways that led among buildings and temples and piles of old stone. Given the smell, they reminded him of capillaries on the face of a cadaver.

His eyes settled on a tall black structure jutting upward, far above the other, lowlier structures, its top swathed in snow—a tower, like a headstone amid a city of the dead.

It was a start.

He began walking.

22/Practicum

▬▬▬:▬▬:▬▬▬

WHEN ZO SAW WHAT TULKH WAS POINTING AT, SHE FELT sick.

He had led her up to the top of a flat, ice-slick slab of rock that might once have been the roof of some unused building. It was dark, but the Whiphid had a phosphorescent glow rod that lit up the night like a thick slice of midday, and in the end she saw much more than she wanted to.

After a long moment of forcing herself to stare at the pulpy thing that squirmed in front of her, Zo realized she was looking at the student from Scabrous's laboratory—the one that had crawled out of the cage. Tulkh must have recognized it; that was why he'd brought her up here to look at it.

The thing's leg was pinned under a pile of rocks, and its head swung at an impossible angle from its upper torso, as though the neck was broken in several places. Yet even so, it writhed and shrieked and snapped at them, thrusting itself forward as if it could somehow break itself in half and attack with whatever portion of its body it could pull off.

The Whiphid poked at it with the spear.

The thing in front of them screamed again, its head twisting snake-like, all the way around. As horrible as it was, Zo thought the final remaining vestiges of humanity on its face were far worse. If she looked hard enough, she thought she could still see a dead teenager in there, fallen into a prison of its own decaying flesh.

"Explain that," Tulkh said.

"Me?" she asked. "You're the one that brought us here. Now we're both stuck in the middle of it."

One finger tapped her firmly in the middle of her chest. "*You're* stuck."

"What about you?"

"I'm already gone."

Tulkh turned away, took three steps, and stopped, looking down off the edge of the overhang. The long, oscillating scream that rose up around them now did not come from the thing smashed under the rock pile. It came, instead, from down below, and when Zo joined Tulkh at the edge of the overhang she could see where he had shone the glow rod.

The others.

Six of them.

Sith students, she saw, the fronts of their uniforms caked in gore, clustered together, their gray faces upturned to show eyes that glittered with that same shared intensity of appetite. When they screamed, they screamed together. One of them was a Zabrak. The others were— had been—human.

Zo snapped a glance back at the corpse whose leg was trapped under the rock.

It's calling them—the orchid's voice broke through in her mind—*summoning them up here, Hestizo*—

When the scream ended, she heard an eager scratching noise. The other students had already shoved forward, grabbing the ragged surface in front of them, clawing at it.

They began to climb.

23/Lowboy

WHERE IS EVERYBODY?

That was what Kindra had asked Ra'at when they were outside, and he'd blown it off, or pretended to, because he didn't have an answer—or because the answer he had was too deeply disturbing to vocalize. But the question returned to him now, down in the dorms, as they went through room after room, finding nothing but empty, silent bunks and vacant corridors.

They had been running for some time, but Kindra didn't even sound as if she was out of breath, and Ra'at realized that he was starting to feel better, too—moving around had helped clear his head, steadying him. Even his arm didn't hurt as much anymore. Being young had its advantages.

Going low had been Kindra's idea, a means of buying time until they figured out what they were up against, and despite Ra'at's avowed intention to go to the infirmary and get checked out, he'd followed her—for now, anyway. They'd run inside a long utility corridor to a place where it branched off in a three-pronged intersection. The permasteel ceiling oozed condensation just above him, and the long tube-lamps embedded in the walls let off a pale, achromatic glow in the hanging clouds of moisture. The opposite end of the corridor intersected another group of dorms, and that was where they'd run into two other students—Hartwig and Maggs.

"What are you two doing down here?" Hartwig asked. He frowned at Ra'at. "Dag, man, what happened to your arm?"

"Training accident," Ra'at said evenly.

Hartwig smirked. "Fail."

"Meaning what?"

"Meaning *that*"—Hartwig pointed at the wound— "doesn't look like any training accident I ever saw. What did you do, fall on a vibroblade or something?"

"I was in the pain pipe." Ra'at held Maggs and Hartwig in the same regard that he did the rest of his classmates, with a kind of suspicious indifference. Their motives were purely selfish, as were his; he had no intention of sharing information that didn't somehow improve his own situation. At this point they all knew something had gone very wrong, contaminating the academy or the entire planet; for the moment they were allies of opportunity. "Have you guys seen anything else down here?"

"What do you mean, anything?" Hartwig asked.

"Or any*body*."

"No." Maggs cracked his knuckles nervously. "Not yet. Weird, huh? It's pretty early for it to be so quiet. I heard there was some kind of assembly earlier, but Wig and I missed it."

"If we're going any farther," Kindra cut in, "we're going to need weapons. Our best bet is dividing up"— she pointed up ahead, where the corridor pronged into three separate halls—"searching these hallways, in groups of two, and—"

"Wait a minute," Hartwig said. "Who put *you* in charge?"

"In *charge*?" Kindra turned, and Ra'at saw that she was staring directly at Hartwig, her gray, almost translucent irises like newly formed frost. "Nobody asked you to tag along." Her eyes flashed off Ra'at. "*Any* of you."

Hartwig shrugged uneasily. "I'm just saying . . ."

"What?"

"We all feel something kind of bad in the air, right? Like maybe some kind of a . . . disease. But who's to say it's not just one of Scabrous's drills?"

Kindra's eyebrows went up. "Excuse me?"

"For all we know he started this himself."

"Why?"

"Maybe it *is* a training exercise," Maggs put in. "Or maybe he's culling the weak students. It's happened before. Remember the unakki eye spiders?"

"This is worse," Kindra said.

"Don't be so sure," Hartwig said. "Eleven students went blind. Two of them died. Remember Soid Einray?"

"Soid Einray was a defective already."

"Maybe, but he still hung himself afterward. And then we found out that Scabrous had reactivated the fertilized spider eggs from the pathogen bank as a nerve-reflexivity drill." Hartwig refused to lower his stare. "I still wake up with blood in my eyes sometimes."

Kindra's expression didn't change. "What's your point?"

"You want weapons? I might know where we could find some. But I'm not gonna risk getting in trouble with the Masters if nobody's actually seen anything." Hartwig waited for a response, looking at Kindra, then at Ra'at, and finally let out a derisive snort. "Yeah, that's what I thought." He turned to go. "I'll see you pus-bags around."

"Wait," Ra'at said. "I saw something."

Hartwig stopped and turned to look at him. Ra'at saw Kindra's tongue come out and moisten her upper lip, listening expectantly.

"Two bodies fell out of Scabrous's tower," Ra'at said. "They hit the ground. I saw them hit, and I heard the noise they made—they were *dead*." He swallowed; his throat was suddenly very dry. "But then they got up."

Maggs and Hartwig were both staring at him now with various degrees of skepticism and outright disbelief. Ra'at discovered that he didn't care. Let them doubt; it would only make them better cannon fodder when the time came.

"Were you all alone when you saw this?" Kindra asked.

"I was sparring with Lussk."

Maggs blinked at him, and Hartwig's eyes grew wide. Maybe it was just Ra'at's imagination, but he thought the mention of Lussk's name brought a paradoxical shiver of credibility to the moment. It was too unlikely a detail to be made up.

"One of the ones who fell was Wim Nickter," Ra'at said. "After he hit the ground, he got up and attacked me. He was dead, but he was . . . still alive. I had to pin him under a pile of rocks to get away." *Out with the rest of it, then,* he decided. "That Sickness in the air that you're talking about—that's Scabrous's doing, up in the tower. I think . . ." He swallowed again, and this time his voice was steadier. ". . . I think he's bringing the dead back to life."

There was a sharp rattle of footsteps from somewhere in front of them.

Ra'at felt a sudden feeling of coolness rising up inside him, as if his skin were being stretched by gallons of cold water. When he spoke, his voice seemed to be transmitting from somewhere far away. "Which way is it coming from?"

Cocking her head, Kindra pointed up ahead, where the main corridor divided into three subcorridors, to the one that branched on the left. "Up there," she whispered. "You hear it?"

Ra'at's ears strained for sound. At first, he heard nothing. Then they all did—a dragging, grating clank. It was advancing down the walkway with a graceless lack of stealth, growing steadily louder with every passing second.

Ra'at began concentrating solely on himself and his own survival, forgetting all the others. The Masters at the academy had trained them to fight as a unit when necessary, but a Sith warrior's true strength lay in his or her own personal will to power. When you could trust no one, fighting alone was axiomatic, a natural state.

Flattening himself to the wall, he felt the Force's dark side coursing through him, a crackling electric chill that rendered fear and apprehension obsolete, and welcomed it. In that moment, he felt only a ready vigilance, weightless and unrelenting. Since arriving here on Odacer-Faustin, it was the closest to happiness that he dared let himself experience. Yet in so many ways it was superior to any happiness he'd ever encountered. It made traditional happiness look anemic by comparison.

All at once he realized that he could see what was coming, not with his eyes but in his mind.

"Relax," he breathed. "It's okay."

Kindra wrinkled her forehead, about to reply, when the droid rattled from the end of the tunnel, stopped, and regarded them dully. It was a bare-bones Sigma series training unit, eight-armed, with belt treads and a force-feedback intelligence implant so rudimentary that it was practically a piece of furniture. Ra'at hadn't seen one like it since he'd run newbie lightsaber drills, not long after his arrival here. Its copper-blue chassis was a dented utility cabinet carbon-scored with hundreds of old marks from countless years of clumsy rookies.

Heaving a sigh, Hartwig came away from the wall, watching the others emerge into view around it.

"What's that thing doing so far down here?" Maggs muttered.

The droid clicked and produced a series of broken-sounding whirs, its equivalent of speech. Equipping such a unit with a vocabulator would have been pointless.

Ra'at reached down and grabbed a loose strip of alloy sealant dangling from its undercarriage, pried it off, and wedged it directly underneath the thing's bulky central processor. He jammed the strip in as far as he could and twisted.

"What are you doing?" Kindra asked.

The processor cowl came loose with a snap. "If I remember right," he said, "this thing's still got a visual mapping system." He eased his right hand between two hot layers of components. "Which means it should still have a playback function. And whatever it's seen lately should still be stored somewhere in its memory bank." He didn't glance up. "Master Yakata used to make us watch our old drills this way, remember?"

"Yeah," Maggs said, "but—"

The space in front of them flickered and brightened with a cone of holographic blue light, the image sharpening, gaining resolution and depth. They all stood back looking at it, pale blue reflecting off their faces, none of them speaking.

At first Ra'at didn't quite realize what he was seeing. Maggs was the first to break the silence. He sounded hoarse, as if he was still trying to whisper but needed to clear his throat.

"What is that?"

Nobody answered. The hologram showed an area somewhere deep inside the tunnels where an indistinct mob of figures was teeming not-quite-randomly in the foreground. From their uniforms, Ra'at realized that they were Sith acolytes—

But there was something wrong about the way their bodies moved, a jolting, uneven pace, and he couldn't see their faces. From this angle it was impossible to tell how many there were. All he could see was that they were hunched together, working over what looked like a massive pile of debris, shoving and piling and dropping it into place in the corridor ahead of them. Within just a few moments the pile in the tunnel had grown noticeably higher. The light on the other side was narrowing to a thin band.

"What are they doing?" Maggs asked.

Ra'at's voice was a nonspecific whisper. "Building a wall."

"Maybe it's some kind of barricade," Hartwig said. "So they can hold off whatever's out there." He caught his breath. "It must be—"

"Look." Ra'at pointed at the hologram. "The angle's changing."

"Maybe they've got weapons we can use." Maggs was sounding excited now. "Yeah, look, that one's got a lightsaber." He was already heading up in the direction that the droid had come. "Let's move."

"*Wait,*" Ra'at said.

"What?" Maggs turned around, frowning. "What's wrong?"

Ra'at was still looking at the hologram. The droid had broadened its field of view, dumping on bandwidth, and the image's signal-to-noise ratio had improved dramatically. Now the blue light-cone showed a huge mob of bodies, dozens of them, more than he could even count, crammed together in front of the barrier. It looked like half the students at the Academy were packed into that part of the tunnel.

Ra'at pointed.

"Their faces."

Maggs came back, hardly paying attention. "I don't see what—" he said, and stopped. "Oh no."

Several of the Sith students in the hologram were turning and looking directly back at the droid. Their faces were slack and vacant, devoid of any emotion—it was the exact same way that Nickter had looked, up on top of the overhang. Ra'at saw that some of them had wounds on their faces and necks, and their uniforms were badly torn, hanging from their torsos like bloody sails. He watched as one of them, a student whose name he couldn't remember, brought his face directly up to the droid's holocam, a sly grin peeling over his lips.

"Like Nickter," Ra'at murmured, and felt Kindra stiffening next to him, in his peripheral vision.

Hartwig said, "What . . . ?"

"There's light on the other side of that barricade," Ra'at said. "But that's it."

"So what are they doing?"

Ra'at looked back at him. "They're walling us in."

24/Seed

▬▬▬▬▬▬ ▬▬▬▬▬ ■▬▬▬■

IT WAS THE ORCHID THAT SAVED THEM.

Looking back, Zo hadn't even been aware of exactly what she was doing, although that by itself shouldn't have been a surprise—a good deal of a Jedi's power was instinctive, a function of the Force. But it didn't make the situation any less disturbing.

The things beneath them had started clamoring up the rock face with a kind of manic agility, clawing their way toward her and Tulkh in spastic bursts of movement. The Whiphid reacted first, drawing his spear and thrusting it straight at the first one, impaling it through the chest and then hauling it upright, using the thing's own weight to drag it down and finish the job. Tulkh swung the spear around with the corpse still on it, bludgeoning the others, driving them back with a series of vicious thrusts.

The plan went wrong almost immediately. Despite the fact that it had been run through completely, the thing at the end of the spear wasn't stopping—it wasn't even slowing down. And Zo realized the other corpses had changed their approach, climbing up onto the overhang from the other side while Tulkh was still struggling to kill the first one. *They can't be killed*, a voice whispered from the back of her mind, *they're already dead, look at them*. At first she thought she was hearing her own thoughts, and then she realized it was the Murakami orchid, roiling in its own guilt and misery, yammering out words that she alone could hear. *Dead but alive, Hestizo, dead but alive, I did this to them, it was my fault, when Scabrous put me into that horrible vat, and now I'm inside them—*

Zo stiffened. That must have been when she made the connection, on some level at least, because a moment later she was staring straight at the dead thing wiggling on the end of Tulkh's spear. Except it wasn't really at the end anymore; it had pulled itself forward until it was almost close enough to grab the Whiphid's face.

I've got an idea, she told the orchid. *Grow.*

What?

You're in them now, she said, *aren't you? You're a part of them. You said so yourself.*

Yes, but—

Then grow.

I can't just—

Don't argue with me! Just GROW.

It might have been that last command, the desperate vehemence of it, that stirred the orchid to action. Zo saw the thing at the end of Tulkh's spear stiffen and then fall abruptly motionless, as if it had just realized something profoundly unwelcome was taking root inside it. An instant later a thin green tendril began to wind itself out of the thing's right ear, extruding a vine that grew steadily thicker as it looped downward. Another vine appeared inside its left nostril, and then a third and fourth—stalks and runners were snaking busily out of both ears now, some of them bearing small clusters of leaves, others tiny black flowers. The corpse's mouth opened, and another stalk, this one as big around as Zo's finger, burst outward from its bloody throat.

Hestizo this hurts, this hurts me—

Grow, she told it. *Grow, just keep growing, just GROW*—

Looking around, she saw the others were experiencing the same effect, sprouting stalks and stems from every visible orifice. Their faces squirmed with thin, wiggling plant life just underneath the skin. Zo knew that it was working now. The orchid was in them, and the orchid was *growing.* She concentrated harder—she could actually see the flora growing inside the things now, driving it harder, farther, faster from within, even as the orchid began crying out, begging her to *stop,* telling her that this *hurt,* it couldn't do it anymore—

She ignored it and stared straight at the thing on Tulkh's spear.

She thought the word again; thought it with all the intensity and determination she could muster, over and over in a smooth and solid thought-wave.

GROW-GROW-GROWGROWGROW—

The corpse's entire cranial vault exploded in a colossal *splat* of red and black and green. In the place where its skull had been, a bright spray of leaves flapped and writhed, winding outward, spilling down, to encompass the entire upper half of the thing's torso. The body fell limp, sagging on the spear.

Tulkh dumped the thing with a brisk shoveling gesture, kicking it so that it barrel-rolled over the edge, and then glanced back at Zo. "You did that?"

"Me, and the flower."

"You better do it again." The Whiphid pointed over the edge of the overhang at the other things. They were still sprouting, Zo saw, but not as quickly, clawing back upward toward them.

Hestizo, please—the orchid sounded weaker now—*no more, not now, I can't, it hurts . . .*

"You have to," Zo said, unaware that she was speaking out loud. "You have to do it, because if you don't they're not going to stop. They're going to kill us, they're going to kill me, do you understand?"

So sorry, Hestizo . . .

Silence.

And it was gone.

A hand closed around her ankle, jerking her forward from below. Zo started to fall, landing on her side just as one of the things lurched upward, fully into view. She tried to pull away but couldn't budge.

Grow, she pleaded with the orchid, *grow, GROW NOW—*

But the flower, wherever it had gone, whatever its abilities had been just moments before, was of absolutely no help to her now. She couldn't even hear its voice anymore. And the writhing, rippling movement under the other things' faces seemed to have stopped. There was nothing more they could do about them now. The orchid was tired, or absent—or dead.

The thing on her leg was dragging her closer.

"What are you doing?" Tulkh shouted. He was stabbing furiously at the others, without much effect. "Stop them!"

"I can't!" Zo shouted back. "The orchid's not there anymore!"

All at once something huge burst up out of the ground in front of them—a monolith, black and featureless, hurling up an enormous corona of rock and ice in its wake. From what Zo could make out, it looked like a turret made of stone and durasteel, taller than the rocky outcropping where she was currently fighting for her life. Lights pulsed within it. As its domed upper mounting swung toward them, she saw the gleam of a heavy turbine—

The blaster pulsed twice, and the corpse in front of her disappeared in an acrid spray. Zo blinked, wiping her eyes, and a massive amount of strength and momentum slammed into her from behind—the Whiphid, she realized—knocking her off the top of the overhang just before the third blast pulverized it completely.

They landed face-first in the dirty snow, Zo's ears ringing, her head splitting from the fusillade of laser blasts behind them. Massive hunks of smoking boulder and snow were showering down from above. Zo stared back at the crater where they'd just been standing.

"Run!" Tulkh ordered.

"What?"

"That way." He jerked his arm toward the long, hollowed-out, tube-like structure twenty meters in front of them, and when she didn't move, the Whiphid shoved her forward just as the laser cannon pivoted again, tracking straight for her.

━ ━ · ━ ·

"STATEMENT," THE HK'S VOICE CRACKLED FROM INSIDE the comlink. "Sir, we located Hestizo Trace."

The Sith Lord paused and adjusted the frequency until the connection became clear. He was standing in the bulkhead of the *Mirocaw*, having just finished a complete inspection of the vessel from top to bottom. Locating the bounty hunter's ship had not been difficult—the tower's sensors had found it crash-landed two kilometers outside the academy, tracking it from the heat signature, and Scabrous had approached it with absolute stealth, on the off chance there might be someone aboard. But there was no sign of the Jedi or the Whiphid who had brought her here. The craft had been abandoned.

"Where is she?" he asked.

"Response: Initial perimeter scan reports positive identification on the northeast quadrant. Scanners registered a ninety-eight point three percent positive pheromone match."

"How long ago?"

"Response: Ten standard minutes, sir. Coordinate vector twenty-seven by eighteen, order of magnitude—"

"Is she dead?"

The slightest of pauses: "Response: Negative, sir, per your orders."

"Good."

"Statement: Our midrange scout systems report that she and the Whiphid bounty hunter are traveling together, headed northwest toward the tauntaun paddock in that near vicinity. They are still on foot and in all probability seeking immediate cover from the initial attack." The HK made a clicking sound, awaiting orders. "Query: Shall I reactivate the perimeter cannons in that quadrant, set for stun?"

Scabrous didn't answer right away, thinking about the terrain that the droid was describing. The tower itself wasn't far from there, of course, and—

And the library.

"That won't be necessary," Scabrous said. "I'll handle it personally."

"Statement . . ." The droid sounded more tentative now. "There is . . . something else."

"What is it?"

"Several local sensors are reporting unverified cluster activity in various quadrants around the academy in general. It's unclear exactly what the source of the activity is. Biorhythm diagnostics aren't reporting any verifiable vital signs."

"Then fix it."

"Clarification: The electronics themselves are online and functioning normally. It's the activity—it shows no sign of life, body temperature, respiration, heart or brain activity."

Scabrous stopped and gazed thoughtfully at the *Mirocaw*'s dented metal bulkhead in front of him. For a moment the only sounds were the low, steady hum of the hemodialysis machine pumping fresh blood through his body, and the susurrus of fluids whisking through tubes, feeding him the cocktail of antiviral drugs.

"How much activity?" he asked.

"Response: Unclear at present," the HK's voice said. "But it seems to be—"

"What?"

"Well, it seems to be spreading, sir."

"I see." Scabrous thought of the apprentice, Nickter, or the thing that had once been Nickter, crawling out of its cage despite the fact that all vital signs registered negative. He thought about how the thing had lunged at him and then gone after Jura Ostrogoth; the appetite that the thing had brought to bear. At that moment, Scabrous had assumed that what he'd seen was a kind of exaggerated nervous twitch, a biochemical accident that the drug and the orchid had triggered inside Nickter's body. But now—

It seems to be spreading, sir, the HK had said.

—he began to reconsider.

"My lord?" the droid prompted.

"Never mind that now," Scabrous said. "I'm going directly to the library. There will be no more need for lasers. Hestizo Trace will meet me there personally, and we shall finish our business together, she and I, as it was meant to be. Have my own ship prepared for immediate departure afterward."

"Yes, sir, but—"

Scabrous cut off the transmission and strode through the *Mirocaw*'s open hatch, down the landing ramp, and out into the snowy night.

26/Subzero

IN THE FIRST HOUR THAT TRACE PASSED THROUGH THE collapsed walls and stone temples of the academy, the blizzard around him only worsened. It was as if the planet itself had read his arrival as a kind of infection on the cellular level and was fighting him off however it could. The temperature, already freezing, continued to plunge until his throat and lungs burned with every breath. The wind roared between the massive boxy shapes of the buildings and substructures, the great slabs and half-submerged corridors. Its scream was wraith-like, endless, the cry of something hungry for more than simple meat. Even the pellets of snow themselves felt sharper, jagging into his skin like tiny bits of shrapnel from an endlessly recurring explosion.

In his peripheral vision, a shadow twitched and slith-ered.

Trace stopped, hand reaching back for his lightsaber, and that was when he saw the man stepping out of the arched doorway to his left. Even before Trace glimpsed the man's face, he sensed the thin, bitter smile twisted over his lips, the threat of violence in those half-lidded eyes. The man's tunic and cloak blew out behind him, snapping whip-like in the irregular gusts of wind, and his voice, when it came across the broken landscape between them, was a low snarl.

"You landed on the wrong world, Jedi."

Trace turned and faced him directly. The man was a Sith Master; that much was readily apparent—perhaps an instructor at the academy.

"I am Shak'Weth, Blademaster here on Odacer-Faustin. I can only assume that you came here seeking humiliation and an unpleasant death."

"I'm here on other matters."

"Ah?" The Blademaster cocked his head slightly, looking marginally intrigued. "But you've found me instead."

Trace nodded. Actually it was only stillness that had found him, clarity of thought, and it came as a blessing. The cold, the darkness, the stinging wind—all of these outside factors had simply ceased to exist. His entire world had shrunk to the exact distance between him and the man who stood before him, an obstacle in the way of finding Hestizo. Trace felt everything inside him beginning to relax and flow smoothly as the Force spread through his nerves and muscles, generating a kind of weightless balance between action and intent. He drew his own lightsaber, felt it blaze to life in his grasp, a perfect extension of himself.

The Sith Master's response was immediate. With a harsh grunt of fury, he flew at Trace, vaulting upward in the wind and angling the blade down with both hands, ripping through the ground where Trace had just been standing. The execution was flawless, a thing of almost organic brutality, as if the Blademaster had become a force of nature, another component of the blizzard that roared around them.

Yet he was still too slow.

Leaping sideways, Trace had spun around with his own lightsaber extended in front of him in a sweeping blow. The Sith Master was there, deflecting the attack and charging him again, hammering him backward with a vicious series of piercing thrusts and jabs, offering no quarter. Twice the blade came close enough to Trace's face that he could smell the scorched stubble on his cheek; the third slash came within millimeters of taking off his head.

Trace realized that regardless of what Shak'Weth had said a moment earlier, the Blademaster didn't intend to humiliate him, to toy with him or prolong the duel any longer than necessary. At this point, the Sith Master was attacking for the most primitive reason imaginable—to slaughter Trace and leave his steaming carcass in the snow. In that split second Trace saw the rest of the duel playing out in two distinct ways, neither of which would last long. Death was hovering over them now like a scavenger, close and claustrophobic—he saw it reflected in the Sith Master's eyes.

When the red blade came at him again, Trace jumped upward. He put everything he knew about Form V's Djem So variation into that jump, leaping over Shak'Weth, spiraling through the flying snow, landing on the other side, and twisting around instantly, keeping his light-saber at throat level with the intention of finishing the duel in a single stroke.

Shak'Weth laughed—a bone-dry chuckle—and deflected the maneuver with mocking ease. He swung at Trace, and this time the Jedi felt a hot, bright stab of pain as the lightsaber seared through his cloak and tunic, slashing into the flesh along his rib cage. Drops of blood fell into the snow, disappearing as they melted.

"Too easy, Jedi." Now the Blademaster's shoulders and back were braced against the slouching stone wall behind him, its outer surface cracked and half collapsed, and he tensed to spring forward. "Now I shall finish you."

As he arched forward, Trace saw a pair of hands shoot

out from the broken wall behind him, gripping the Blademaster by the throat and jerking him backward. Shak'Weth slammed into the cracked stone hard enough to drop his lightsaber, and Trace saw a ghastly white face burst up through the open hole in the wall, a *screaming* face, suctioning down on the Sith Master's right cheek and eye, teeth bared, gouging into his face.

Trace took a step back, still holding his own lightsaber up, watching the thing that hauled Shak'Weth through the hole in the wall where it could more easily devour him. Great arterial eruptions spurted from the ragged perforation in the Sith Master's throat, spraying up over the wall and down into the snow and ice, painting the whole world red. Inside the wall, the thing lifted its face up and Trace saw its eyes—flat and without the slightest spark of life—yet they had once been human, even youthful. A Sith student, he realized—a teenager. What had happened?

The thing shoved its mouth back down into the ragged red cup that had once been Shak'Weth's right eye socket, slurping noisily. When it paused a moment later, the noise that it made was a high-pitched, ululating scream, and Trace realized that there were other screams, countless screams, a threnody of them rising up along with it, coming from every direction at once.

The night was full of them.

27/Paddock

ZO AND TULKH DUCKED THROUGH THE ENTRANCEWAY OF
the long, tunnel-like structure, and the bounty hunter
stopped and raised his head, sniffing the wind as if picking up on some obscure scent.

"What was that out there?" Zo asked, gazing back
out through the way they'd come. Her own voice
sounded distant to her, and her ears felt as if they were
plugged with soft wax from the force of the explosions
outside.

"Turbolaser," Tulkh grunted. "Heavy artillery."

"It's Scabrous, isn't it?" she asked. "He's looking
for us."

If the Whiphid heard the question, he ignored it; a moment later, he sidled on, deeper into the foul-smelling recesses of the building. Reluctantly, Zo followed. She was
still processing the attacks, the laser cannon that had
erupted up out of the ground, and the even more horrify-
ing assault that had come before it—the screaming, undead things that had been intent on devouring them.

"The orchid," she said, for want of a better place to
start.

Tulkh said nothing, kept walking. The smell around
them was getting decidedly worse with every passing
step.

"It was the only reason I could fight those things off. It's because of how Scabrous used it in that experiment. I think it's inside their bodies somehow. I told it to grow. But . . ." Zo shook her head. "It's not there anymore. Now I can't get it to respond to me at all. It might be dead."

The Whiphid responded to all of this with a grunt. "You finished?"

"I just thought you might want to know how I saved our lives back there. You were the one who asked me for an explanation, after all."

"My mistake."

"Really?" she said. "Oh, I'm sorry. Maybe you should have thought of that before you abducted me and dragged me out here to a planet full of walking corpses."

No reply from the Whiphid.

"Where are we going, anyway?"

"Taking shelter. Waiting out the storm. In the morning, I'm going back to my ship."

The conversation ended there. Almost without meaning to, Zo found herself reaching into the bounty hunter's thoughts, tentatively exploring his mind for some idea of what he knew about where they were headed. Normally her telepathic abilities weren't particularly strong when it came to nonplant life-forms, but the Whiphid was what she thought of as a relatively easy read. In fact, from within, his mind resembled nothing so much as the trophy room aboard his ship where she'd first awakened: a place of death, a de facto display space for grotesque trophies and old kills. Some were alien species that she'd never seen before. Others were human. All were brought together in universal expressions of pain, desperation, and helplessness that they'd worn as the bounty hunter had delivered the coup de grâce. His mind had become a storehouse of their dying moments. This crypt of suffering, this reliquary, wasn't just what he carried around in his head every day—it *was* his head.

Undaunted, Zo plumbed deeper and realized that, with some effort, she was able to pass through these thoughts into another chamber of the Whiphid's consciousness, into his more distant memories. She saw faces rising up around her, others of his species, family perhaps, early enemies from his home planet of Toola. The atmosphere here felt very still and long undisturbed, almost as if it were hermetically sealed, and she wondered if she'd arrived in some part of Tulkh's past that he himself rarely visited. Certainly she had such places in her own mind, aspects of her life she'd walled off in vain hopes they'd die of suffocation or neglect. Zo could almost feel the membrane that enveloped this part of his thoughts beginning to constrict over her.

Then she heard breathing.

There was something alive in here.

She shifted her focus away from the older memories and saw the man gazing down at her, utterly calm and pleasant. His gray eyes were clear, sparkling with intellect. Wide, almost sensuous lips seemed perpetually on the verge of speaking, but instead they only twisted into a bemused smile. It was the Sith Lord.

"Get out of my head, Jedi!"

Tulkh's snarl boomed through the memory-caverns around her with devastating force. Zo recoiled, drawing back, staggering as she retreated, and, looking around, saw that they were standing in a wide, bare-metal chamber facing a series of tunnels that branched off in different directions. Icicles spiked down like semi-translucent stalactites from the long, low ceiling. She couldn't breathe. It took a second to realize why. The Whiphid had one hand locked around her throat, clamping her airway shut between his thumb and forefinger. His tusked face loomed just centimeters from her own.

"The next time I catch you in my head," he said, "you'll lose yours. Is that clear?"

Zo nodded, and he released her, allowing her to stumble backward, regaining her bearings. Somewhere across the room, in one of the adjoining tunnels, she could hear a high-pitched whining beep going on and on, not an alarm necessarily, but some incidental mechanism, maybe as simple as a light that had already started overheating and would eventually burn out.

Right now, however, this area was still brightly lit. Presumably that was why Tulkh had chosen it. As far as temperature went, the space was an ice locker, but at least she could see what was around and between each of the broad utilitarian pillars holding up the ceiling.

The Whiphid turned, head cocked and listening as he lumbered back up the corridor. Zo, who at this point had spent a good deal of time looking at his back, noticed a difference in his gait, the way he carried his shoulders: they were stiffened, tense with anticipation. Without breaking stride, he reached for his bow and started to draw an arrow from his quiver.

"Is this the way we came in?" Zo asked.

"What do you think?"

"I think you're not sure. And you're trying to cover for it." She paused and sniffed the air; the feral, ammonia-foul odor was growing thicker around her. "Are we staying down here all night? What's that *smell*?"

No answer from Tulkh . . . at this point, had she really expected one? She went after him, down the concourse, in the general direction of the exit. The lights were trembling even more erratically here, spluttering on and off for a second or two at a time.

The acrid stench had become eye-wateringly intense. Zo covered her nose and mouth. It didn't help at all.

"This isn't the way we came in." She coughed. "I would have remembered—"

Tulkh stopped. Off to their right, she saw a row of stalls. Something inside one of the stalls was swinging itself around, chuffing out volumes of air. Listening, Zo heard it let out a low, restless groan. There was a silence, then a sound of feet rustling, followed by a bronchial squabbling honk.

The Whiphid replaced the arrow that he'd taken out, and took a step forward.

The thing inside the stall let out another nasal, braying squawk and thrust its long head outward. Its muzzle drew back and Zo saw two pairs of nostrils, large and small, flaring to let out another blast of moist breath. It swung its shaggy head sideways, its curved horns nearly gouging Tulkh's face before he drew back.

"Are they . . ."

"Tauntauns." The Whiphid made it sound like a bad word about somebody's mother. "At least it explains the sm—"

A thick gobbet of spit hit him squarely in the face, and Tulkh lunged forward, wiping it off, meeting the tauntaun eye-to-eye. He and it were almost the same height. The snow lizard's lips were already working up another load of saliva—Zo thought the thing actually looked like it was smirking at him—when Tulkh abruptly broke into a grin. It was the first time Zo had seen him express anything other than impatience and indifference, and the effect was disconcerting.

"Good girl." Tulkh brushed one hand over its snout, ruffling the fur beneath one of its horns. "I bet there's probably some mook fruit for you around here somewhere." Then, glancing back at Zo, his smile faded. *"What?"*

"If I'd known that spitting in your face was the key to your good graces," Zo said, "I would have done it a long time ago."

Ignoring her, Tulkh returned his attention to the creature. "You're a foul old girl, aren't you?" he said affectionately. "I used to hunt with one like you, back on Toola." He glanced at the thick harness tethering the thing in its pen, and turned to look up ahead at the source of another noise, lower and more dissonant.

Listening, Zo heard it, too. The stalls in front of them were full of an increasing din—braying and squabbling—getting louder every second.

"Something's got them spooked," she said.

"Yeah." Awareness dawned in the Whiphid's face. "I think you're right."

In the stables, the tauntauns sounded as though they were screaming now, stomping in their paddocks.

The lights went out.

The blackness that engulfed them was crushing and total. Zo felt Tulkh's hand reach out and seize hold of her arm, just below the shoulder. "Stay close," his voice rumbled in her ear, and she heard the creak of the leather quiver on his back. "Keep back."

Zo felt her vision adjusting, straining after whatever slender traces of light she might find at the other end of the paddock, but there was precious little available, and what there was only created a myopic swamp of deep gray shadow. She could feel her senses reaching out into the recesses, pinging off the walls and ceiling. Her pupils ached from trying to pull something of substance out of the darkness. Immediately in front of her, she heard Tulkh suck in a sharp breath of air.

"What?" she whispered.

He jerked her forward so hard that her teeth snapped together and all at once she was moving blindly, half running, half dragged through a black and sightless sea. The bounty hunter's grip on her arm was like a manacle. Swinging forward, losing her equilibrium and then regaining it, she felt the floor skid out from underneath her feet. She wondered how he could see at all, or if he was navigating by sense of smell, or plain dumb luck.

Then she felt them, coming up from behind.

One or many, she didn't know, but the presence felt massive, an unwelcome intrusion of breath and motion and stinking flesh that bulked through the dark corridor, filling it.

She heard a scream, a sound like she'd never heard before.

—EEEEEEEEEEEEEEE—

It rose, a piercing shriek, pressurized and skating upward into the highest registers of audible sound, thousands of vibrations per second, until she expected it to burst apart, splintering into ragged strands and threads of individual voices. But instead it held together, compressing somehow, overwhelming the cries of the tauntauns and everything else.

—EEEEEEEEEEEEEEE—

Zo sensed a probing, almost prehensile quality to that note; it was the echo-locating noise of something—some *things*—investigating the blackness around them with a desperate, mindless voraciousness.

As quickly as it had started, the scream broke off. The tauntauns' cries had strangled away as well, leaving a void of utter silence in their wake. Zo drew in a breath, summoning the Force. What came next was a mental image, no longer than a second or two at the most, like a flash grenade exploding in her head. In that moment she glimpsed the perimeter in front of them, the stalls, and the space behind them. She had just enough of a view to sense what she had to do, *now*.

She swung one leg in front of Tulkh's ankle, planted her foot, and felt him trip over it, tumbling sideways with a snarled curse into an empty tauntaun stall to their immediate right. Zo collapsed on top of him. The night vision that the Force had given her was already gone. She felt something long and smooth jabbing painfully against her cheek and realized later that it must have been one of the Whiphid's tusks.

"What—" he snapped, and this time she took hold of him, squeezing hard, digging her fingers as hard as she could into the bounty hunter's scaly, sweat-slick hide. In surprise, or maybe realization, he went quiet.

The events of the next few moments weren't simply a matter of sound or smell but some collusion of both sensory and extrasensory perception. With the Force guiding her, Zo realized that she could *feel* the stalls alongside them, still pitch black, filling with the noxious stirring of many bodies, packed close together, piling past.

Searching.

At one point, Zo sensed them lumbering by so closely that if she'd reached one hand out of the stall, she could have touched them.

And they could have touched her.

They weren't screaming now, weren't even breathing. Instead the things, whatever they were, made little incidental grunting noises, the sound of bodies pushing themselves along for the simplest of motives—hunger, hatred, rage.

She held her breath, didn't move.

After what felt like forever, the grunting noises trailed off, until all that was left was a putrid cloud that made her want to breathe through her mouth.

Beneath her, Tulkh stirred, straightened, and shoved her off him.

"If you ever do that again, I'll kill you myself."

Zo glanced off in the direction that the things had gone. "Seems a bit redundant, given the circumstances."

"I don't run. And I don't hide."

"*Listen,*" she said. "We saw what those things are. I

can't fight them off, and neither can you. So for the moment that leaves us with running and hiding."

To her surprise, he didn't argue. Climbing out of the stall, they made their way forward through the dark, toward the strange pewter-gray light she'd noticed earlier. It grew slightly brighter by degrees until she realized that she could see the exit taking shape in front of them. The air was colder, and she saw the first big flakes of snow drifting in from outside.

Tulkh stopped and tilted his head back, the wind blowing the fur from his face.

"This isn't where we came in," he said.

"How do you know?"

He raised one hand. Zo looked where he was pointing. It took her a moment to realize what she was looking at. Once she did, though, she couldn't look away.

They were back at the tower.

28/What the Sickness Said

IN THE DINING HALL, LUSSK WAS WATCHING THE DEAD awaken.

He saw it with two sets of eyes: the ones he'd had when he'd been alive, and the strange new vision that the Sickness had given him. On some intuitive level he understood that the first set was fading, going blind, and that was fine with him, absolutely fine. The Sickness had given him everything he'd hoped for, everything he wanted, power and strength beyond all imagining. It had altered the midi-chlorians in his bloodstream, telescoping his natural abilities, enhancing them exponentially.

He had been here, of course, when the things burst out of the kitchen, and he'd defended himself adroitly with a series of Force pushes and acrobatic jumps while weaker and less skilled students had fallen and been devoured. Within minutes the things from the kitchen had transformed the dining hall into a charnel house of untrammeled butchery. Now the floors were slick with blood.

The newly dead were rising slowly, shuffling to their feet. Rising up with them, Lussk stared into their faces, faces that he recognized from the academy, now contorted into something utterly new. He felt no fear at the sight of them, no sense of foreboding—only a slick dark fascination.

I'm looking at my future, he thought, and shivered with anticipation. It was a *good* future, he realized, an endless future, a place of unfathomable possibility.

He saw it all now. The rumor was that Darth Scabrous had been experimenting with an immortality drug, a remedy for death itself, and Lussk saw now that the Sith Lord had been successful beyond his wildest dreams and most deranged nightmares. These things *had* transcended death. The power they held was beyond anything taught here at the academy. Before it, both Jedi and Sith were nothing, less than nothing, infinitesimal crumbs in the vast expanse of the universe.

Lussk saw the things around him crowding closer.

And that was when he realized it.

It wasn't enough just to be transformed, to see the world with these new necroscopic eyes. The Sickness had given him its gift, but it wanted something in return, something crippling and enormous, and now, belatedly, Lussk grasped what it was. The Sickness wanted that part of him that made him who he was, that exceptional set of skills and memories and quirks that had made him unique. The Sickness meant to siphon all of that away, so that it could make him part of the greater, swelling organism of the dead.

The Sickness wanted his soul.

No, Lussk told it. *It's too much. Even for what you offer, even for immortality itself, the price is too high.*

I will make you the last one, the Sickness promised. *Of all the others, you alone shall endure. That is what I have to offer you.*

No.

The Sickness paused within him, considering. *That is too bad,* it said finally, *because you no longer have a choice in the matter.*

Placing his hand over his chest, Lussk felt his heart stop beating. All around him, the newly dead were screaming, screaming.

He threw back his head and opened his mouth.

And he, too, began to scream.

Ra'at FOUND THE WEAPONS CACHE JUST BEFORE THEY reached the barrier.

He'd heard that these tunnels were lined with sub-chambers and cysts, some of them hundreds of years old, as old as the academy itself. According to the rumors, generations of Sith Lords had used them for storage or hiding places for things they never wanted found.

He and Kindra had found the first of the chambers twenty minutes after the group had finished watching the training droid's hologram. Nobody had spoken much since then; they had moved in silence, listening.

"Look," Kindra said, pointing at the badly oxidized metal sign bracketed onto the wall. It read:

ARSENAL 1174-AA

"Give me a hand," Ra'at said, taking hold of the handle. It was a rudimentary side hatch whose stubborn refusal to open was less a matter of security and more a result of the moisture and grit that had accumulated inside its components over the years.

Maggs grabbed one edge and Hartwig and Kindra took the other, and it came open with a metallic clang. They all stood for a moment peering in.

Hartwig whistled.

"That's the most beautiful sight I've seen in a long time," he said.

Ra'at had to agree with him. The bin in front of them was loaded with gear—some basic melee weapons and body armor for training purposes, headpieces and blast-dampening chest plates, and in the back, in a separate wall mount, three lightsabers.

Kindra reached past him and grabbed one in each hand. As Ra'at took the last one for himself, he wondered why she'd taken two, and guessed she was just optimizing her chances of getting a fully functional weapon. Although the power cells were supposed to hold an almost indefinite charge, there was no telling if any of them still worked, or even how long they'd been stashed down here. As often as he'd trained with them, lightsabers still held an arcane sense of mystery that made them both fascinating and vaguely unsettling, a link to the Sith's ancient past.

Ra'at thumbed the activation plate, and the scarlet blade sprang to life. He could feel it vibrating up from hand to elbow, the sheer authoritative power of it humming through his entire arm, giving it purpose and strength. He brought the blade up in front of his face, admiring it, feeling the small fine hairs stiffen on the backs of his arms. Next to him, Kindra had switched on both of hers as well. After a moment of comparison, she deactivated both lightsabers.

"Maggs," she said, and tossed him the one in her left hand. He caught it effortlessly.

"Thanks."

Hartwig frowned. "Wait a second. Where's mine?"

"There were only three."

"So what, I'm out of luck?"

Kindra shrugged, and Ra'at realized the other reason she'd grabbed two instead of one: it had allowed her to decide who carried the third. She had given it to Maggs, who—while not the most proficient duelist—was probably the least likely to snap under pressure and take one of their heads off either by accident or in a fit of poor judgment.

"Flay *that* noise," Hartwig said. "We should draw lots to see who gets what. Otherwise . . ."

"Otherwise what?" Kindra asked. She was still holding her remaining lightsaber in front of her, regarding Hartwig coldly from behind its blade. "You'll leave? Good riddance. It's everyone for themselves anyway."

Hartwig glared at Kindra with a glint of righteous indignation that Ra'at guessed was eventually going to get him killed. Kindra, however, had already seemed to have lost interest in him: she deactivated the lightsaber, clipped it onto her belt, and began eyeing the corridor ahead of them. "Come on, let's keep going. There might be another weapons dump up this way."

"Don't turn your back on me," Hartwig said.

"Is that a threat?"

"Just a warning."

She unclipped the lightsaber. "Then I guess I'll just kill you now, won't I?"

"You—"

Kindra's arm whipped upward. The blade was already ignited, sweeping up in a lethal blur, halting centimeters from Hartwig's throat. Stepping back, Hartwig glanced over at Maggs and saw him waiting to see what would happen. For a long moment, neither of them moved or spoke, and the only sound inside the tunnel was the faint steady hum of the lightsaber itself.

"You won't do that," Hartwig said. "You need me too much." But what he'd obviously intended to be defiance came out as little more than a strangled-sounding squeak. Kindra didn't answer, just stood riveted to his gaze. The blade stayed where it was. Ra'at saw how its light reflected off the beads of sweat that had begun to accumulate on Hartwig's upper lip.

"Kindra," Ra'at started.

"Shut up."

"He's right. You saw those things in the holo. We're outnumbered. We need every—"

"I'll tell you what I *don't* need." She still hadn't taken her eyes off Hartwig. "I *don't* need to constantly be looking over my shoulder." She nodded, seeming to decide something in that moment. "No, Hartwig, I think I'm going to have to finish your sorry carcass off right now."

Hartwig's lip twitched, trying to make words that wouldn't come for what seemed like a long time.

"Do it then," he rasped. "Make your move."

Ra'at's hand slipped downward toward the handle of his own lightsaber. Things were deteriorating even faster than he'd anticipated—yet somehow he wasn't surprised. Perhaps it was better this way anyway.

You really want to take sides now? he thought, and for the moment at least he willed his hand to stay where it was.

"Uh, guys—?" Maggs said from behind them. "You're going to want to see this. It's—"

He broke off in a sloppy cough that sounded too loose and wet, as if he were struggling to keep himself from gagging.

Maggs whistled. "Anybody else smell that?"

That was how they found the wall.

30/Taste

▬▬▬❙▬▬❙▬▬❙▬▬

SCABROUS ENTERED THE LIBRARY THROUGH THE NORTH-west side, as was his habit. There were five main entrances, but this one led directly to the underground chamber where he'd first found the Holocron, so it held a certain degree of emotional resonance. Also, it was closest, and he had begun deliberately conserving energy. According to the hemodialysis counter on the shoulder pack, his whole-blood reserves were down to two units now. He wasn't worried about running out, but he wanted to make sure that he was sufficiently able to enjoy everything that would come next.

Stepping out of the storm, he walked beneath the high, icicle-dripping stone archway and strode briskly down the corridor that led to the main stairwell. These walls were thick, but he could still hear the wind whooping and shrieking outside, and after a moment of standing absolutely still, he heard another sound, the low crack of shifting rock and stone. It sounded like something making its way through a pile of brittle old bones.

"Dail'Liss," Scabrous said. "Come out."

At first, there was no response. Then a long branch slithered from the crooked crack in the wall above him, sliding sinuously downward, and the Sith Lord looked up to see the face of the Neti, its ancient, wrinkled eyes peering wearily at him.

"My lord," the librarian said. "What brings you here?"

"I need something from you."

"Anything, my lord."

Scabrous started to speak again, and something in the Neti's voice stopped him. In the past its tone had always been respectful, even reverential, but now it sounded outright frightened. Its fear was the fear of the old and infirm, the apprehension of a thing that couldn't protect itself properly from some nebulous but very real threat.

"You feel it, too, then?" Scabrous asked.

"What, my lord?"

"Do not play ignorant with me."

The Neti quavered visibly but did not answer right away. Then it said: "You refer to the Sickness, yes?"

"Is that what you're calling it?" Scabrous asked. "A sickness?"

"If it pleases my lord . . . it is a disease, some kind of uncontrollable infection that has been let loose."

"The academy has been exposed to worse things in the past."

"I speak not simply of the academy." Another pause, then one even longer. "I sense it within *you,* my lord."

Scabrous stared up at the tree creature's face, looking deep into its moist and measuring eyes. As he looked, he felt something stir inside him, a chasm opening, as if some second, chiseled set of jaws were spreading apart in his chest. It wasn't a painful feeling, not at all—if anything, it was profoundly *tactile.* For a moment he actually looked down at his body, expecting to see his abdomen stretching beneath the broadcloth of his tunic, the rib cage broadening, gaping open to reveal . . . what? Something new? Something that transcended even his vast realm of experience?

Scabrous drew a breath, trembling with anticipation, and allowed the feeling to recede.

"Come down here," he said.

"My lord?"

"Now."

The crack in the wall widened and the Neti's thick trunk slithered tentatively downward through it, wood grain creaking in sinuous little crackles as it twisted closer to where the Sith Lord stood waiting. Now there was no mistaking the fear in the librarian's face; it bordered on panic.

"My lord, please—"

"I want you to send out a message."

"*Yes?*"

"There is a Jedi here among us, on this planet."

The librarian waited.

"The Jedi's particular talent is botanical telepathy, plant language. Right now she is communicating with the spirit of an orchid, a flower whose presence she trusts implicitly, and . . ."

Scabrous paused. He could hear the words that he was saying, but his voice sounded different to him. As he spoke, he became aware of that hollow, gaping feeling again, except this time it wasn't confined to his chest and abdomen—it was radiating through his entire body systemically, enveloping his arms and legs and head.

"My lord?" the Neti prompted.

Scabrous still didn't respond. For an instant, certainly no longer, he could actually feel the presence of transformation pushing up against the corpuscles of freshly infused blood, fighting against it, invading and overtaking it. And again, as before, there was no pain, only a feverish red aura spilling outward to encompass his vision from within. He was deeply conscious of his own breathing, in and out, a hot coppery taste in his mouth, and a peculiar wave of euphoria rushed over him—a promise of power beyond comprehension. Yet miraculously, he remained lucid, wholly self-aware.

"The Jedi's name," he said at last, "is Hestizo Trace. I want you to speak to her in the voice of the orchid, do you understand? You will *summon* her here to the library in the voice that she trusts, so that I shall deal with her, and fulfill my destiny. Is that clear?"

The Neti garbled out a sound that wasn't quite a word.

"I asked if you . . . ," Scabrous began, and then he saw why the tree creature wasn't answering. A huge chunk of pulp, the Neti's woody flesh, had been ripped out just below its mouth, leaving a hole the size of Scabrous's fist. Thick amber-colored sap dribbled from the wound, oozing down its rough bark, trickling over its branches.

Scabrous licked his lips and smiled, still tasting the strange sticky blood of the tree creature on his tongue and the roof of his mouth. *I did that*, he marveled. He'd attacked it without the slightest conscious intent—it had been that thing within, that mouth. On some intuitive level he understood that this explained the vast explosion of strength he'd felt.

"My lord . . . ," the Neti managed at last, its voice trembling. *"Please . . ."*

"You do understand what I'm asking," Scabrous said, "or do you not?"

"Yes . . . my lord."

"Excellent. Then I await her arrival."

He left the Neti stretched from the ceiling, a pool of semi-translucent sap already spreading underneath it across the library's floor.

31/Flesh Blizzard

Zo stood with snow falling in her face, staring up at the tower.

"I don't understand," she said. "How did we end up back here?"

The Whiphid didn't answer. This time, though, any response would have been gratuitous. She *knew* why they were here. Somewhere inside the paddock they'd lost their sense of direction to a Sith illusion, crude but effective, and now they were back out where they'd begun.

Then she saw the figures.

They were poised like carved grotesques along the uppermost walls of the tower, life-sized statues illuminated by the irregular stammering red glow from the top. At first, she thought that was all they were. Statues. Gargoyles.

Except they were moving.

Crawling, swarming over the others' backs like some hideously overgrown version of the flesh-eating boski beetles she'd seen aboard Tulkh's ship. And when the light caught their faces, she could see that they were—or at least once had been—human. Their uniforms, which Zo realized must be the black robes and tunics of the Sith acolyte, were tattered and ragged, and they billowed behind them in the screeching wind. She watched as a cluster of them began to clutch and lever their way closer to the tower's viewports. One of them threw back its head and began to hammer one fist on the surface with awful ape-like determination.

"What are they doing?"

Tulkh grunted. "Looking for a way in."

"Why?"

A scream came shearing down from above, the single compressed blast that she remembered from inside the supposedly deserted barracks, and the bounty hunter stepped back, hissing some obscenity under his breath.

"They—"

Before he could finish, one of the things fell from far above, whistling down in front of her.

She looked back at Tulkh. ·

He was gone.

Zo jerked back and looked up again. Overhead, another of the things on the tower had detached itself and was plummeting downward like a renegade slab of darkness itself, some broken chunk of the universe, falling fast, still screaming, through the flying snow.

The screeching thing slammed into the ground on all fours, and even though its back was to her, Zo could see the hole where its uniform was ripped open to reveal the architecture of exposed ribs and scooped-out portions of vertebrae. Snowy air whistled through the hole, and she saw clumped loops of intestine, blackened with a crust of dried blood, flapping alongside the torn fabric. Part of its lungs seemed to have been jolted loose in the fall, leaving one of them dangling, inflating and deflating raggedly like some small panting animal.

Tulkh. It drove him down into the snow when it landed on him. And now it's trying to get him out.

The second thing stalked over toward the snowdrift, its head slightly inclined, seeking an angle of attack. Zo heard another scream from above, and the two corpses in the Sith uniforms shrieked back their answering cry.

Tulkh's arm burst up and out of the snow, holding his spear, and thrust it forward. An instant later the Sith-thing on top of him reared back, staggering blindly, the tip of his spear embedded in its face. Its right cheek was a suppurating cave-in of demolished bone structure. The long shaft protruded from its head like a clumsy over-sized horn.

Tulkh sat up, spitting snow.

"Juddering yank-wit," he snarled. "This should teach you to jump on me."

He knocked the thing backward with one foot, held it down, and jerked his spear loose from its face. Then using both hands, he brought the spear tip down hard, directly into the thing's already-demolished torso, hard enough to pulverize the spine, cutting it completely in half. The upper and lower segments squirmed listlessly in the snow, then fell still.

"Hold on." Breathing hard, he glanced up at Zo. "Where's the other one?"

"I don't—"

"*Down.*" And without waiting for her to comply, he fired the spear directly at her. Zo dropped to her knees, feeling his spear whisk through her hair, just across the top of her scalp. From behind, something landed on top of her, a landslide of meat, flattening the air from her chest, blocking out sight and hearing, driving her into the snow. She felt cold, clutching hands and the sticky-oily drip of partially coagulated fluids seeping down over the skin of her neck, where her collar didn't quite cover her flesh. It, too, began to scream, and then the scream broke off with a choked flapping noise. It was followed by a series of sharp chops, and the flapping stopped.

"Get up." Tulkh's voice, muffled, came from above her.

Zo dragged herself upright. The bounty hunter was standing in front of her. The severed head of the thing he'd just decapitated hung from the top of the spear at an almost jaunty angle, the tip jetting upward through its broken jaw to protrude from one empty eye socket. The gray lips sagged, dangling thick strands of ropy pink drool, and its one remaining eye wobbled back and forth, somehow managing to look both sly and stupid beneath the swollen lid.

"A teenager," Zo said. "Seventeen, eighteen at the most." She watched the yellow eye. "It's still looking at me."

"They're dead." Tulkh shrugged down at the other body he'd left in the snow and shook his head. "Forget about it."

There was another klaxon-like blast of noise from up above. Zo looked up as far as she could.

It was like a rallying call.

The snow-choked darkness that surrounded the tower was suddenly filled with falling bodies, more than she could count. They came tumbling in twos and threes from the top of the tower, eyes blazing, teeth shining, slamming into the ground in every direction, some almost close enough to grab her from the point of impact. They brought their screams with them so that they seemed to land on a cushion of sound.

In front of her, Tulkh fell into a fighting stance.

"Jedi trained you to fight, didn't they?"

She nodded once.

"Then fight them!"

The Sith-things were all around them now. Their screams were constant, ululating everywhere, the air itself seeming to stiffen with their shrieks. Zo realized that she couldn't see Tulkh anymore.

There's no way we can take them all.

And then something else spoke.

Yes, you can.

Zo paused, brought up short by the voice. It sounded true and strong and clarion-clear. At first, she thought it was the orchid. Then she realized that she was hearing the voice of her brother Rojo.

But that's impossible, he's nowhere near here—

And it wasn't really Rojo—the words were coming from her memory, from the storehouse of encouragement that he'd given her in the past, when she'd been training at the Jedi academy. There had been times when she'd felt exhausted and hopeless, and he had spoken to her, encouraged her to stand up, to be strong and be true.

Listen, Hestizo. The Jedi taught you much more than simply how to fight. They taught you how to live. How to live within the Force, and uphold the bond that you share with it.

With these words, Hestizo Trace felt a deep and voluminous feeling of rightness booming through her. At the Jedi Temple she'd heard others in the discipline try to describe the experience, saying it was like this or like that. But for her it was simply the experience of being alive, of wild and ecstatic belief, but amplified. All the encumbrances of frustration and anxiety fell away, filling her very essence with an entire universe of pure, sustaining energy.

She looked around again and saw the Sith-things crashing to the ground on all sides of her, raising their heads and opening their mouths.

And everything.

Slowed.

Down.

"*Get . . . ,*" Tulkh was saying, one arm sludging back to pluck a meter-long arrow from his quiver, moving so slowly that he seemed to be underwater. Zo sprang up into the air like a woman moving through a gallery of wax figures. She came down just behind one of the Sith-things, grabbed its greasy, partially decayed skull in both hands from the back, and wrenched it hard to the left. The cervical spine popped and gave with a crunch, the entire cranium coming loose as she ripped it free from the shoulders. The head was still screaming as she threw it underhand into the next shambling thing, hitting it hard enough to knock it back into the side of the tower. A third she grabbed by the throat and crotch, hoisting it up and pile-driving it straight upward in the direction it had come.

Behind her, she heard the twang as Tulkh's arrow finally left the bowstring. Without glancing back, Zo reached out and lifted the flying arrow out of the air. She did this effortlessly, without a thought, like someone taking a book from a shelf. Behind her, across the depths of motionless snowflakes, Tulkh stood with his lip still curling to form the last part of his first word while the five remaining Sith-things perched like statues barely moving in various aspects of attack.

Springing forward, snapping the arrow in two, Zo buried the halves of the shaft in two of their skulls hard enough to impale them permanently together, face-to-face like horrific lovers melded for all eternity. She grabbed the arm of the grinning, mossy-faced Sith acolyte who appeared to have gnawed through his own lips and the interior of his mouth up to his hard palate. Twist. *Pop*. The arm came free at the elbow and she swung it down like a club on the skull of the walking corpse in front of him.

She sensed events moving faster now, her hold on the situation loosening again. The snowflakes were coming unstuck from the air, starting to confetti down in reckless profusion. The Sith-thing that she'd flung upward earlier was finally coming back down. As the last of the things shambled toward her, she heard a dull whacking thump, the kindling-sharp crack of a dozen fractured bones.

". . . *down!*" Tulkh finished, only then seeming to realize that the arrow was gone from his bow and that the Sith-things were all on the ground now, torn apart. He looked up at Zo. His nostrils twitched.

"Leave any for me?"

She pointed at the two bodies writhing in the snow between them. Tulkh drew his spear, raised it up, and rammed it down through them both. His eyes were blazing, saturated with red, almost glutted with pleasure, and there was no misinterpreting the grin that twisted over his face. Zo thought that she'd never seen any living thing, human or otherwise, extract such shameless pleasure from the act of killing.

Hestizo . . . ?

This time the voice of the orchid was unmistakable.

Hestizo, come . . .

She stopped and listened, felt herself smiling, overcome by a sudden surge of hope. From somewhere in the falling snow, Tulkh was staring at her.

"What is it?" he wanted to know.

"The Murakami," she said. "It's alive!"

"I thought you said—"

"I know! But I can hear it! It's calling me!"

Tulkh scowled, unconvinced. "Where?"

She peered back through the blizzard, pointing.

"The library."

32/Flametown

IT WAS A PLEASURE TO BURN.

The Neti saw it now—latched onto this simple tautology in a way that he had never grasped anything in his long life. Within moments after Scabrous had left him here with his mission, to call out to the Jedi, to summon her here, everything within his ageless wooden mind had begun to grow wonderfully, gloriously clear.

And oh, it was a pleasure, a *pleasure* to burn.

Clutching rows of holobooks with one long branch-hand, the librarian flung them into the rising flames. And the flames surged higher.

After the Sith Lord had bitten him, Dail'Liss had endured a brief but agonizing spasm of physical weakness and distress, the pain compounded by the brooding fear that had been growing in his mind throughout the day. This was what he'd felt outside the walls of his sanctuary. The Sickness was in here now, it had violated the barriers of safety and security, and it was inside *him*—running through his roots, spreading through his branches and leaves.

And the Sickness was *laughing*.

At first that laughter had sounded so mocking, so bitter and cold, that the Neti had only cowered before it.

Even the Sith themselves couldn't match the dark malevolence in its voice.

Old fool, it had said, *foolish old creature, your life has been wasted here among your books.*

The Neti had tried to respond, to tell it no, that these scrolls and texts *were* his life, but the Sickness hadn't shown the slightest bit of interest in that. It had more to say, and the Neti realized that he was a captive audience.

It's not too late, the Sickness said. *I have given you new life, and a new purpose, and you will know it if you seek my face. Will you, old tree? Will you seek my face?*

What is it? the Neti asked. *What is your face?*

Mine is the face of blood and fire.

And with those words, everything changed. Looking around now at the contents of the library, the countless scrolls and ancient texts, the holdings and stacks that he had spent his lifetime accumulating here, organizing and cataloging for a thousand years or more, he saw them for what they were.

Fuel.

The flesh is our fuel, the Sickness counseled, and its voice was like thunder now, *and the books are our fuel, and this planet is our fuel, all things are fuel, they exist only so that they can be consumed by us.*

Yes, yes—

They are meat for the beast.

Yes.

And the beast is you.

Yes.

From there, the Neti discovered that everything came to him with oily, gratifying ease. Giving himself up utterly to the Sickness, he had started the fire without the slightest hesitation. There were years of fuel here, plenty here to burn. Within minutes, the central wing of the library was ablaze, and the seeping, maddened grin of the Neti shone with reflected orange firelight.

Although there were no mirrors here, no means of seeing his reflection, Dail'Liss knew that the Sickness had changed him. Whole chunks of its once-proud bark had begun molting, dropping off in patches, its branches curling and blackening, dripping with thick, foul-smelling drainage that gathered around its roots. But the most profound transformation had happened within him. The Sickness had taught him. He had sought its face. And now the Neti laughed into the fire—its once-kind eyes were twisted now, tightened into knotty slits, its mouth coiled into a wide, salivating grin as it spoke out in the voice of the orchid.

Come, Hestizo Trace. Hurry. Come to the library.

More scrolls, more holobooks, tumbled into the fire. Sap boiled in the coals.

I await your arrival eagerly, I wish to see you here, I have urgent need of you—

He stopped and turned, branches whispering.

She was already on her way.

33/Redwall

"LOOKED BIGGER ON THE HOLO," MAGGS SAID, HIS VOICE muffled by his hand.

He and Ra'at and the others were all standing in front of the wall, covering their noses and mouths. The end of the tunnel was filled with a smell so rancid that it almost transcended the definition of the word. In the single breath that Ra'at had inadvertently sucked in without covering his lips, he'd actually been able to *taste* it on the back of his tongue and the roof of his mouth. It was the horribly organic ripe-rot-reek of once-living tissue whose life force had evacuated it, leaving only a mass of stinking weight.

"What's it made of?" Maggs muttered.

"Looks like scavenged metal, debris . . ."

"Metal doesn't stink like this."

"It's not just metal."

"So what is it?" Kindra asked.

"Well . . ." Ra'at pointed at a white blade-like shaft sticking out. "I'm pretty sure that's a shinbone."

"Human?"

Ra'at nodded.

Hartwig swallowed. It took him a few tries. "Gah."

"Looks . . . ," Ra'at started to say, and stopped. He was going to say *partially digested,* and decided that

that observation probably wouldn't bring anything helpful to the conversation. If the expressions of the others were any indication, they were holding just this side of gastric mutiny.

"The exit's on the other side," Kindra said, and activated her lightsaber.

"Hold on." Ra'at turned and looked back. He'd felt something—not much more than a ripple in the fabric of the Force, but he'd long ago learned to trust such quirks of perception as far more meaningful than anything gleaned by eyes and ears. He shot a glance at Maggs. "Lightsaber. *Now*."

Instantly Maggs joined him and Kindra, and Ra'at pointed silently into a pool of shadow just beyond a bank of massive metal cases that looked as though they'd been turned into storage for droid parts. Something was moving visibly on the other side of the storage bins, and an instant later it came staggering into view.

"What in the name . . . ," Hartwig said. It was the first thing he'd said since the confrontation with Kindra over the lightsaber. "What's wrong with him?"

"What's wrong?" Maggs made a sick noise. "What's *right*?"

Ra'at recognized the Sith acolyte making his way toward them, but only barely—he was the fifth-year known as Rucker. The left side of Rucker's face had been ripped cleanly away to reveal the gleaming infrastructure of cheekbone and jaw. His gelid eyes quivered in their sockets like a pair of infected red eggs. He was naked except for a pair of black breeches torn open at the front, and the massive bulge of his swollen abdomen was so badly distended that he could hardly carry it forward.

He—it—stared at them for a long beat. Then it threw back its head, jaws wrenching open, and screamed.

"Kill it!" Hartwig said. *"What are you waiting for?"*

Still screaming, the Rucker-thing whirled and staggered toward the wall. Ra'at saw its mouth open even wider, the mandible popping loose from its hinges completely now, and the scream became a gargled gush as it disgorged a flood of reddish gray directly onto the barrier, its belly shrinking visibly as it did so.

Watching helplessly, Ra'at felt a nauseating roundelay of terror swerve through him, like the shadow of some far-distant flying object—a latecoming refusal, despite everything he'd seen so far, to fully accept this monstrosity at face value. *Am I seeing this?* he thought. *Am I really?*

Still dribbling, the thing flung its hands up to pack the mess together, working it tightly into the wall. Almost despite himself, Ra'at thought of the cosm-wasps he'd read about, and the way they built nests by filling their bellies and regurgitating the pulp.

We're pulp, too, he thought, and the smell hit him in the most vulnerable part of his own stomach, making his gorge rise. The only thing that stopped him from losing total control of his gag reflex was the even more potent realization that the thing was swiveling back toward them, moving much faster now.

"Take him down," he heard Kindra murmur, almost to herself, and she, Maggs, and Ra'at himself advanced in a single coordinated strike. Kindra sliced its head off with one sweep, while Maggs took out its legs. Ra'at's blow slashed down the front of the body, cleaving it almost perfectly down the middle. Less than five seconds later the Rucker-thing's corpse lay on the floor, drawn and quartered, still twitching.

"What happened to the others?" Maggs breathed, gesturing at the empty space.

"Good question," Ra'at said. "It's a dead end here. Where'd they go?"

"Forget it." Kindra turned to the wall. "Let's get to work on this."

Ra'at nodded but didn't move. His gaze went back to the steel droid bins, near the shadowy area where the thing had originated. He was still thinking about that scream it had let out, high and shrill, like the blast of a living air horn. What if it had been a signal to the others, some kind of—

One of the steel droid bins fell over with a clang.

And Ra'at saw.

The students of the Sith academy of Odacer-Faustin were gathered here after all, had been here the entire time. They'd just been waiting in silence, watching.

"How many?" Maggs murmured.

"Ten," Ra'at said, "maybe twelve—"

The silence exploded in a scream, and the things came spilling forward in one coordinated wave, surging into the open tunnel like a single organism.

"Precision killing box," Kindra snapped. "Right and left." She flicked a hand at Hartwig and Maggs. "Get us through that wall."

Ra'at broke right, as directed, letting his lightsaber lead him like a natural extension of his will. He pivoted and swung it down into the head of the first Sith-thing that he came to, splitting its skull down to the tonsils. But its hands flung upward blindly toward him like a pair of carrion birds, and it kept fighting. Turning, he came up from below and took out its legs just above the knees, leaving the thing in a slimy mess of its own dissolution. Two more came at him, and he chopped them down with an absolute economy of motion.

To the right. To the left. Behind. Move. Move. Move.

Ra'at unplugged his mind and let his training take over. It was just like the drills in Master Hracken's pain pipe. He'd already begun to see the fight through the mirror-bright lens of a warrior, reducing the battle to a sequence of movements, like a series of doors he had to pass through to get to the other side.

The things were screaming around him again, that pulsing, deliberate scream. Like the smell, it blanketed everything and made his skull feel as if it was going to pop. As he chopped another of the things in half, a white-hot shock of pain sprang up through his right shoulder. His hand went numb, just like that, the last three fingers dead around the handle of his lightsaber, and he spun around, snatching it from the air with his left hand before it hit the floor. Everything was happening with crazy tricked-out speed, and he both saw and didn't see the thing that had attached itself to his biceps, grinning up as its incisors raked his flesh. Blood splashed around its lips like tawdry lipstick.

Kindra flashed into his peripheral vision and thrust her blade crosswise through the thing's upper thorax, slashing it down in a meaty spray. Its jaws stayed locked onto Ra'at's arm, until Ra'at swung his own blade down on top of it, working left-handed, cutting the thing's head apart. Across the tunnel he glimpsed Maggs hacking his own hole through the group, his blade a fan-like blur, but the tide of bodies was too thick. If they kept coming like this, the things would have him cornered. Ra'at saw the black oval of Maggs's mouth shouting something, but he couldn't make out what it was.

We're losing, Ra'at thought, and then: *How can we be losing?*

A sudden crash of electricity exploded across the cave. Ra'at saw one of the Sith things go rag-dolling backward into the wall as if it had been jerked away on invisible wires. Now Ra'at could smell the ozone in the air, along with the unmistakable smoky odor of burned hair and skin.

In front of him, Hartwig lunged into view, eyes bulging, his forehead a map of veins, but the look on his face was pure confusion.

That's not possible, Ra'at thought, *only Sith Masters can use Force lightning, how—*

"*Stand back!*" a voice shouted, and when Ra'at looked behind Hartwig he saw Master Hracken standing there. Hracken's arms were thrust out, with both hands extended. "Down, now!"

Maggs and Kindra had taken down three more of the things between them, and stepped over the bodies as the Combat Master flung his hands up and outward, hurling out streams of Force lightning. The tunnel shuddered, erupting with an electrical firestorm so intense that for an instant Ra'at couldn't see past it. He smelled his own scorched eyelashes. Even after he shut his eyes, the afterimage of the cave, the bodies, and the others lay imprinted on his corneas in bleeding plaid patterns of red and black.

The Sith Master kept his hands in front of him, muscles straining, jaw clenched with fury. For a moment he disappeared yet again behind a vast crackling hood of electricity. It shattered the length of the tunnel with a massive, ear-rending *KRACK* that rocked the entire structure to its foundation and sent loose particles of building materials skittering down the walls.

Ra'at rubbed his eyes, waiting for what he saw to make sense. Part of the permasteel ceiling above his head was torn loose by electrical shock and dangled on a slew of cables. All around him, the floor was filled with smoking corpses, severed limbs and heads, still writhing as if trying to find a means of knitting themselves back together. Some of them were actively on fire. Others lay blind, their eyes cooked in their sockets. The heat from the Force lightning had literally melted off their skin, leaving webs and rivulets of liquefied tissue trickling from piles of blackened bones while the things shifted and squirmed, tried to stand and collapsed back into their own murk.

In front of the foul-smelling wall, Hracken stood trembling. A tendon twitched and jigged in his jaw, and Ra'at saw that the Sith Master had bitten his lip hard enough to draw blood.

"Through this way," he said.

Kindra pointed to the wound on Ra'at's arm. "How bad is it?"

"Not bad."

"Did one of those things do that to you?"

"I'm fine." Ra'at tore a scrap of his pant leg loose and started hurriedly tying it around his upper arm as a make-shift tourniquet. But the blood was already soaking through the fabric, sluicing down his elbow to his fore-arm with alarming eagerness. Kindra was looking at that, too, along with Maggs and Hartwig and Master Hracken, and Ra'at realized the power dynamic of the group had already shifted. As quickly as the battle had ended, he, Ra'at, had become a liability. Weight to be carried.

Or cut loose.

Out of the game, just like that.

"I can fight just as well with my left," Ra'at said weakly. "You saw. You all did."

Kindra just nodded, her face inscrutable, a map of un-spoken strategy. Master Hracken said nothing, didn't even seem to be paying attention. None of the others spoke, either. Ra'at ignited his lightsaber again in his left hand and swung it down on top of the wall that the things had built here, slashing deep into the pile of scrap metal and congealed viscera, driving it home, carving out a massive chunk of debris and kicking it loose. It dropped to the floor with a soggy clank.

"See?" he said.

None of them commented. Next to him, on either side, Kindra and Maggs also fell to work, cutting into the wall. Ra'at attacked his part of it as if he were still working alone. The smell of cooked meat was stronger than ever, and the pain in his right arm had become a dull, pounding drumbeat. He tried to put it all out of his head, to no avail. He thought of Nickter, how fast he had changed. They would leave him behind, too, unless he showed them that he could still fight.

Use the Force. Let the dark side strengthen you.

Yet at the same time, something cautioned him about using the Force in his current state of mind. Something told him it was a bad idea. No, not just bad—a *terrible* idea. Who knew what he might be invoking if he summoned it now?

What is your state of mind right now? a voice inside asked.

Dying. I'm dying.

No, that was crazy. It was a flesh wound. He'd lost some blood, yes, but he was young and strong. Trained. Conditioned. He'd suffered worse injuries in the pain chamber, for that matter, even today.

What if those things were infected?

Ra'at realized that he was too dizzy to stand. A clammy layer of sweat had already crept over his forehead, one or two drops venturing down the small of his back. His vision broke into a series of yellowing ocher bands and shadows, streaking through everything, staining it. He couldn't breathe. It felt as though someone had slammed a durasteel restraining band across his chest, the pain shooting down his left arm.

Gasping, he fell to his knees. Shut his eyes. There was the desire to scream, but he couldn't muster a breath. Helpless, no longer having a choice, he invoked the power of Sith alchemy, the Force itself.

Abide in me now. Fill me with the strength to stand and fight, to—

It smashed into him at full volume, a vast black wave, torrential beyond all reckoning. Too late Ra'at realized what he'd invited into his brain.

It might have learned to mimic the Force.

It might have answered as the Force.

But it was not the Force.

Ra'at shuddered. The others were all staring at him now. It didn't matter. In a penultimate moment of clarity, he could actually *see* a skeletal black fist clamping over his heart, squeezing it until the muscle burst. He could feel his body shutting down, whole systems crashing, blood pressure and respiration failing, as this contaminated version of the Force took over.

Mine now, the Sickness said. *Mine body and soul.*

Not killing him.

Transforming him.

Ra'at felt a dark, orchestral surge of relief rushing through him. Released, he felt weightless, towering, godlike. A horrific smile gnarled over his face. He began to weep—big bloody tears of gratitude running down his cheeks and dribbling off his chin.

I can scream now, he thought. *Oh thank you, I will scream and they will hear me, bless you, I can scream and they will know how it feels to have an entire galaxy spread out like an open grave at my feet.*

The thing that had been Mnah Ra'at jerked its jaws wide. In that instant he saw, of all things, a pyramid, as black as the tide that had obliterated all conscious thought, a thing resting in a pair of pale hands.

All at once he knew his place in the galaxy.

He knew everything.

And he screamed, and as he did, he saw Combat Master Hracken standing directly in front of him with his hands outstretched.

"Good-bye, Ra'at," Hracken said.

Ra'at lunged forward. A white-hot explosion of Force lightning exploded through him, and he knew no more.

34/Reboot

IN THE END, IT TOOK TULKH LESS THAN A MINUTE TO RE-
alize how much trouble he was truly in.

The Whiphid had never believed in fate or any kind of
mystic galactic justice: in his experience, whatever happened, happened. The innocent suffered while evil
thrived, and to the victors went the spoils. Even so, when
his own personal circumstances went from bad to worse,
he couldn't help wondering if this were some kind of cos-
mic comeuppance for abandoning the Jedi at the library.

She'd been so certain that the flower was summoning
her from inside there. Maybe it had been, but Tulkh saw
no advantage in going in after it, not when he could return to his ship and put this whole forsaken planet in the
past. And so he'd let her go alone. After all, he owed the
Jedi girl nothing. All right, she had saved him, but he'd
saved her at least once as well and that made them even,
didn't it?

A new kind of darkness had risen up from the landscape now like some night within the night, so that the
academy's snow-swept ruins glowed faintly in what little light emanated from within them. In the distance,
Tulkh heard screams. They were not random, these
screams—they rose up and swooped down, oscillating
in the wind, rising from different directions.

Yet it was the silence in between that made him the most uneasy.

He thought about the things that had dropped from the tower, and how many more of them seemed to be out there now, screaming into the storm. Tulkh gripped his spear, checked his bow, counted his arrows, and listened to the screams grow louder—closer. With numbers like those, he couldn't help but wonder how many he would encounter on his way back to the *Mirocaw*.

He didn't have to wait long.

He was detouring around a long, curved, hangar-like structure on the western outskirts of the academy's grounds when they came at him.

Crushing waves, one from either side, poured in on his right and left. Tulkh smelled them, heard their screams, the lurching stomp of their advance, seconds before they would have ripped him limb from limb.

He'd already kicked open the hatchway behind him and dived inside, pivoting to get his first look at the high, brightly lit curved-rib structure that surrounded him. The students must have used this place, he thought— some wit had left a handmade sign painted over the entranceway. It read:

WELCOME TO THE PAIN PIPE

Tulkh looked around. It appeared to be some kind of training simulation chamber, a wide, high space full of elaborately machined devices that protruded from the floor and walls, even down from the ceiling—pillars, pinions, retracted coils, and battering rams. But that quick impression was all that Tulkh was able to absorb before the hatch burst open behind him, allowing the flood of bodies to come spewing into the space with him.

The Whiphid's evolutionary process had optimized his killing skills. Now he called upon the full extent of his genetic heritage. The hatchway forced the things to enter singly, and Tulkh brought the first and second ones down with arrows, firing point-blank into the space between their eyes with enough force to embed their skulls directly into the walls. The arrows alone didn't stop them, but they held the things down long enough that he could charge forward and gouge their heads off with his spear. The headless corpses dropped to the floor with a gurgle while the heads hung in place from the walls, gnashing and twitching and rolling their eyes like hideous masks from some dark gallery of death.

That was when he'd looked around and realized how many more had come in.

Dozens.

Teenage Sith zombies, Tulkh thought—how in the moons of Bogden had it all started? Every so often, the universe must just get bored and decide to really cut loose. Like the corpses that had come after them from the tower, most of them had already started to rot. Others were missing whole pieces of their faces and outer musculature, turning them into walking pathology lessons without the common courtesy to lie down and die. All of them surged forward with the lurching, eager speed of things whose appetite—for flesh, or for death—would never be fully slaked.

Tucking his spear into the quiver on his back, Tulkh jumped for one of the overhead support struts and swung himself up onto it, shimmying toward the control booth that he'd noticed up above. Anything that could climb to the top of the Tower and crawl over the glass would have no problem scrambling up one of these girders. But he had noticed something else up here, and although it probably wasn't enough to tip the battle in his favor, it might give him the edge.

And the edge was all he needed.

Tulkh punched one claw through the booth's view-port, gouging out a hole large enough to drag himself through, and turned around to face the wide, curved instrumentation panel that he assumed controlled the entire training facility below.

The dead things were swarming in even more thickly now, crawling all over one another in an attempt to move forward. Some of them had already started trying to grapple their way up into the booth after him. Tulkh reached for the simulator controls, found one labeled SWING-ARM 17-155, and hit the switch.

The simulator responded instantly. Two massive pillars swung down from either side of the ceiling, slamming straight into the swarm of bodies, smashing them aside and sending them flying. Tulkh grunted, not entirely satisfied with the result. This wasn't his favorite way to hunt, but the numbers were against him and he needed every advantage he could marshal in his defense. He activated another sequence, choosing one at random. Slots opened up along the ceiling, spitting loops of razor wire from both sides of the room, stretching out as the things staggered and stumbled and caught themselves, screaming.

Tulkh glanced back down at the controls. The monitor screen to his right was glowing bright green, outlining the entire suite of possibilities for him in a clean, ray-traced diagram, the cursor awaiting its next command. Tulkh chose one called PONJI STICK and tapped the EXECUTE key.

The right half of the floor whipped open and a spring-loaded row of gleaming hydraulic rods burst up from below, where—by all rights—they should have rammed the Sith student-things straight backward, or possibly impaled them through the feet.

But something else happened instead.

The things jumped back, en masse, just a split second before the rods had burst up. It was like watching a single prescient organism reacting to a perceived threat. They moved with unbelievable speed and agility, as if they'd known exactly what Tulkh was going to do, even before he'd known he was going to do it.

Tulkh gaped down in disbelief.

Are they using the Force? Or their version of it?

The question didn't have time to percolate long in his mind. Now the things were swinging up the pendulum arms that Tulkh had released, dodging the obstacles from both directions—they knew he was up here, and were intent on finishing him. Even the ones that he'd knocked aside had already recovered, and they seemed to have done so with unprecedented speed. Tulkh's frown deepened. For the first time in memory, he actually felt his confidence waver.

He took a step back, evaluating his options, and felt something strike his shoulder from behind. Pivoting, already prepared to rip apart whatever had snuck up behind him, he saw the bright metallic eyes fixating on him from the chromium casing of their processors. It recoiled with an electronic burble of surprise, and Tulkh realized that he was looking at Scabrous's HK protocol droid.

"What are you doing up here?"

"Response: Excuse me, sir, I certainly didn't mean to disturb you, I merely—"

"Shut up."

"Acknowledgment." The droid's yellow photoreceptors swiveled with recognition. "Tulkh the Whiphid?" The droid's vocabulator expressed a mixture of surprise and confusion. "It was my impression that Lord Scabrous already dismissed you quite some time ago. Did you have difficulty finding the exit?"

"You could say that, yeah."

"Clarification: It's just across the—"

The Whiphid let out a low growl, grabbed the droid's arms, and pulled it to the viewport overlooking the simulator below. "Look," he said, pointing: "You see what's down there?"

The droid's head pivoted toward the open space below, seething now with hordes of undead Sith students. They were all attempting to scale the support struts, swinging their arms up. The closest ones were near enough now that Tulkh could smell them.

"Response: Indeed sir," the droid said dutifully, "but I hardly see what—"

"Your boss is the reason why all this went haywire in the first place."

"Query: I fail to see why—"

"Here's why." Tulkh wasn't bothering to look at the HK's photoreceptors anymore. His attention was completely devoted to the components on its breastplate. "You're an HK model."

"Confirm: A Czerka Corp HK series, yes, sir, but—"

"You know what *HK* stands for?"

"Response: It's an industry term, sir, but—"

"Hunter-killer."

The droid made a scandalized chirp. "Correction: Respectfully, you're mistaken, sir. I am a protocol droid. Proficient in millions of galactic languages and—"

"Czerka built you special to get around local laws banning assassin droids." Tulkh was gritting his teeth now. "Those flip shields over your eyes—that's a combat modification. When Scabrous brought you here, he put a restraining bolt on you, but if I do this—"

He yanked the bolt off. There was a brief, hissing sizzle as the HK's processor muzzle shorted out. Tulkh felt his skin tighten, his fur standing on end. He cast a grim look at the droid. "Remember now?"

The HK didn't bother to answer. Weapons slots opened on its forearms to reveal an augmented laser array bristling from both limbs. A second later the control booth came alive with blasterfire. The Sith-things recoiled, spun backward, pitched, and pivoted off their feet by what appeared to be a nonstop fusillade of hot plasma. Somewhere to the left, Tulkh ducked as the HK completed a full circle, laying down a line of fire so fast and dense that it seemed to create a single ballistic wave. He jerked his head back as a laser bolt ricocheted off the wall, then bounced past him in the opposite direction.

"Stand aside," the droid said, having apparently abandoned its customary method of speech along with its former programming.

"What—"

Its left leg rotated outward to reveal a wider-barreled object extruding from the port. A massive jet of blue flame roared straight across the room, igniting several of the Sith-things, and they staggered, blazing, screaming as the flamethrower erupted a second time.

Through the sea of burning corpses, Tulkh could see a clear corridor to the exit at the back of the simulator. One of the Sith-things was slashing its way toward him, jaw sagging hideously, its face on fire. Tulkh yanked his spear from where it was still strapped against his back and rammed it as hard as he could into its wide-open mouth.

Jerking the spear back, the Whiphid glanced in the opposite direction.

"Where are you going?" the droid asked.

"Back to my ship." Tulkh was already halfway across the floor. He turned and looked back at the droid. "You staying here?"

"Here? With them?" The HK didn't hesitate. It followed the Whiphid down through the simulation chamber, out of the pain pipe, and into the snow.

35/The Anatomy Lesson

"IT'S COLD," MAGGS SAID, SHIVERING AND LOOKING around as if for verification from the others. "Feels good though, doesn't it? After all that?"

Kindra didn't say anything. They had just stepped out of the tunnel, she and Maggs and Hartwig with Master Hracken silently bringing up the rear. Hartwig had taken Ra'at's lightsaber, scrubbing the handle with the first handful of snow he could scoop up, but no matter how hard he tried, he couldn't get the stain to go away.

"Are we gonna talk about what happened back there?" Maggs asked.

"What," Kindra said. "You have something you need to say?"

They all turned around to look at Hartwig, standing several meters behind them, still inside the tunnel so that half his face remained in darkness.

"With Ra'at," Maggs said. "He—"

"Ra'at got turned," Hartwig said, emerging into the vague gray glow of the twilight air, breath pluming from his lips. It was the first time he'd spoken since they'd chopped their way through the barrier, and his voice sounded different, thick and strange. "He changed into one of them, and Master Hracken boxed him. And I got his lightsaber. End of story."

"What about us?" Maggs asked.

"None of us was bitten, as far as I can tell." Hartwig looked around as if waiting to see if the others would contradict him. "You okay?" Maggs nodded. "Kindra? You have something you need to come clean about?"

She didn't look around.

"Kindra?"

Silence.

"Hey." Hartwig walked over, pushing past Maggs, and grabbed her shoulder, swinging her hard toward him. "I'm talking to y—"

Kindra snapped around on him, her eyes brittle pellets.

"I'm clean."

"You sure?" Hartwig hadn't lowered his hands. "What's that on your neck?"

"Very funny."

"You think I'm joking?" He waited while Kindra reached up and touched her throat, perhaps a centimeter lateral to the jugular. She winced at the open wound, drew back her hand, and looked at the scarlet stain on her index finger.

Standing apart from them, a little distance away, Master Hracken watched without saying anything.

"Just a cut," she said. "A piece of the electrical fixture—"

"You don't know that," Hartwig said.

"You don't think I'd remember being bitten?"

"I *think*"—he held her gaze—"that there was a lot of infected blood flying around. And if some of it splashed in there—"

"Then I'd already be screaming and ripping your guts out," Kindra snapped, "which I'm not . . . no matter how much I'd like to. So if you're done casting baseless aspersions—"

"You were ready to kill *me* back there over a lightsaber," Hartwig said. "Seems to me that it's in the group's best interest if we took you out of the equation now." He glanced at the Sith Master. "Right, Master Hracken?"

Hracken didn't have a chance to reply before Kindra cut in again.

"Is this really what you want?" she asked Hartwig, blade ready. "We've sparred enough times in the training arena. You know how it's going to go down."

Hartwig didn't answer, just stared at her, shoulders rising and falling with every breath, his face betraying no trace of emotion. The wind flung another thin gust of snow between them, and Kindra felt the cut beginning to ache on her throat.

"Make a move," she said.

"You first."

"Wait," Maggs said. "Nobody knows what the incubation period for this thing is, right?"

Hartwig didn't take his eyes off Kindra. "Seemed pretty fast with Ra'at."

"Yeah, but Ra'at got tagged firsthand. Maybe accidental exposure takes longer." Kindra could hear Maggs's voice growing more confident as he spoke, warming to his own argument. "Point is, *we don't know*. So before somebody does something stupid, how about we all take a step back, strip down, and make sure nobody's got any open cuts that could have gotten contaminated blood in them." He looked back at Combat Master Hracken, who still had not spoken. "What do you think?"

Hracken nodded. "Yes," he said.

"Strip down?" Kindra's expression had already gone from bellicose to incredulous. "You're asking me to take my clothes off?"

"It's the only way to be sure." He glanced at Hartwig. "You agree to that?"

"Why not?" Hartwig shrugged. "I've got nothing to hide." He yanked off his tunic and the uniform shirt beneath it, then shoved his pants down to his ankles. In front of him, Kindra had already slipped out of her coat, keeping her bare arms crossed over her chest, gazing back defiantly at the others.

"That's as far as I'm going."

Hartwig rolled his eyes and turned back to Maggs, who stood shivering in his shorts and boots, clutching a wad of balled-up clothes against him like a small child that had gone to sleep. Behind him, bare-chested, stood Master Hracken. The Combat Master had also stripped to the waist, without being asked, revealing a broad, well-muscled physique hardened by scar tissue, strange tattoos, and decades of intense physical conditioning. His head was bowed, as if he was inspecting something in the snow.

"Looks like we're all clean," Hartwig said. "So I guess that means we—"

Master Hracken raised his head. The crooked slash of the grin on his face seemed to cut almost diagonally across the entire width of his head. Blood had already started streaming down on either side of his mouth where he'd gnawed his own lips open.

There was nothing human in his eyes.

With a shapeless noise that was half shout, half gasp, Hartwig fumbled for his lightsaber and dropped it in the snow. He bent down, scrambling to pick it up, but succeeded only in pushing it deeper.

In less than a second Hracken was on him. He grabbed Hartwig's head and buried his teeth in the student's throat, ripping out a mouthful of tissue and cartilage. Kindra watched wild, looping parabolas of blood spurting high in the air around him like a miniature fountain that had been turned on directly beneath Hartwig's chin.

Hartwig staggered backward, hands up, blinking at

the Sith Master as he whipped around to face him. His nerves were gone. Hracken's hands flew up, preparing to fire off a burst of Force lightning, when its head toppled sideways off its shoulders and rolled, still spurting, into the dark snowdrifts.

Hracken's decapitated body collapsed, seizing and twitching, and Maggs saw Kindra standing behind it. She gripped the lightsaber in both hands with absolute steadiness.

"Thanks," Maggs breathed.

"Forget it." She walked over to Hracken's still-snarling head and chopped it straight down the middle. "That one's all yours."

Maggs looked back around at Hartwig's corpse, its ripped-open throat spilled out sloppily across the snow like a losing hand of pazaak. The thing was already starting to come back. It was squirming in place, shifting its arms and legs, preparing to sit up again. Listless bubbling and gurgling sounds issued from the hole in its neck.

"You going to take care of that?" Kindra asked.

Maggs took a breath and swung his own lightsaber down on Hartwig's corpse, carving its torso open from throat to groin. Gazing down at him, Kindra realized she could see the black, still-pulsing gristle of the thing's dead heart laboring stupidly onward, grasping for one more beat. What she felt more than anything at that moment was revulsion at the human machine's mindless commitment to endure and endure and endure.

"Is it down?" she asked.

Maggs didn't answer.

"Is it down?"

Maggs went to work with the lightsaber again, and this time it took the Hartwig-thing's head off at the shoulders. The head dangled for a moment on one remaining ribbon of flesh, then dropped away. A few listless dribbles of boiled blood leaked like tears from the sheared-off arteries, black as used oil, before they cauterized completely.

"Now it's down," he said.

Kindra nodded but kept her own lightsaber drawn.

"What now?" Maggs asked.

"I'm leaving," she said. "You're staying here."

Maggs blinked. *"What?"*

Kindra's lightsaber slashed out from the back, catching him across the hamstrings, shearing through tendons just above the ankle. Maggs shrieked and slipped, arms pinwheeling, all balance gone. He was screaming at her, asking her why she did it, what did she think she was doing, but by that time Kindra had already turned and started running—not walking, but *running*—as fast as she could in the opposite direction.

"Wait!" Maggs sat up and tried to stand, but his lower legs refused the job, the severed Achilles tendons dumping him forward again into the snow.

When he lifted his head up, he heard the noises coming up from behind him.

No, Maggs thought, *no, this was all a mistake, just a big mistake*—

He looked back, and they fell on him.

36/Drear

■■■—:■■■—:■■■

AFTER TWENTY MINUTES OF WANDERING THROUGH THE LI-
brary, Zo had to admit that she was utterly lost.

At first, the voice of the orchid had drawn her onward
as she'd entered the high doorway and followed the
main concourse through room after room, some with
ceilings so high that she couldn't see them, others so
cramped that she had to bend down just to pass through.
Irregularity was the only design here, symmetry fractured by age and weather. With every step, the subterranean air had grown steadily colder, and Zo was
acutely aware of traveling not just forward but *downward,* as though the library's depths sank without
boundary into the very core of the planet. She could feel
the air in her lungs, and taste the oxydized flavor of
metal shavings. The only remaining light came from the
torches and lamps mounted high overhead; the only
sound was the crunch of her footsteps. Even at these
depths, snow had found its way inevitably through the
cracks and broken places, stirring wraith-like and restless in the low whine of the wind. When she looked
back, she saw her footprints leading down the hallway,
one lonely set of tracks gleaming in the torchlight.

Who lit these torches, she wondered, and who kept
them burning?

Tulkh had refused to follow her here, leaving her to go alone. When she'd confronted him about it and said, *Let me get this straight, you'll walk into a Sith Lord's tower, but you won't go into a library*, he'd merely nodded and planted his feet, telling her that he knew a trap when he saw one. Zo had protested—she knew the sound of the orchid's voice calling to her—but now she was beginning to wonder if he was right to stay away.

The orchid would never deliberately put you in danger. You know that.

Yes, she did. And yet . . .

Up ahead, a vast cathedral-ceilinged room spread open, flickering in the light of a few sparsely placed torches. Faintly, she thought she smelled smoke, and burning flimsiplast. She looked right and left, allowing her attention to be drawn upward and upward farther, straining to encompass the shelves and their apparently endless holdings. Another gust of wind whipped through the open space, stirring the old, dry snow that lay here and there in random accumulations along the tiled floor.

Zo paused. She hadn't heard the voice of the orchid in several minutes. Not for the first time, she wondered if she could find her way back if she had to. She supposed that she might be able to follow her own tracks back out, if the draft from the cracks in the walls hadn't already smoothed them away. There were plenty of hiding places here if she ran into trouble—but what if the trouble was waiting for her in one of them?

Something touched her face, cold and knowing.

Zo froze and held her breath, staring into the empty space immediately in front of her nose. There was nothing visible there . . . yet she felt its presence, an unseen leather-gloved hand stroking her cheek, running over the length of her jaw and down to her throat, searching out her soft areas with the intimacy of a lover. Her chest squeezed and clamped shut over the skittish tremolo of her pulse.

A noise behind her scraped through the silence, very close.

Zo whipped around and looked back up the way she'd come. Her tracks were still there, leading away into the distant edge of vision—

And now she saw them.

A second set of tracks, running parallel to hers.

The prints stopped, perhaps ten meters away, and cut sideways, disappearing behind a sagging half wall, its dimensions buried in shadow. Within its depths, something was standing, watching her. Zo felt the weight of its presence settling over her, anchoring her to the spot.

Tensing to run, she saw Scabrous step out from behind the wall and into the half-light, so that almost exactly half his face was illuminated. Zo glimpsed the gem-edged hardness in his eye. His face was a mottled quilt of gray flesh and exposed muscle, and the clenched grin on his face was somewhere between madness and rigor mortis. He'd been infected, she realized—yet somehow he'd managed to stave off full transformation, at least temporarily. Her gaze fell to the pack of medical equipment, monitors, tubing, and depleted reservoirs of blood that dangled from the angular arch of his shoulders. This new version of him looked gaunter but somehow more imposing, as if the bones inside his body had swollen and remade him from the inside out.

"Hestizo Trace," he said, extending one hand. "It's good to see you again. I hope you won't bother trying to run."

She opened her mouth to speak and realized she couldn't breathe. Scabrous gestured with one hand, and she felt herself yanked forward, down the corridor, and into his grasp. Within seconds she was so close to him that she had to look up to see his face.

"This library," he said, "is the oldest part of the academy, older even than the tower itself. It was constructed over a thousand years ago by a Sith Lord named Darth Drear. He founded the academy, back when the planet itself was young. The ancient writings tell about how he used his first students as laborers. For hundreds of years, the Masters at the academy believed that a good many of those students died down in these very chambers, using the Force to move hundreds of tons of snow and ice and dig out these corridors and chambers to house Drear's vast collection of . . . specimens. It was thought that Drear worked the students until they died from exhaustion." He smiled without the slightest gleam of humor. "The true genius of the structure lies beneath it. Under these floors, Drear built himself a secret temple, where he practiced the rituals and rites of the ancients, encoded in the Sith Holocron."

Zo's lungs began to unlock enough for her to sip in a small breath. *Grow,* she called out to the orchid, *oh please, if you're there, if you're there at all, grow, grow in him, grow now—*

But there was nothing.

"When I first discovered the Holocron," Scabrous said, "I did not fully understand its protocols." He gestured to his face, at the horror of its ongoing decay. *"But I understand them now."*

"What do you want from me?" Zo asked.

"Ah." Scabrous's cheeks sucked in, and he licked his lips so that she could see the dead gray surface of his tongue like a lizard coiled against the yellow stones of his teeth. "Darth Drear wrote that he had found an elixir for staving off death itself, the ingredients of which he recorded in the Holocron—including, of course, your beloved orchid. The mixture was complete in and of itself, with a single flaw—" He gestured at his own face. "The inevitable dissolution of the tissue. It struck immediately upon exposure, spreading first through the brain, where it drove the victim into a state of homicidal madness, and then through the rest of the body, shutting it down. The flesh would remain animate, but insensate—living only to hunger, to feed and kill."

"If you knew all that," Zo asked, "why would you ever try to re-create the experiment yourself?"

Scabrous's grin seemed to dangle from the sides of his face, a prehensile thing all its own. "Before he died, Darth Drear wrote of the final stage of the process—the step that he himself was never able to achieve. He dispatched his sentries to a nearby planet to abduct a Jedi and bring him to the secret temple underneath the library. After ingesting the elixir, in the final hours before his body gave in completely, under exactly the right circumstances and conditions, Drear planned to use a ceremonial Sith sword to cut open the Jedi's chest while he was still alive, and eat his heart. Only then, with that final infusion of midi-cholorians still warm from the Jedi's blood, would the decay process be held back—granting the Sith Lord his ultimate immortality."

Zo stared at him. She couldn't move, couldn't breathe.

"Unfortunately," Scabrous said, "the sentries failed to bring back a Jedi with a suitable quantity of midi-cholorians in his bloodstream before Drear's disease overtook him. But tonight, with your assistance, I am in the unique position of being able to fulfill that destiny personally."

Zo felt something curl around her arms, snapping them back with a sharp jerk and forcing her shoulder blades back. Thick green vines had looped over her elbows and squirmed up her sides. She craned her neck to the right, and when she looked around, she saw them.

The dead ones: the corpses that she had faced on the rocky overhang, outside the tower. Their heads were still gone, blown off their shoulders. Instead, the riot of catastrophic vegetation that she had coaxed from inside their skulls had grown more profuse since she'd seen them last, grown with utter abandon. These were the runners and vines that had ensnared her now, stretching from the stumps of their necks, dozens of slick green ropes gripping her arms and holding her fast.

As Zo stared at them, she saw, to her immeasurable horror, that the stems were topped with dozens of tiny black orchids, budding everywhere. In her mind, she could hear the flowers hissing and shrieking, crackling hysterically, hungrily, insanely. They pricked her arms like thirsty syringes, questing after her blood.

No, she thought. *No, no, please*—

"You grew them," Scabrous said. "How lovely that they recognize you."

The headless, vine-stricken corpses pushed in closer, groping and shoving, until Zo realized that she could smell them. They stank like a freshly disinterred grave, full of black dirt and mold and rotten meat. She felt their cold skin pushing against her even as the vines constricted tighter around her arms, squeezing, twisting, pinching her skin.

Scabrous stepped forward, shoulders rising up until he towered over the things.

His mouth opened wide and he screamed.

His breath was fetid, the breath of a thing that had already died and was decaying from the inside out. Zo felt the things responding immediately to the scream, recoiling, pulling her back with them. And when they screamed their response, it was a terrible, throatless noise that came throbbing up from their severed necks, vibrating up and out of the stalks, one solid blast of high-pitched sound that rose, shifted frequency, and dropped again, a message composed entirely of high-pitched, almost ultrasonic oscillation.

They swung her around.

In an act of pure desperation—some part of her must have already known she would fail—Zo tried to use the Force on them, tried to reach out and connect with the plant-presence inside them. At the instant she made contact, a sharp jolt of toxic energy crackled through her, slamming through her brain like an ice ax and making her cry out loud. The inner landscape of her eyelids swirled with sere colors, shades of burnt bronze and anemic yellow.

The vines were dragging her down the corridor of the library, across the cold floor. Zo's eyes widened. Up ahead, a great rectilinear hole gaped open in the floor to reveal a shadowy pit whose depths seemed bottomless, even from here.

Yet there were strange lights below, shimmering from deep within.

And she knew where she was going.

Under these floors, Drear built himself a secret temple, where he practiced the rituals and rites of the ancients . . .

Scabrous gestured, and they pulled her down.

37/Some Kind of Nature

TRACE CROSSED A LONG DESOLATE STRETCH OF NOTHING-
ness between two high featureless walls, the night's
storm barreling down over him like a demon with a debt
to collect. Up ahead—still perhaps a hundred meters in
the distance—stood the tower. He was almost there.

Despite his urgency, he knew he had to move more
carefully now. Since the death of the Sith Blademaster,
he'd seen no more of the things like the one inside the
wall, but he'd known they were there. Extrasensory perception, telemetric ability, was no longer necessary. He
could *hear* them screaming. And the screaming got
louder the closer he came to the tower—more intense,
somehow. And hungrier.

He had never seen anything like the abomination that
had ripped the Blademaster apart: a living corpse, a
dead thing whose flesh and muscle still moved, even as
it decayed before his eyes. He sensed their presence
around him, below and behind the unseen temples and
stone outbuildings. Could a lightsaber dispatch a creature like that, or would it merely tear it into individual
pieces that would, in turn, continue to pursue their prey?

And what about Hestizo? Had the things found her as
well?

He stopped again, stretching out with his feelings, the

Force casting a wide psychic net in search of any sign of his sister, but it retrieved nothing. He still believed that she was here—perhaps in the tower, perhaps not—but the silence within him was far more disturbing than the screaming in the distance.

Keep going. You will find her. You will.

For another ten minutes, he scrambled forward. He took another step and faltered again, raising his head slightly, sniffing the air.

He smelled smoke.

Clamoring to the top of a broken pillar, he looked in every direction until a glint of firelight in the distance caught his eye, a flickering orange glow inside a vast half-sunken stone structure, perhaps a quarter kilometer away. Trace watched it for a moment. He wanted to be sure. By itself, a fire would have meant nothing, especially on a planet of ruins where the Sith ruled and the dead had been restored to life.

But he also suddenly felt his sister's presence inside.

She's in there. She is.

Leaping down off the broken pillar, Rojo Trace began to run.

Twenty seconds: the time it took him to reach the entryway, shoving his way through, unmindful of the darkness, the snow and clutter, and the thickening stink of smoke. Loose objects lay strewn randomly around the floor—books, scrolls, unidentifiable debris. Rows of low stone tables like marble slabs. It was some type of vast library. He kept going.

Hestizo, it's me, are you there? It's Rojo. I'm coming, I'm—

An arm hooked him from behind, lurching him upward.

"Have a care, Jedi."

An ancient voice, it croaked in front of him. Each word came out deliberately, as a glottal, sawdusty reverberation that seemed to move the air molecules themselves. "You seem to have forced your way into my sanctum sanctorum. Perhaps a modicum of restraint is in order."

Trace felt himself being swung up into the air, and realized that he was hanging from the limbs of an immense tree. Looking down, *far* down, he saw the warty knuckles of its roots plunged deep into the floor itself, causing its variegated tiles to buckle and bulge. The thing's trunk rose upward to spread dozens of sinuous gray limbs throughout the cavernous and gloomy room around it. Its upper branches clutched his wrist tighter than ever, swinging him around, and Trace observed that the walls around him were lined floor-to-ceiling with shelves of holobooks, scrolls and grimoires, and various cluttered arcana crammed back in every available notch and crevice.

"This is my dwelling place, yes?" the tree creature's voice burbled up from somewhere inside its trunk. "And you have intruded here."

Trace's hand eased back for his lightsaber. There was a sharp whip-crack and a sting as one of the branches slapped it aside, and Trace saw the lightsaber go pinwheeling away. It landed below the shelves, in the corner, by the outer edge of a glimmering hearth, where the orange coals of a fire seethed and flickered.

"No need for your weapon here," the voice said. "Not in this place of learning. We *are* both learned beings, are we not? Enlightened and informed by the written word. No need for the encumbrances of physical violence." It uttered another bulky, dusty chuckle. "Look upon me, if you like. *Seek my face.*"

Trace smelled a tangy, musty odor pass beneath his nose, and turned to see the librarian's enormous wooden head craning toward him between its barren branches. It was a Neti, he realized, and it was sick. Whatever contagion had infected this planet had spread to it as well. Along its back side, the plant creature's once-majestic form had taken on an altogether different cast. The formidable branches hung like clumps of atrophied muscle. Clusters of open sores had devoured the bark, and the exposed heartwood oozed a steady trickle of dark leakage that had collected on the floor around its roots. Whole shoals of holobooks and Sith texts floated like skiffs in the sprawling puddle of fluid. Whatever had befallen the Sith students here, it had jumped across species without losing any of its virulence.

"I'm looking for a Jedi named Hestizo Trace."

The Neti didn't respond right away, except to shift his branches. Trace saw now that the creature's limbs were loaded with mountains of holobooks, hundreds of them, some piled so high that whole avalanches went spilling in one direction or another whenever he moved.

"Of course I know about her," the Neti replied. "You are her brother, yes?" The branches trembled, and more books fell. "Alas. She is lost."

Trace felt a sudden chill run through him, as if he'd just been poisoned and was only now beginning to realize it. "How do you know?"

"What does it matter? Through the bond of leaf and vine." A faint pause. "I summoned her here at the request of Lord Scabrous, and he killed her."

"You're lying."

"Am I now?" The withered face didn't seem overly offended by the accusation; if anything, it looked intrigued. "You don't sound so sure of yourself, Jedi. Not so sure at all. I have lived for more than a thousand years, and now I have come to glimpse my final hours. Perhaps before I pass into the next stage of my evolutionary development, you would like to peer inside my mind and see whether or not I'm telling the truth?"

Trace started to say something, but his voice broke

off. The branch around his wrist clasped harder, turning him idly around, gouging into the bone. Archaic limbs rustled behind him, and he smelled a different odor coming out of them now, something far worse than the thing's breath. It was the enormous boggy stench of the disease, something deeply and profoundly wrong.

"Go on," the Neti said. It sounded almost giddy now. "Look into my mind, Jedi. See what awaits you there. *Seek my face.*"

Trace felt something encircle his right leg at the ankle and pull tight, even as the branch tugged harder at his wrist, exerting a steadily increasing tension.

Seek my face.

The Neti repeated itself, forgoing speech entirely now, shouting the words directly into Trace's mind.

Seek my face!

Helpless, Trace felt himself sucked into the mire of the thing's thoughts. It was like plunging his hand into a vat of warm black ooze. He groped for a moment in total blindness, trying to make some sense of the random shapes and impressions swimming around him in the Neti's palatial memory.

And he saw.

It was a different part of the Sith library, the holo-books and archives neatly arranged. Trace understood that he was seeing it through the Neti's eyes *before* it had gotten sick, and now he grasped the true dimensions of the librarian's collection—it didn't fill just this single room, but a series of other halls winding off in manifold directions. For the millennium or more that the Neti had held court here as the academy's librarian, it had been accumulating holobooks and charts, records and ephemera.

Scouring the inner landscape for any sign of Hestizo, Trace's inner vision glided down one of these halls, moving as the Neti's limbs had moved, winding around a corner, beneath the shadowy recesses and through gigantic horseshoe archways. The architecture changed here, becoming less monastic and more ornate, resembling more of a battlement than a library. The winding, incorporeal branches of the Neti's mind carried Trace deeper, past a recessed gallery, over a parapet, pausing here or there over endless accumulations of texts and writings. *This is my fortress,* the voice inside him intoned, *my bastion of knowledge acquired over the millennia, but now it is my FUEL.* And always the echoing, mindless call for acknowledgment: *Do you see, Jedi? Do you understand FUEL?*

And Trace felt himself nodding in perfect understanding. He *did* see. The Force help him, he did. Whether or not he had actually *become* the Neti in that moment, he wasn't sure . . . but their consciousness had melded, the two of them sharing a fundamental commonality that transcended simple thought and expression. He heard strange noises in his head, plosives and sibilants, making a somehow-familiar name.

Dail'Liss.

It was the librarian's name, Trace realized, his patronymic, and somehow he knew that on his home planet it meant "lover of knowledge," a perfect choice for—

All at once the quality of light changed.

The memory grew brittle, harsher, more severe: an opening in the floor, a chasm of immeasurable depth leading down into silent gray volumes of cold subterranean space. Here, at the bottom, Trace saw a hooded silhouette standing in a dusty shaft of overhead light, surrounded by piles of rubble. Part of the wall had collapsed, or been torn away, to reveal a hidden chamber inside it—a hidden Sith temple. The cloaked figure fell to his knees and knelt there, face hidden from view, galvanized by whatever he saw.

Trace watched as the man reached in with both hands

to take out a large gray case, ornately filigreed with hieroglyphs glinting in the meager light. A moment of stillness shivered past. Then the figure turned the case on its side, smooth pink hands. They slid over it to find a recessed release-switch.

And activated it.

The box sprang open, and in that instant Trace caught sight of a black pyramidal shape, its depthless surface reflecting back no light, only the pale face of the man gazing raptly into it.

A Sith Holocron, Trace thought. *Here in this library, this is where Darth Scabrous found—*

The pyramid was vibrating ever so slightly, and Trace saw the man's reflection change as his lips moved, murmuring words he couldn't hear. The pyramid began to vibrate more steadily, practically purring in the man's fondling embrace.

The image hit him head-on, cannonballing him out of the Neti's thoughts and back into the present moment with all the impact of unrestrained collision. His eyes throbbed in their sockets. Pain racked his chest, ribs, and pelvis until they felt as though they were being pried open by hooks. Somewhere amid the dying branches he could hear laughter, the mindless, jabbering laughter of the Neti surrendering itself to madness.

Smoke, I smell smoke—

Trace fought to clear his mind. *Heat.* His skin blazed. Smoke assaulted his bronchial passageways, scorched the inner lining of his sinuses. The vision of what he'd seen in the temple pit was still glued to his consciousness, and he understood now that this was where the Sickness had first originated. Its source had been the library in whose labyrinthine depths Darth Scabrous had discovered a Sith Holocron, forgotten perhaps for more than a millennium, and unleashed something that even he was unable to control.

Trace felt the blood vessels in his head bulging with the sudden reversal of hydrostatic pressure. Wrenching agony took hold of his spine and hips. He looked down and saw that the Neti's branches were squeezing him harder until his muscles howled for release. Behind the tree creature and below it, great ragged bursts of flame had started licking upward through the piles of fallen holobooks and sacred Sith texts, rising to engulf the library.

"Ought to have run away from here when you had the chance, Jedi." The Neti's branches, blazing now, swung across the shelves, knocking hundreds of holobooks into the fire. "Ought never to have sought my face. I told you I had entered my final days here. Now we'll perish together . . . yes?"

"Wait—"

"There is nothing left for me here. Nor you. We will go now, both of us, and join your sister, yes?"

"*No.*" But his limbs felt leaden, miserably weak, as if the smoke in his lungs had solidified, dropping massive hunks of ballast into his extremities. He had the awful suspicion that if he didn't start moving them soon, he'd never be able to move them again.

Above him, the Neti-thing was having exactly the opposite reaction. Impending death had transformed it into a frantic, slashing version of itself. It flung its branches violently from side to side, twisting and heaving as if caught in a fiery hurricane, ripping its roots up from the floor.

Somewhere in his own mind, Trace could feel the creature's last grasp on reality coming totally unmoored, even as it ripped itself from the floorboards. On either side, shelves were shuddering and collapsing with frightening speed, dumping their contents like squadrons of fiery angels falling into the abyss. The holobooks crackled, hissing showers of sparks as their circuitry burst apart in the widening blaze. How long did he have until the fire brought the roof itself down on top of them? Five minutes? Less?

HELP ME PLEASE HELPMEHELPMEHELPME—

He recoiled as if slapped. It was Zo's voice, screaming through his mind. The thought went rocketing through him, snapping him back to a state of total awareness.

Trace breathed, clearheaded again and grateful for it. The reprieve wouldn't last forever, wouldn't even last very long, he knew, but it might be enough to do what needed to be done.

Closing his eyes, he let his body fall motionless in the grip of the Neti's branches, surrendering all resistance. He took one last deep breath and held it. That single lungful of air would have to last him . . . or else his last hope of helping Zo wouldn't amount to more than suicide.

He created a small bubble, not much bigger than his own body, and sealed it shut, evacuating the air from inside it as he did so. The flames on his clothes, oxygen-starved, guttered and died.

Step one done. Now get busy.

Jolting himself free from the Neti's branches, he lurched forward inside the bubble as hard as he could, his momentum knocking it loose and letting it fall down into the landscape of the library's floor.

The bubble spun and slammed into the heaps of burning holobooks, pitching him sideways inside it as it continued to spin. The library reeled around him.

Then, next to the Neti's trunk, he saw his lightsaber.

It lay among the creature's winding snake-like roots, in front of a large ragged knothole that had already started charring black. Steadying himself inside the bubble, Trace placed both hands along the inner curvature of its surface, spread out his fingers, and waited. A burning branch as big as his body swung down from high above, crashing off the top of the bubble, the Neti's twig-fingers clutched rigidly as they twisted and burned in front of him. Trace almost breathed in and caught himself. His body ached for oxygen, for even an ounce of fresh air, but he knew that if he dissolved the barrier now and tried to inhale, the surrounding heat would flash-fry him in seconds, starting with the lining of his lungs.

He looked at the lightsaber, laboring to evacuate every other thought from his mind. At the Jedi Temple, they had taught that it was never a matter of manipulating the object, but of eliminating the space that separated you from it. Yet at this moment, the object in question had never felt so far away.

To me. To me.

The lightsaber remained where it was.

Closing his eyes, he felt the bubble shift forward like a reluctant animal roused from hibernation, and begin rolling over the mountains of burning books, toward the Neti's scorched trunk. When he opened his eyes, the lightsaber lay right in front of him, poised near the ragged knothole less than a meter away. Trace centered himself, drawing up his composure. The timing of what happened next was critical. Deactivating the bubble, he opened his hand, and the lightsaber flew into it. Its handle was almost too hot to hold, but the solidity of it had never felt better in his life.

It didn't take long to find what he was looking for. His eyes followed the thing's trunk back down to where it met the floor. It had yanked its roots almost entirely out of the structure's foundation, and its balance now hung on by the slenderest of threads.

Trace waited until the creature was about to fling itself forward again. Then he swung the lightsaber's blade in a single crosswise motion, slashing the remaining roots to the quick.

The Neti-thing pitched forward, no longer even remotely anchored to the library's floor. It swung loose and kept falling, a captive of its momentum. It hit the floor hard enough to thrum the entire structure on its foundation, throwing up whole blinding swarms of sparks and ash in its wake.

Trace staggered forward, waving away the smoke in front of his eyes. From here, he saw a gaping hole that the tree had torn through the library's outer wall, and through it, the frozen surface of Odacer-Faustin's snow-covered landscape. He could already hear the hiss of steam as the flaming architecture met the subzero air outside.

Help me . . .

Trace felt his sister's scream go burning throughout his entire body. This wasn't just an impression, some random emotional flash—he actually *felt* her pain as it wrenched through his right arm, throbbing into his shoulder and chest, blasting up to the roots of his teeth. Tears boiled up in his eyes and the wind whipped them away. His legs went numb and he stumbled, almost falling over in the snow.

He shook it off. He couldn't explain what he'd just experienced. It was as if everything he knew about his sister and the Force itself had suddenly been inverted, corrupted on some fundamental level. All that remained now was a sense of evil so intimate, so profoundly *personal,* that it made him want to crawl out of his own skin and leave it lying here like a heap of soiled clothes.

She was close . . . so close . . .

He took a step back toward the burning hall of the library. Snow was blowing in furiously now, swirling with smoke and ash, as he staggered through the ruined stones. If he had to go back into the fire for her, then so be it. If he had to give his life—

A bloodstained arm burst up from the rubble underneath him and seized him around the ankle, pulling him down. Then a second and a third. One of them hooked around his right wrist, the others around his waist. Two others punched upward, clamped down over either leg. Claw-like fingers plunged into one corner of his mouth and drew it back into a hideous, involuntary half grin. The debris around him was roiling with activity now, of half-buried shapes clawing their way upward from below.

They were covered in vines.

Gravity took him, and he fell.

38/Cold Caller

ALTHOUGH HE'D NEVER CONSIDERED HIMSELF A LUCKY man under the best of circumstances, Pergus Frode had had the presence of mind over the past several hours to realize that he was very fortunate indeed.

The cargo hold of Dranok's cruiser, where he was hiding, had obviously been built to smuggle contraband. All around him, in the half-light, empty swing-bins and hidden storage spaces stood open, exhaling the damp and fragrant residue of illegally transported spices that had been piled up here over the years.

Frode squirmed a little, lifting his head, stretching his legs and back, allowing himself to straighten up just enough to restore circulation to his extremities. There was tingling through his feet and toes, pins and needles as the leaden heaviness of numb muscle tissue began, reluctantly, to reawaken. He was going to need the full use of his feet, he knew, in case he had to run again.

He hoped it wouldn't come to that. He'd run enough tonight already. Although it certainly did beat the alternative.

It had started hours ago. How many? He wasn't even sure now. He'd just finished removing the flight computer from Dranok's ship, and had hauled it back into the shop to run some basic diagnostics on it. All that time, his unconscious mind had been wrangling with the issue of how he was going to handle the incoming heat signature from the unknown vessel heading straight for Odacer-Faustin's landing hangar.

To inform Darth Scabrous, or not to inform him—that had been the question he'd been pondering when a bloody palm had slapped and squeaked off the control booth's glass.

Jarred out of his thoughts, Frode had sat up and spun around just in time to see something—it might once have been human—in the process of ripping the hatch off the booth. That face was like something out of a nightmare, a gray and grinning mask: whole chunks of viscera had begun to pucker and peel around its lips. Staring at it, Frode's brain had flashed back to a corpse that he and another mechanic had once stumbled across inside the cockpit of a speeder they'd been salvaging.

Except *this* corpse's eyes were wide open, and staring at him hungrily.

If he'd stopped and given it even an instant's thought, Frode would already have been dead. Luckily for him, rumination was not his natural tendency—his first reaction was to run. He got one leg free and kicked out the front plate above the booth's instrument panel. The plexi popped loose and he'd gone slithering out, hitting the hangar bay and running faster than he'd ever run in his life.

The hangar was largely empty and presented extremely limited possibilities for protection. Acting on his gut, he'd reared around toward the nearest vessel—the cruiser that those two doomed bounty hunters, Dranok and Skarl, had arrived in—and went bolting up the still-extended landing ramp, reeling around to slam the ship's hatch shut behind him.

Frode had piloted his share of ships before becoming a mechanic, and this one looked like as good an escape vehicle as any. Whatever the thing was that had tried to attack him, he had no intention of sticking around to fight it. No job was worth that.

He'd started to power up the ship, ready to activate the flight computer, and realized his error.

The hole in the instrumentation panel gaped at him like a slack, empty mouth.

No, he thought, remembering the components that he'd yanked out with such enthusiasm just an hour or so before. The flight computer was still sitting on the counter in his booth, and he couldn't fly without it, any more than he could—

The thing landed on the cockpit in front of him, grinning hideously, and began pounding and scratching at the transparisteel. Frode screamed. He couldn't help it. He didn't think he'd ever screamed that loud in his life, certainly not in his *adult* life, but terror was booming through him now in big, wide, frantic waves. He felt dizzy with it.

And then he saw something worse.

Outside, the hangar bay was filling with the living dead.

Sith students—Frode realized only now how much he truly hated them—were shambling in the direction of the ship from all sides, jerking and scrambling and lurching forward, their mouths scooped open in big shovel-faced grins. Behind them, a sprawling, gangling thing that looked like a living tree was dragging a long mesh of dripping black roots and branches toward him. Its eyes reflected only madness. As Frode—who'd never once set foot in the academy's library, and would never have recognized the infected remains of its arboreal curator—stood crouched in the cockpit, one of the branch-arms had swung up and slapped at the transparisteel viewport. It connected hard enough that, for a second, he almost thought he'd heard the port crack. Impossible, but . . .

That was when he'd run back into the rear of the ship, down a landing ramp, through a hatch, until he'd landed here, in the safest place that he could find, the smuggler's bin, and curled here, and hadn't moved since—

"Pergus?"

He sat up a little, uncertain if he'd heard the voice or simply imagined it. He was not a particularly imaginative person, and the voice—a female—sounded very real. After a moment he realized it was coming from the comlink mounted above his head. Frode reached up and keyed the mic.

"Pergus?"

"Who are you?" he asked aloud. "How do you know my name?"

"Kindra."

"How come I can hear you—"

"The Force, Pergus. You're up there. I know."

Frode listened to the voice. There was something unsettling about it, as if the speaker, Kindra—whoever *that* was—was trying very hard to sound calm and easygoing, as if nothing was wrong. Underneath it, though, he detected a strong undercurrent of . . . what? Fear? Terror?

"Where are you?" he muttered.

"*Hangar,*" the voice said. "Get out. Get me out."

"What about those things? Aren't they still out there?"

No answer. He wondered if it was because something had happened to her that he couldn't hear her talking anymore.

"Kindra?"

"Just . . . open the hatch of the ship, Pergus. Open up and let me in. I'll be quick. We'll both fly out of here together. We can't stay here. But hurry. I'm right outside."

"I can't," he said. "I took out the ship's flight computer . . . it can't navigate without it. We wouldn't make it three klicks in this weather. We'll crash right back into the snow."

"I'll . . . I'll help us. We'll get away somehow, I promise. Please, Pergus. Just . . . let me in . . . please. Hurry."

Frode grimaced. One of the reasons he'd ventured all this way to the far end of the galaxy was his rotten luck with women, specifically his inability to deny them anything. Yet here he was again. Hating himself already, he stood up inside the storage bin, lifted off the steel plate, and crawled up onto the main landing ramp. In truth, he wasn't sure why he was doing it. He *knew* it wasn't right—there was definitely something wrong about opening the hatchway—yet the voice, the girl's pleas, her desperation, motivated him forward, drew him along in a way that he couldn't quite comprehend, and maybe she could help get them out of here, maybe . . .

The Force, a faint voice of reason piped up deep inside him, from somewhere hopelessly deep within himself, *she's using the Force on you, to manipulate your actions,* and although he knew it was true, he still couldn't quite seem to resist.

He reached the main hatchway, placed his hand on the lever, and turned it, pushing it forward.

"Look," he started, "I don't think this is—"

And stopped.

Beyond the hatch, the hangar was completely dark.

Frode stood clutching the bulkhead behind him, pupils dilating, trying to make out even the vaguest of shapes, but without success. It was as if whatever was out there had destroyed the lights and ripped out the power, burying the vast space around him in utter blackness.

But he could hear them.

Holding his breath, he could hear the sounds of many bodies rustling together, the faint moist sound of their shoulders and arms and torsos packed together in the dark. They weren't breathing, but they were making hollow rasping noises that could have been some obscene attempt at speech.

Then, all around him, the lightsabers started coming on.

They activated individually and in clusters, red humming spikes of light, dozens of them, shooting upward, filling the air with a low, oscillating hum that shook Frode's molars in the back of his mouth. His eyes began to adjust, and at length he began to make out the blades shining off the starved dead faces of the students that held them upright, their blank expressions, the bleak and rapacious eyes that gaped back at him. Drool gleamed on their lips. Dried red gore encrusted their teeth and lips.

No, Frode thought. *Oh no.*

Staring out at the things, he felt something inside him loosen, turn to liquid, and swirl away, something both abstract and at the same time terribly visceral, like the blood supply to his heart. Everywhere he looked, more scarlet streaks continued to crosshatch on top of one another, springing up in all directions, as if something were clawing its way out of the dark and the dark was bleeding.

And looking closer, he saw the girl.

She was standing at the bottom of the gangway amid a shifting prison of red blades, surrounded by the rotting corpses of her classmates, their hands clutching her arms and legs, holding her captive. Lightsabers crisscrossed in front of her, hovered over her head, immobilizing her. One of the things had its open mouth pressed up against her bare throat. Another's teeth were bared and ready to attack a small, exposed part of her shoulder. A third and fourth stood waiting behind her, their jaws open so wide that it almost seemed like they could have devoured her entire head in one huge, all-consuming bite.

"*I did what you wanted!*" Kindra shouted at them. "*He opened it! Now let me go! Let me—*"

The things fell upon her, the red blades slashing her to pieces as they ripped her apart. Even from where Frode stood, the crunching noises were thick and juicy and glottal, like the sound of someone biting into a particularly ripe apple. Several of the corpses broke free from the group and started thundering up the gangway, toward the open hatchway, just as Frode slammed it shut again.

He decided he could fly the ship without the flight computer after all.

39/Down in It

ZO AWOKE TO A TIGHT BAND OF PAIN ACROSS HER CHEST and shoulders, twisting in her joints like ground glass. When she tried to shift her position to alleviate the pain, she realized that she couldn't move at all.

The pit where she lay was settled at the bottom of a deep shaft, its high onyx-colored walls shining up as far as the eye could see, in some unfathomable expanse of glassy black. Her head spun. She realized that she had been tied down here, strapped to a large stone slab by wide leather bands and iron rings that crisscrossed her chest and looped over her wrists and ankles, pinning them in position. Torches burned on either side of her, rows of them in the hundreds, leading upward, flickering up over the walls, gleaming off tiny, ornate lines of script and filigree that moved across it like rows of programmer's code.

She breathed, coughed a little, and tried to summon moisture onto the back of her tongue. The air down here tasted metallic, dusty, and very old. It was like inhaling through a hole in some archaic stone tablet. Oily tallow from the torches dripped on the floor around her, and the greasy black smoke wafting up from their flames only made her throat feel more parched.

From somewhere behind her, she heard movement,

the scuff and rustle of footsteps, the soft clink of objects being arranged outside her peripheral vision.

"Look up," Scabrous's voice croaked.

Zo turned and moved her neck, straining to tilt her head as much as the straps would allow. The Sith Lord was gazing down. The decay process had accelerated drastically since she'd last looked at him. The Sickness had taken over his face completely now, remaking it into gelid, shapeless soup from which two bloodshot eyes gleamed at her with terrible scrutiny. Gray strips of gristle quivered from the exposed bone of his skull, and when he spoke she saw the tendons swing inside his throat.

He was holding a sword.

Not a lightsaber, but an actual Sith sword. Its shining blade seemed to have been forged from the same black durasteel as the walls around them, and stretched as long as Scabrous's arm. As the Sith Lord raised it up, Zo realized that the designs from the walls of the pit had been echoed along the blade's entire length, great thorny rows of script and inscription gleaming in the torchlight. The resulting weapon seemed almost to blur and merge with its surroundings, its lethal edge shimmering and disappearing again as the Sith Lord swung it overhead.

"This blade," Scabrous said, "belonged to Darth Drear. It was forged exclusively for him, to ensure his immortality. So today, in accordance with his legacy, I will use it to slice out your living heart, and devour it while you watch."

Zo tried to answer—with no idea of what she might say—but the knot in her throat blocked out all speech. Terror, bright and uncontrollable, had fastened itself over her conscious mind, and she could not stop staring at the sword. At this moment, nothing in her past, her training, or her aspirations for the future seemed as real to her as its blade, the inarguable geometric equation that connected its edge to her flesh.

Hestizo—

There was nothing she could do.

The sword plunged down.

40/Wet Work

"THERE'S ONE," TULKH SAID. "BEHIND THAT WALL. SEE him?"

The HK pivoted unhesitatingly, firing two quick blasts at the openmouthed Sith-thing as it stalked around the corner in front of them, arms thrown open. It went down screaming.

"Your turn," the HK replied. "To your left."

The Whiphid turned and flung his spear into the space between the building and the statue rising before it. An instant later, a Sith student lunged out, the spear embedded in its chest, roaring toward them until Tulkh fired an arrow into its head.

"Nicely done," the droid said. "But it's still coming."

With a grunt, Tulkh ambled forward and picked the Sith student up by the spear hanging from its ribs. Lifting the thing completely off its feet, he wrenched it around sideways and hammered it into the stone wall alongside them. The tip of the spear twisted loose, and he used its serrated edge to rip off the thing's head.

He held the head out on the end of the spear, offering it to the droid.

"Keepsake?"

"No."

"What happened to *No thank you, sir?*"

The droid gazed at him. "Look out behind you," it said drily. "Sir."

Tulkh looked back at the side of the structure where he'd just beheaded the Sith-thing. The ground began to tremble. He saw a flash of motion inside the half-open hatchway, something big, and heard a scream . . . a great torrent of gargling screeches. It didn't sound like the ones that he'd heard before. But the smell was hideously familiar.

"Watch out," he said. "This is gonna be bad."

The first undead tauntaun came charging out, smashing the door of the hatchway completely out of its housing with the bulk of its body. From here Tulkh could see that half its thoracic cavity was ripped away, the remains of its internal organs flapping from its ribs. A large section of its head was gone as well, but it was still screaming as it flung itself toward them. Its eyes were clouded and pinkish, like milk mixed with blood.

"Burn it," Tulkh said.

The droid's flamethrower roared across the open ground, and the bounty hunter saw the snow lizard's oily pelt come alive with flames. Howling, the thing spun around, trampling furiously, rolling in the snow, trying to extinguish the fire, and the HK fired into it, blasting its carcass to shreds.

"You have anything bigger than a laser?" Tulkh asked.

"Mortar rounds. Why?"

The Whiphid gave a nod back at the open paddock. The herd of infected tauntauns was already thundering out, half a dozen or more, all producing that same indefinable shrieking noise. The front-runner had a gaping hole in its flank, the ragged edges of the wound quivering as it galloped so that the hole slapped open and shut like a second, stammering mouth. Something was wrong with its upper torso—Tulkh could see a heavy shape writhing around inside the snow lizard's belly.

He slammed his spear into it, and the thing burst open in a thick welter of fluid. From inside, the blood-soaked form of a Sith student came spilling out into the snow. The Sith-thing stood up grinning from inside its sticky web of blood, shook its head from side to side violently, and screamed.

Tulkh speared the Sith student, ramming its body back into the snow lizard's carcass and pinning it against the thing's spinal column. He looked back at the droid. "They're hiding inside the tauntauns," he shouted. "They—"

The hard metal of the HK's arm swung back and shoved him over, forcefully enough to knock him down in the snow, just as a slick bullet of bloody spit flew out of the infected tauntaun's mouth. Another centimeter to the right and it would have hit Tulkh directly in his open eye; as it was, the gobbet of mucus stuck to the side of his head and clung there. Looking up, Tulkh saw the animal's gore-soaked muzzle puckering, summoning up another mouthful.

"They're notorious for their aim," the droid said.

"Thanks."

"I suggest another plan."

"They're faster than us." Tulkh saw the other undead tauntauns behind the one he'd gutted, their hollowed-out chests and underbellies swelling and bulging with the Sith students hiding inside. Already he could imagine what it would be like, the snow lizards pounding up behind him at fifty kilometers per hour, only to eject their flesh-starved passengers on top of him. "Any ideas?"

"Only one," the droid said.

It was already taking aim. An instant later the HK's mortar round flew directly into the center of the herd. At close range, its twenty-meter blast radius was a sight to behold, even to Tulkh, who had seen the end result of such weapons many times before. He shielded his eyes as chunks and fragments of cold tauntaun fat, human flesh, and bone came raining down on top of them.

"Is there anything else we can kill?" the droid asked.

"Ourselves, if we don't move."

The HK turned to regard the landscape where they stood. Something inside its processor made a low, steady whirring noise, as if it was processing the recent developments, or experiencing a memory. When it spoke again, its voice was unhurried, almost introspective. "Have I told you how much I hate the Sith for enslaving me here for so long?"

"Only about twenty times." Tulkh stepped around the still-twitching tauntaun hindquarters, idly admiring the knob of exposed hip joint. As trophies went, it would have made a fine addition to his collection, but it was going to have to stay here. He sighed. "Let's go."

They turned and started walking. The Whiphid's fur was wet and dirty from the snow, and it clung to the side of his head in thickly plastered strands that made his flesh both clammy and numb. He was exhausted and distracted and more than ready to get out of here. Neither he nor the HK noticed the bloody, gelatinous glob of infected tauntaun sputum that the snow lizard had fired at him, but it was still there, still trickling steadily down the side of his brow, making its way toward the corner of his eye.

Arriving at the *Mirocaw*, Tulkh saw something that stopped him cold. There was a second ship—one that he didn't recognize—crashed forty or so meters away from his own, its nosecone crumpled, half embedded in the snow.

The HK beeped. "That's Dranok's ship."

"Who?"

"Another bounty hunter."

"What's it doing all the way out here?" Tulkh asked.

"According to my scanners, there are no life-forms on board," the droid said. "But—"

"Let me guess." The Whiphid raised his spear. "You're picking up a positive reading in *my* ship."

"How did you know?"

Tulkh pointed at the tracks leading across the snow in front of them, from one crashed ship to the other.

"Come on," he muttered. "Looks like we've got at least one stowaway to scrag before we get out of here for good."

41/World's End

SCABROUS SWUNG THE SITH SWORD DOWNWARD. WITH the first cut, the blade slashed through the dirty outerwear and animal skins that Zo had been wearing since her arrival here, exposing bare skin. She looked down and saw the shallow white trough that the sword had gouged through her flesh, a pale streak of pain, the cut turning red as it filled with blood.

Scabrous grinned at her, staring down at the wound, actually salivating now as he raised the sword a second time, extended high over his head, clutching its handle with both hands for maximum leverage, angling its tip directly toward her chest. His eyes rolled madly, utterly lost to the Sickness that had overtaken them. Zo went rigid, yanking at the straps, knowing even as she did it that there was no way she could get loose.

Not with your muscles, Hestizo. Reach out with the Force.

It was the same voice that had called out to her just a moment before. She drew in a breath and fell absolutely still, closing her eyes, surrendering her mind to the moment so that time itself seemed to fall motionless, settling down around her like silt. And when she raised her arms up again, in one smooth motion this time, the bindings fell loose beneath her—it was as if she'd passed *through* the leather straps without a whisper of resistance. Her wrists swung outward, her torso and legs suddenly, shockingly free.

Snapping upright, Zo swung her body off to one side of the slab.

"No!" Scabrous roared from the other side, the blade still held up high in the air above him. His voice was shrill, and as he shouted, Zo realized that she was hearing two voices, one forming the words in her ear while the other emitted the piercing, ululating scream in her mind. "You shall not! You *dare* not!"

She scrambled farther back. She was upright and on her feet for the first time, and the confines of the temple where she stood were only now beginning to register to her—an oblong room centered on the sacrificial altar, the stone floor beneath her cluttered with braziers, casting shallow pools of shifting firelight.

The Sith Lord charged at her, angling the sword downward, its blade whickering past her so closely that Zo heard the steel hissing crosswise through the air, shearing molecules from their bonds. It clanged off the wall and he spun around with sickening, eye-watering speed, slicing sideways for her.

Hestizo, it's me—

The voice in her head again, the one that she still couldn't identify, although its words continued to waft upward through her mind, resonating outward, ripples in a pond. Even as she lurched backward again, the corner of the temple pressing into her back so that there was literally nowhere left to turn, she heard it calling out.

Hestizo—

Where are you? her brain cried back. *Who are you?* A remote possibility, wild but somehow impossible to ignore, burst into her mind fully formed. *Rojo? Is that you?*

"Jedi trash." Scabrous appeared in front of her, raising the sword between them, the sticky ruin of his face glinting off the engraved steel. He moved forward to administer the death blow but in that same moment a crash erupted behind him, clanging deafeningly across the temple, followed by the rolling tinny clatter of an upset brazier.

The Sith Lord whirled, sword still raised, lips drawing backward, and glared at the man standing before him. The man wasn't even looking at Scabrous. He was looking at Hestizo.

"Get behind me," Trace told Zo. "*Now.*" Not waiting another instant for her reaction, he sprang upward, arcing around and landing on the floor in front of Zo so that he was face-to-face with Scabrous, locked directly into the Sith Lord's stare. His lightsaber pulsed to life, its beam humming. "This is over."

Scabrous's answer came in the form of a scream. The Sith sword slashed downward in his right hand while his left swung upward, gripping his own lightsaber. He flung himself forward, both blades whirring in front of him, spinning outward, flashing steel and pure blood-red energy lashing out, the long, terrible scream still stretching from his jaws.

From the first thrust, there was no art to his attack, no evidence of grace or form. It was already too late for that, and both Trace and Scabrous seemed to know it. They went at each other viciously, head-on, like animals with no air between them, slashing and blocking, edging around the open place in the floor. Every time their blades crashed together Zo felt it in the hollow of her chest and the roots of her teeth.

She watched as Trace probed the Sith Lord's weak places, or where he must have hoped they'd be, but Scabrous seemed to anticipate each move. The Sickness had made him incredibly fast, insurmountably strong. For every attack that her brother made, one of Scabrous's two blades had an effortless reaction, as if he already held the outcome of the duel in the palm of his hand.

Yet for some reason he was still allowing Rojo to force him backward, across the temple, back toward the sacrificial altar, his movements almost ethereal behind the constant reckless smear of blue and red and steel blades all carving through the air.

Scabrous was poised in front of the altar now, standing before the slab where he'd laid Zo out for her sacrifice. He stepped lithely between the braziers, even the one that Rojo had knocked over when he'd landed, maneuvering without the slightest effort past the rising bank of flames where the fire had started to spread. It was climbing the black wall, orange peaks and tongues flickering upward, rising.

Zo watched her brother press forward again, keeping the duel tight and close, but the Sith Lord made no move to back away any farther now. Even as he continued to deflect Trace's blade, his lips were moving. Zo couldn't make out what he was saying, and when Rojo brought his lightsaber up for a final attack, she saw that Scabrous wasn't just smiling; he was actually *laughing*.

Trace swung down again, one final blow, the coup de grâce that was intended to finish things between them permanently. Just then, Scabrous glanced up and gestured, a small, insignificant flick of the fingers in the direction of Trace's lightsaber.

There was a slight airborne tremor in the space above his arm.

And Trace's lightsaber went out.

"Did you really think," Scabrous's voice was saying, "that after all that, I would trust the outcome to a duel?"

Trace didn't even bother looking at the deactivated lightsaber in his hand. He tossed it aside and pivoted backward as Scabrous's blade slashed across the open space where he'd been standing a split second earlier. The red blade crashed into the floor, shaking it under Trace's feet.

Everything had gone wrong. The Sith Lord had laid a trap, and he'd walked right into it.

Scabrous swept toward him, triumphant now. The remains of his eyes were huge and dead, bulging in their sockets. At first he looked as though he was going to scream again. But when he spoke, his voice was oddly mellifluous, almost a purr.

"Tell me a story, Jedi. Tell me about the Force and how it binds everything together. Tell me how it protects the good and sacred in life." The Sith Lord's lips drew back to show all his teeth. *"Tell me all your lies."*

Trace raised up one hand. He'd intended to levitate the stone altar behind Scabrous into the air—he could probably flip it around and drop it on top of Scabrous fast enough that he wouldn't have time to react. But Scabrous sprang forward with the lightsaber, and when Trace moved to dodge it, he thrust himself directly onto the waiting edge of the Sith sword.

Trace looked down and saw the blade plunge through him. He felt a peculiar weightlessness pass over him, as if the gravity in the room had been suspended, as if—by lifting his feet off the floor—he might dematerialize completely.

When he looked down again, all he could see was blood.

Zo was staring at her brother when Scabrous's blade sliced him apart. Trace staggered back, wobbling on his feet, and as he wheeled around toward her she saw that he'd been cut wide open from neck to belly.

"No." It came out like a choke. *"No."*

Trace stumbled again, fighting to keep on his feet. The

wound in his abdomen was even deeper than she'd first thought, pouring out whatever remained of his life. From where she stood, she could see pigtails of small intestine poking visibly from beneath his ribs. Trace's cheeks had gone chalky white. Blood pattered on the floor between his feet, and he skidded in the puddle and fell, first to his knees, then to his back, where he lay motionless in front of her. He looked like a dancer for whom all music had permanently stopped.

He stretched out one hand. "Zo . . ."

And then nothing.

No. No. No.

"That was easy," Scabrous snarled, and turned to her. "You're next."

Zo shook her head. It wasn't going to happen like this, she wanted to say, it didn't get to end this way. He didn't get to win.

But Scabrous was lumbering toward her, circling the pool of blood and the hole in the floor. The last dregs of his humanity had drained from his face, and now he was a shambling skeleton, a thing like those things that had dropped from the tower.

When he opened his mouth again to speak, all he could do was scream.

His transformation was complete.

Hestizo . . . ?

She closed her eyes and heard that voice again, ringing out, growing steadier, like a sleeper awakening from a deep and disorienting coma.

Are you there? she asked the orchid. *Are you alive?*

Silence, and then: . . . *felt the Sickness for so long . . . thought I was dead . . .*

Never mind that now, she thought. *Just grow.*

Hestizo, please—

Grow.

Not sure I'm strong enough yet to—

GROW, Zo cried out, shouting at the orchid, needing more than anything to be heard. *GROW. GROW! FOR THE SAKE OF MY BROTHER AND ALL THAT HE LOST, FOR MY SAKE, JUST—*

The Scabrous-thing stopped in its tracks.

The rotting chamber of its skull cocked slightly to one side, as if it had just heard an unfamiliar sound, a voice shouting out from a far-off room. With one gnarled, spade-claw hand, it reached up and clutched at its left ear, working the finger around inside and wincing at the results.

Zo could see something inside the gray shell of his ear, just a glimpse.

But a glimpse was enough.

Something was inside there.

And it was green.

The Scabrous-thing made one final effort at speech. At that same moment an abrupt, brilliant javelin of pain sprang across the demolished remnants of its face, like a glint of light from a broken mirror. Then its head—its entire upper body—lurched forward. Its right hand opened, releasing the Sith sword, dropping it, letting it rattle to the stone floor. When the thing slung itself around sideways, Zo saw the thin green tendril sprouting out of its ear, spreading downward to trace the exposed mandible that made up the jawline.

Its mouth fell open. Just beyond its teeth and tongue, she saw another flash of green, darker, thicker, a stalk poking upward in the back of its gullet.

The thing that had once been Darth Scabrous began to convulse, producing not a scream now but a milky gagging cough as if to expel the green, to *get it out,* but the stalk only grew farther, stretching outward over the rag of the corpse's tongue. A second runner was sprouting up alongside it, twisting down over its chin. As Scabrous's head went backward, Zo saw the vine reaching down out of its left nostril. The vine began stretching straight out, oddly curious looking, with a single petal from its tip, like a tiny hand reaching for the sky.

An orchid blossom.

The Scabrous-thing fell to its knees in front of her, next to Rojo Trace's body. No more sound came out, not even a rasping wheeze. Its temples were bulging now, rippling with what looked like veins, except the vein-shadows were moving under whatever remained of the crepe-paper skin, shifting and squirming around its eye sockets.

Hands opening and closing randomly at its sides, Scabrous made a soft, hiccuping whimper. The right half of its skull bulged, the skin splitting open.

Grow, Zo told the orchid, one last time, no longer an order or even an instruction but just a word. *Grow.*

The Sith Lord stared up at her, its one remaining eye filling with blood. Its lips puckered, twitched, and fell still.

Its skull exploded in a thick nest of vines.

The corpse slumped the rest of the way down, right arm flopping bonelessly to the floor while the left was tucked under it in a mock-protective gesture. The next time Zo looked at the thing, she saw only the severed neck teeming with mad floral life, dozens of small, black blossoms erupting amid the demolished kettle of the thing's skull.

The vines were already stretching out toward her, screeching and hissing in her mind.

Can't hold them back, the Murakami told her. *I can grow them, but I can't control—*

Zo shook her head. "I can."

And reaching down, she picked up the Sith sword.

The blossoms screamed as she hacked them off at the vine, the arms of the Scabrous-thing still groping blindly for her as she swung the sword, the floor beneath her littered with shrieking black buds and petals. She stepped on them indiscriminately, crushing them under her feet as she forced the Scabrous-thing backward toward the wall, the blade still swinging until every vine had been cut down to the stump of the neck.

This is for Rojo, she thought, and rammed the Sith sword through the torso of the thing that had once called itself Darth Scabrous, plunging it home as hard as she could with both hands, embedding it in the black wall behind him, pinning him there.

The Sith Lord's body trembled once.

Zo staggered back, hair dangling in her face, chest on fire, trying to recover her breath. Her arms hung at her sides, limp and exhausted. Heat crackled behind her, orange flames from the toppled brazier spreading along the far side of the wall. Her lungs weren't the only things that were burning. In her mind, the orchid was making its enervated clicking noises, warning her that she had to get out of here now.

She was starting to turn away from Scabrous's headless corpse when it sprang at her again, arms outstretched, jerking the Sith sword halfway out of the wall with the suddenness of its attack. The raw green ends of slashed vines bristled up from the hole in its neck as if it were still, against all odds, trying to scream at her.

As the hilt of the sword struck its breastbone, halting its advance, Zo grabbed her brother's lightsaber and switched it on, even as the shriek of rage burst up from her lips.

"Enough!"

She slashed the lightsaber across the corpse's torso, hacking it cleanly in half, so that its lower body dropped to the floor while the chest, arms, and neck remained pinned to the wall. Still shrieking, inarticulate now, she cut through the legs and pelvis, chopping them to pieces, and then turned her attention to what was left on the wall, swinging Rojo's lightsaber back and forth, reducing the upper torso to chunks of smoking, twitching flesh. Only when she realized that she was literally unable to cut it down anymore did she finally deactivate the lightsaber.

She looked around the temple. The fire had now spread across a full two-thirds of the floor, still rising, the flames reaching shoulder height, heat rippling visibly in the air. It was already starting to creep this way, as if drawn to the chopped-off petals and vine sections scattered over here.

Take them, she thought. *Burn it all.*

Hestizo, the orchid's voice murmured in her mind, *I'm so sorry. I was sick, and I couldn't . . . I just couldn't . . .*

I know.

Bending down, she gathered her brother's body in her arms and lifted him up, pressed his cold cheek next to hers. Pulling his eyelids shut, she looked slowly upward, up the seemingly endless wall toward the faint gray promise of daylight.

I'm sorry.

She kissed his cheek, crying a little, and released him, laying him slowly back down.

Then she went to the far wall, running her hands over it. Again she saw the lines of inscription that had been carved deep into the sleek black stone, row after row, going all the way up. Scabrous had told her that Darth Drear had built this temple to achieve immortality, engraving the walls with writings, plans that signaled the end of the Jedi.

Instead, it would be her salvation.

Hooking her fingertips into the chiseled letters, using the carved words for a toehold, she drew herself up and began to climb.

42/Crawlers

TWENTY METERS FROM THE TOP, SHE SAW THEM STARING down at her.

They were crouched on all sides of the rectangular opening of the pit, gripping the edge, their faces peering over, eyes shining and hungry in the flickering orange light that shimmered up from the bottom of the pit. Thin pink liquid trickled down from their half-open mouths.

So, so many of them.

For an instant Zo stopped and clung there, shuddering, her fingertips numb and bleeding from the endless trek up the wall. Every centimeter of her body was dripping with sweat. Her hands had cramped so badly now that it felt like someone had hammered nails through the knuckles. The muscles in her calves trembled and twitched, begging for release. If it weren't for the Force, she knew she never would have made it this far, but now that she saw what was waiting for her up above—

They opened their mouths as one, and screamed.

Zo turned away with a grimace, feeling the ghastly, infected wind of their breath washing down over her as she stared down to the bottom of the pit. Flames had overtaken Drear's ancient temple now, smoke rising so that she could no longer see her brother's body or the remains of what had once been Darth Scabrous.

Then she looked up again.

They were starting to crawl down the walls toward her, corpses of the Sith students of the academy on Odacer-Faustin, scurrying down over the walls in her direction with that clutching, fly-like speed. The appetite in their faces was unmistakable now.

Hestizo, the orchid's voice murmured, *I'll try to grow in them, I'll try, but when the vines come, I don't think—*

Zo nodded once, grimly. There was nothing else to do. She tried to summon the Force, sought out that sense of refuge and peace that had come immediately before she'd slipped free of the straps on the table, and found only a numb, mute absence, like the phantom sensations from an amputated limb. She was too preoccupied, she had let fear invade her too thoroughly and couldn't concentrate.

The closest of the things was almost on her now, its mouth peeling back in anticipation. It was going to scream again, Zo realized, and then it was going to leap at her. She started to recoil, and her toes slipped from the crack in the rock where they had been planted.

Zo felt a silent gasp escape from her lips. For one dizzying, gut-shrinking second she was dangling by her fingertips, feet kicking out in empty space, unable to find anything to catch on to. The thing crawling down toward her was now nearly close enough to touch, the rabid urgency blazing out from the center of its stupid, dead face.

Hestizo, the orchid shouted out, *Hestizo, don't let go— Can't hold on, I can't hold on—*

Her fingers slipped, and she felt herself starting to fall.

At that same moment the wall-crawler sprang down at her, gripping the carved inscriptions in the black glossy surface with its left hand while its right swung down to clamp around her throat. Something popped in Zo's larynx and she felt the cold, slippery tension of its thumb and forefinger pinch tight over her neck like an iron clamp, hauling her back upward.

It screamed again, so loud that she actually felt it pushing in her eardrums, surging into her skull like warm wax. They were *all* screaming, scampering downward, filling the inside of the long shaft with their bodies as they crawled toward her, so that Zo's watering eyes could no longer make out the surface itself, nor the words chiseled on it. Now the wall was just a solid layer of rippling flesh.

The thing that had her by the throat swung her upward with impossible strength, hoisting her toward its salivating mouth. Zo flung her hands up, an instinctive defensive gesture, hands slapping off the cold skin of the thing that was crawling over her current attacker, possibly with the intention of getting at her before the other corpse could. It grabbed her right arm; the other seized her left. They began to yank her back and forth, her arms jerking in their sockets—here, clinging hundreds of meters over the burning remains of Scabrous's temple, she was going to be ripped to pieces.

Grow . . .

Zo wasn't even sure if it was the orchid, or she herself, who thought the word, but it didn't matter anymore. Through faint and fading eyes she saw green tendrils spreading out from their ears, pushing out from their nostrils, but it was too late, there were too many of them.

That was when the blaster bolt tore down from above, ripping a hole in the wall.

When Zo looked up again, she saw it plainly. It was brilliant white light so full and intense that it brought tears flooding up into her lids where they welled over and spilled down her cheeks.

What . . . ?

A second blast pounded off the wall, several meters above, shaking the entire passage. She threw one hand up and gripped the craggy edge of the crater it had left in the wall, elbowing her way until she had something like a solid grasp. Now the light was pulsing down everywhere, filling her vision, flooding it from above.

By the time the third blast struck, she had crawled completely into the rough-hewn hole, tucking her legs up behind her. The great pit reverberated violently around her. Bodies were dropping from above, shaken from their perches and plummeting downward past her, still screaming, shrieking, clutching together as if somehow the infernal bond that death had forged among them might save them.

She watched them tumbling down into the fire.

Turning her head upward, she saw how many were left—dozens, still, but they were slithering back up toward the top of the pit, clambering away so that they wouldn't fall.

Zo blinked. Something was dangling in front of her face from up above, long and slender.

It's a vine, she thought, *another vine, and if I never see one of those again, it will be too soon.*

But it wasn't a vine.

It was a tow cable.

43/Under the Gun

■━━■:■:■━━■

ZO LEANED FORWARD OUT OF THE BLAST CRATER AND seized hold of the cable with both arms, clutching it tight to her chest, then looping it about her waist and tying it clumsily around herself, somehow managing to knot it under her arms. She didn't trust her mangled fingers to grasp anything for another second, even with her life depending on it. Her hands felt dead and numb, like cold roast nerf that had been grafted to her wrists.

She pushed herself off with her legs, tumbling free.

She dropped and then the cord snapped tight, constricting just above her breasts, her body dangling, swinging from side to side like a pendulum in the middle of the shaft. Then, slowly, she felt herself being lifted up toward the bluish white lights from above. Zo let her head tilt back. Wincing, pupils straining against the brightness, she could just discern vague shapes above her, oblong rectangles and long tubes that she assumed were part of the library's ceiling.

As she came up out of the pit, her mind registered several things at once. This portion of the roof had been completely blasted away, exposing the open space and the shaft to the elements. Snow was blowing down through the streams of white light—landing lights, she realized now. What she'd assumed was the high ceiling was really the underbelly of the spacecraft whose hatchway stood open, the towrope pulling her up inside it.

After a moment she recognized it.

It was the *Mirocaw*.

As the cable drew her inside, something reached out of the darkness, and Zo felt cold talon-like claws fasten over her shoulders and hips, dragging her up. Abruptly she realized that she was too weak to fight anymore, too fatigued—whatever had taken the effort to drag her out, she couldn't resist it anymore.

"Get in here," Tulkh's voice growled.

Zo opened her eyes and saw the Whiphid crouched down in front of her, squatting on his haunches, face half hidden in shadow. On the other side, a droid—Darth Scrabrous's valet, the HK, she realized—was peering at her with that incurious, analytic gaze unique to highly developed artificial intelligence.

"She seems all right," the HK said. "I need to run a diagnostic scan on her to make sure she's not infected." It paused, and a small steel panel slid open in its breastplate, extruding a slender syringe. "This might sting a bit."

Sting? Zo would have laughed if she weren't so completely undone by terror and exhaustion. After everything she'd been through, the needle hardly registered. She allowed the droid to draw its blood sample, and for a moment there was no sound except for the whir of its processors and the low steady rumble of the ship's turbines.

"Sample is clean," the HK reported dutifully. "She's uninfected."

The Whiphid didn't say anything, just grunted and made the shrugging gesture of one who'd expected no less, then hoisted himself up and began to lumber away.

Zo levered herself up on her elbows. "Tulkh?" she managed. Her voice was hoarse; she could scarcely produce more than a scraped-out-sounding whisper. *"Tulkh?"*

He stopped without turning around, looking slowly back over his shoulder.

"Thanks."

Another shrug. "Wasn't my idea."

"Yeah, I bet." Zo let out a breath, allowing herself to sink back down against the cool metal skin of the *Mirocaw*'s hold. The HK was still hovering over her, its visual receptors pulsing and blinking in the half-light of the glowing maintenance arrays.

"Who's flying this thing?" Zo asked.

"Someone named Pergus Frode. He—"

"Who?"

The HK didn't respond right away.

"I'm picking up some form of contamination," it said. "Very close by."

Zo stared at it. "I thought you said I was clean."

"*You* are." The whirring sound had grown louder; now it sounded alarmed. "But something else onboard this vessel is—"

The ship slammed sideways, tilting hard to port, throwing Zo backward against the bulkhead. Klaxons blared and whooped up above, accompanied by the wild swirl of blue lights. She sat up just in time to see the HK rounding the corner, heading for the steel rungs that led upward through the oval hatchway to the main flight deck.

"Wait, what's happening?"

The droid didn't answer, even as she chased it upward, following it through the gangway and into the cockpit. By the time the second explosion struck the *Mirocaw,* she didn't need an answer. She already knew.

They were under attack.

44/Raw Feed

THE BROWN-HAIRED, HAGGARD-LOOKING MAINTENANCE engineer in the pilot's seat had both hands locked on the ship's controls, his expression stretching somewhere between worry and outright disbelief. Outside the *Miro-caw*'s hull, another blast rocked the vessel backward. Over the shrill whooping of the ship's collision alarms, Zo heard steel splintering off the underside of one of its wings.

"What's shooting at us?" she asked.

"Scabrous's perimeter cannons," the man shouted, jerking his head forward. Red and white emergency beacons pulsed off his face. "Down below."

Zo gripped the back of the pilot's seat and stared out through the canopy's viewport. What she saw below was enough to freeze her blood. They were still hovering over the planet, no more than half a kilometer above the blizzard-smothered surface of Odacer-Faustin. Between the fallen temples and stone buildings, the heavy guns that had come thrusting up out of the ground itself were turreting back around, tilting upward, energy beams hammering the ship in heavy bursts of artillery.

"Get us out of here!" Zo shouted.

"It's not that simple! They're laying down a solid wall of restraining fire across the upper horizon!"

"What?"

"They don't want us to leave!" Frode whipped back around and met her gaze. His eyes were surprisingly blue. "And I can't maintain the deflector shields on this piece of junk!"

"Where's Tulkh?" Zo asked.

"Who?"

"The Whiphid! The guy that owns the ship!"

The HK didn't respond right away. Zo fought the urge to grab the thing by its processors and shake it. She couldn't imagine the Whiphid idly standing by while Sith cannons blasted his ship to pieces, but she hadn't seen him since he'd stalked off, and if the droid knew something about that—

"Can you deactivate the cannons?" she asked.

The HK emitted a low, resigned buzz. "Not by remote . . . not anymore."

"How can we stop them? They're going to blow us out of the sky!"

"The main control system is inside the tower," the droid said. "I might be able to override the system manually. But that would mean—"

BOOM! Another fusillade of blasts, the biggest yet, hammered the *Mirocaw* from below, almost hurling it sideways. Zo toppled into the copilot's chair and strapped herself in, fastening the restraining web around her shoulder and waist. She saw whole rows of durasteel turrets protruding up from the snow now, their cannons flinging wave after wave of red pulses up at the ship.

"Take us down," she shouted at Frode, pointing across the landscape where Scabrous's tower rose up like a single black accusatory finger stabbing back at them. Frode, for his part, didn't argue, ramming the stick hard to the side so that the *Mirocaw* shot down and over, dipping across the academy's buildings and then angling upward again. For an instant the top of the tower appeared beneath them like a flat black disk encircled in lights from below, and there was a sharp, scraping cough of metal on metal as the *Mirocaw*'s landing gear settled on its roof. Another round of blasterfire strafed the air directly in front of them, the last of the bolts slamming into the ship's side, ricocheting off. There was a new, steady, high-pitched whine siphoning down to silence as the last of the deflector shields failed.

"Hurry," Frode snapped grimly. "We're not going to last another thirty seconds up here."

The HK had already disappeared from the cockpit, angling back down the hatchway to the hold below. A moment later, an alarm shrilled, announcing an open hatchway. Zo and Frode stared out of the cockpit at the top of the tower.

"No," she rasped.

"What?"

Zo pointed, a terrible coldness spreading over her as her throat tightened with revulsion. Gazing out into the first tremulous gray swirls of dawn, she could already see the first of the things crawling up from inside the tower's upper chamber onto the roof, squirming through the broken windows of its top level, closing in on the ship. The tower was infested with corpses, she realized, packed solid with them. Her mind whirled back to what the droid had said.

"Is there anybody else aboard?"

"Just that Whiphid bounty hunter." Frode scowled. "Why?"

"The HK said there was an infection aboard."

"*What?*" He looked down at himself, hands patting his flight suit as if searching for some indication of illness. "Where?"

"It didn't say, but—"

THOOM! A massive blast of energy smashed into the side of the *Mirocaw,* hard enough to knock it off its landing gear and send it skidding crookedly across the roof of the tower, right toward the edge. Through the cockpit, Zo saw the front end of the ship spin forward, slashing into the mob of corpses clustered in front of it, shoving them off the roof and sending them spilling down off the roof of the tower in waves. The ship kept sliding, lurched, tilted, and dropped nose-first into free fall.

Suddenly Zo realized she was looking straight down at the surface of the planet hurtling up toward them.

We're going down, her mind cried out, *we're going to—*

Frode punched the engines and the *Mirocaw* swung violently upward at the last possible second, skimming off the rocky outcropping of Sith architecture and pulling up, streaking skyward.

Spinning in her seat, Zo looked back at the tower, clearly visible now in the morning light. Its roof was crawling with the Sith-things, every student at the academy who had been infected, seething up from the windows and surging forward to fill the empty space where the *Mirocaw* had just been. They were out there, open-mouthed, screaming together, and although Zo couldn't hear their cry, some part of her *could* feel it resonating through her chest cavity, through her mind and heart. She knew it would be a long time before that scream faded completely from her memory, if it ever did.

"The droid must have gotten to the main controls," Frode said, pointing down. "Look."

Zo turned to see Scabrous's ground-based turbolasers pivoting back around. At first she thought they were targeting the ship again; then she realized they had continued to rotate, until at least a dozen of the cannons had trained their digital crosshairs on the same central target.

The tower.

The droid, Zo thought, *the HK, it's still up there—*

The laser cannons fired together, each one of them spitting a solid beam of energy directly at the top of the tower. The blasts collided simultaneously, and the tower exploded in a blinding spray of shrapnel and flame, a vast cloud of secondary combustion spreading out from inside, widening in a vast, all-consuming ring as the main and secondary reactors blew.

The report was colossal, world-shattering. Up in the cockpit, Pergus Frode, who knew precious little about combustion or reactors, but grasped the fundamentals of self-preservation on a very personal level, had the presence of mind to open the *Mirocaw*'s thrusters all the way. It was the only thing that kept the ship from getting sucked back into the shock wave, and it was enough.

Hitting escape velocity, penetrating Odacer-Faustin's atmosphere and already preparing herself for the jump to lightspeed, Zo could still feel the tremors shuddering through the ship. When she looked down at her fingers, she saw that she was gripping the armrests of the copilot's seat hard enough to blanch her knuckles white. With some deliberate effort, she let go, cleared her throat, and held out one hand to the man flying the ship.

"By the way," she said in a shaky voice, "I'm Hestizo Trace."

"Pergus Frode." He let out a breath and took her hand. "Pleased to meet you."

"Nice flying."

"I've done a bit of it in my time," he said, and a faint frown line appeared above his right eyebrow. "Wait, where are you going?"

"Back into the hold," Zo said. "I need to go check on something."

45/Mazlot

SHE STEPPED SLOWLY INTO THE TROPHY ROOM, PAYING AT-tention to every detail. The chamber where she'd first awakened was just as she remembered it—the bones and pelts, the skulls on the wall, the Whiphid's arrays of kill-trophies, all surprisingly ordered and organized de-spite the ship being slammed and tossed by the blaster attack. It was as if someone, or something, had just come through and straightened everything up. The closed-in air was thick with the stink of spilled liquid fat, oily fires, and the cloying, constant reek of dried blood.

She took another step, ducking under a row of rusty meat hooks dangling from pulleys over her head, and paused, staring deep into the far corner. There was something huddled there, crouched away from the light, a low, bulky form whose outline eluded shape or detail. She could hear it making low breathing sounds.

"Tulkh?"

The form shifted, squirming slightly, just enough that Zo glimpsed one of the glassine eyes looking up at her. The Whiphid, she realized, had bolted himself to the wall, clamping himself into an array of heavy chains and cables, with an additional metal brace—a type of slav-ing collar, it looked like—pinned around his massive neck. Thick red clots and seeping sores had already taken root in the fur around his face.

"What happened?" she asked.

Tulkh snorted, raised his head, jaws creaking open. "What's it look like?"

Zo drew in a sharp breath. Despite everything she'd seen so far, she felt a thin stiletto of shock slide through her at the sight of the Whiphid's ravaged face. The right eye, the entire right side of his head, had swollen up horribly, ballooning with infection and necrotic tissue working busily within. Weeping pustules across his brow and cheek trickled with syrupy-thick discharge down the front of his chest. Even the tusk that jutted up from the right side of his jaw had turned a sickly yellow shade, like a cavity-rotted tooth.

"You?" she asked.

Tulkh made a guttural croaking noise, gesturing at the restraints that he'd placed on himself. "Locked myself in," he managed. "I can feel it. It's coming on."

"How did—"

"Snow lizard."

"*What?*"

"Infected one. It spat on me." Tulkh made a rueful sound that might actually have been a wry chuckle. "Must have gotten blood in my eye. After everything else that's happened . . ."

"Maybe . . ."

"Here." He raised one hand, and Zo saw that he was clutching the broken end of his spear, the one that he'd been carrying with him. Perhaps half a meter of the shaft remained, tipped with a flinty arrowhead edge that looked just as razor-sharp as it had the first time she'd seen it. "Keep that. Might bring you luck."

"Listen," she said. "The sickness affected you differently. You're still alive. Maybe there's a way we can—"

"Mazlot."

"What?"

He jerked his head back at the two-meter wall to which he'd bolted himself, and Zo saw the black rubberized seal encircling it, its outer edges slightly rounded like the curves on an old-fashioned monitor screen. "This whole back panel drops away. Blow the seal with that switch on the far wall."

Zo glanced back at the switch plate that the Whiphid had gestured to, on the opposite side of the hold. She remembered seeing it the first time she'd been here, seeing the writing but being unable to make it out under the scrum of moss that had grown over it. The moss was thinner now, and she could see the single word in all-capital sans serif letters:

MAZLOT

"It means 'air lock,'" Tulkh said, nodding. "Go ahead, do it."

"Maybe—"

"*Now.*" Tulkh lunged forward hard enough to make the chain snap tight, the bolts creaking in their studs. He thrust the spear at her, business-end-first this time, hurling it, and Zo dodged out of the way as it clattered off the far side of the chamber, then fell to the floor amid a pile of skulls.

Tulkh slumped backward, seemingly exhausted by the effort. When he raised his head at her again, light had shifted in his eyes, thin and slanting, a shade that she didn't recognize. A burbling snarl escaped his lips.

Backing off, Zo went to pick up the broken spear, bent down and curled her fingers around it, and returned her attention to the air lock switch. There was precious little mercy shown here in the past day. If the Whiphid asked her for a quick death, she thought she'd seen enough to grant it. But—

The shriek came from behind her, a deafening blast.

Spinning around, she saw the thing in the doorway of the trophy room lunge at her. A Sith student, one she'd never seen before, was flinging himself at her, its corpse-mouth gaping open in an oval rictus. The thing's eyes were bright green and wild, like emeralds on fire, and long strings of orange-red hair dangled back over its shoulders, swinging and snapping wildly around its face as it tried to bite her. Its academy tunic was a stiff apron of gore.

Thwack! Zo slammed the spear into its face, driving it backward, but not nearly far enough. The thing bolted at her a second time, and when it screamed Zo could hear Tulkh screaming behind her in exactly the same pitch and volume. The Sickness, she knew, was fully awake inside him; there wasn't anything she could do about it now.

Use the Force . . . It was the orchid's voice in her head, faint but distinct, guiding her. *Focus, Hestizo.*

She nodded to herself, her hands already moving up, reaching forward the way they sometimes did when she was deeply attuned to the great energy field surrounding her. The Sith-thing—she somehow knew that its name had once been Lussk, and that it had been promised this ultimate role by the Sickness that had overtaken him— rammed into her. Zo grabbed it by the front of its blood-stiffened uniform and thrust the body straight upward, into the air. She swung him up and over, face-first, into the meat hook dangling over her head, so that the underside of his jaw dropped straight down onto the hook's rusty barb, impaling him up through the mouth.

The Sith-thing twitched and thrashed in the air, legs kicking furiously, arms jerking but unable to get itself free.

Now, Hestizo. Now!

She circled behind it, got her footing, and shoved. The

hooks and their pulleys were on tracks running from one side of the hold to the other, and the Sith-thing went careening forward across the hold, still dangling by its jaw, and crashed directly into Tulkh. The Whiphid yanked one arm free, threw back his head, and screamed again.

Now—

Zo threw one arm up, found another cable dangling from above, and wrapped it tight around her arm. With her free hand she reached backward, fingertips extended toward the plain rectangular switch plate.

MAZLOT.

There was a sharp whooshing hiss, like a canister of compressed air being ripped open, and the entire back wall of the hold blew off, the sealed panel vanishing, just gone, sucked out in the void. The Whiphid and the Sith-thing went flying out with it in a frantic cyclone wash of skins, pelts, and bones spilling out into space. Zo held on. The cable bit into her forearm. Behind her a cauldron of liquefied fat sloshed over sideways, spraying along the floor, and her feet slipped, legs whipping forward toward the open air lock. She held on. Gripping tight, she pulled herself back until she touched the hatchway leading out of the *Mirocaw*'s hold and levered herself through it, then managed to hit the console outside, sealing it shut.

Her last glimpse of the hold was a bare metal chamber, its contents gutted in a matter of seconds by the vacuum of space. Every scrap of the Whiphid's gruesome trophy collection was gone, along with the vegetative growth that had marked her brief stay here—all of it sucked clean into the relentless and insatiable void.

In the end, Zo wasn't surprised.

The galaxy, she had learned, could be a very hungry place.

46/All Down the Line

When she arrived back on Marfa, Bennis was waiting for her on Beta Level Seven, standing behind a copse
of Onderonian bamboo. "Hestizo, welcome back." He
smiled when he saw her approaching, stepped away
from the pale pewter-colored stalks rising up from the
growth lights overhead, and held out his hand.

Zo hugged him instead, probably too tightly, and released when she felt Bennis wince a little. "Sorry. It's
good to see you again."

"You as well," he said, patting his chest. "Remind me
to show you my scar when the bandages come off. It's
quite impressive."

"You're all right now?"

"Soon will be. The Force is a strong healer." His smile
slipped, edging into darkness. "I heard about Rojo. We
all did, of course. Hestizo, I'm . . . so very sorry."

She nodded, and for a moment neither of them spoke.
There were times when no amount of speech could con-
vey the heart's grief, and silence was the most articulate
response. After a time, she felt Bennis tentatively reaching for her hand.

"Come, I have something to show you."

She followed him through the long greenhouse, past
familiar plants and species, their stalks and branches

leaning up over her, some whispering her name, along with the other Jedi who were at work here. Up ahead she saw the incubation chamber. Bennis opened the hatchway, and they stepped inside.

Hestizo?

She stopped and looked at the Murakami orchid rising up in front of her, its petals wide, practically quivering with expectation and excitement, and she smiled.

Hello there.

Hestizo, I've heard much about you, let us talk, we shall—

"The second of its species," Bennis said. "It arrived here just this morning. Suffice it to say, it's been anticipating your return here with great enthusiasm."

"I'm sure," she said, reaching out to touch the flower's petals.

You were with my seed-brother, the orchid said, arching toward her. *Is that true?*

Yes, I was, she told it, and thought about the voice of the first orchid, the one that she still heard in her mind. *I still am, in a way. He saved my life.*

Really?

Bennis smiled again, the indulgent smile of a proud parent, and gave the orchid a small pat. "Easy," he said. "There will be plenty of time for that once Hestizo has settled back in with us, I'm sure."

"Actually . . ." Zo met his eyes. "I wanted to speak to you about that."

"Oh?"

"I'm going to go away for a while."

Bennis waited.

"I'm considering returning to the Jedi Temple at Coruscant to continue my studies. Not that I don't love it here, of course, but I feel—there is more for me to learn."

He paused for a moment, then nodded as if he'd expected no less. "I had a feeling you might say that."

"When I was away, I saw things . . ." Zo drew in a breath and held it until she was fairly certain that her voice was steady again. "You have heard about what happened on Odacer-Faustin?"

"Some," Bennis admitted, "yes."

"I have nightmares about it now. I probably will for months. And I think . . ." She shook her head. ". . . what if it isn't over? What if the Sickness that Darth Scabrous created . . . got out somehow?"

Bennis didn't respond, just gazed back at her steadily, until Zo sighed and managed a thin smile. "I made a friend, an unlikely ally—a mechanic, actually. Named Pergus Frode. He's a good pilot. He'll take me to Coruscant. From there . . ." She shrugged. "Who knows?"

"I hope you'll stay in touch." And then, with absolute sincerity: "Hestizo?"

"Yes?"

"May the Force be with you."

Zo smiled at that old refrain, words that she'd heard all her life, whose meaning she was still learning to understand on a personal level. "And with you."

They stood together for a moment without speaking. Zo reached down and brushed her fingers gently over the orchid, then turned and walked out of the incubation chamber, through the research level where she'd spent so much of her adult life. She didn't hurry. She knew that when she arrived at the hangar, Frode would be waiting for her with the ship, ready to take her back to Coruscant, and whatever might be waiting for her there. The mechanic would be good traveling company, she sensed—there was a low-key air about him that bespoke dozens of untold stories, events that had made up his life and taken him to the unlikely destination of Odacer-Faustin. She felt herself already beginning to trust him.

Making her way toward the turbolift that would take

her up and away from all this, Zo thought about taking one last look back at the plants, the greenery that made her life here. This was the world she knew. Perhaps she should reconsider, give herself time to recover her bearings before moving on to something else.

The doors of the lift opened, and she stepped inside, finger hovering over the button just long enough to take in a last, fragrant breath of the vegetative life she was leaving behind.

That was enough.

The future was scary, but you couldn't avoid it, anymore than you could outrun the past.

She pushed the button and didn't look back.

Acknowledgments

When your debts run as deep as mine, there's the tendency to say, "You know who you are," but when you're dealing with something of this magnitude, that doesn't quite cover it.

For all their guidance, inspiration, and encouragement all along the way, I owe much appreciation to my agent, Phyllis Westberg at Harold Ober Associates, my editor, Shelly Shapiro, along with Erich Schoeneweiss, Keith Clayton, and the rest of my Del Rey/Random House family.

At Lucasfilm, major kudos to Sue Rostoni and Leland Chee for saving my bacon within the universe of continuity and the Holocron. And of course, to George Lucas, for knocking my socks off when I was seven years old and instilling a sense of awe from which I never recovered.

I want to extend a special thanks to the 501st Legion, whose generosity and commitment made the *Death Troopers* book tour unforgettable—especially the Southern California Garrison, the Golden Gate Garrison, the Cloud City Garrison, the Midwest Garrison, the Bloodfin Garrison in Indianapolis, the Great Lakes Garrison, and Garrison Carida in my own backyard—you guys rock. And an extra loud shout-out to the Empire State

Garrison, who came to Manhattan on a hot summer day to shoot Del Rey's *Death Troopers* trailer and didn't forget the blood . . . or the beer.

To everybody who came out to say hi on the tour, or plunked down your money to buy any of my books, thank you. Without you, this whole enterprise would start and end on my desktop.

As always, I have to reserve my greatest thanks for my family: my amazing kids, and my wife, Christina. Your love, encouragement, and profound sense of the ridiculous are constant reminders of the everyday magic, which is the most important kind of all. A guy couldn't ask for more.

Read on for an excerpt from
Star Wars: Scourge

by Jeff Grubb

Popara started to say something else, then stopped, repeated himself, and let out an indecorous belch that
took the Twi'leks aback. He started to say something
else, but stopped again, even as he seemed to sway for a
moment on his repulsorlift. Then his eyes widened in
pain and horror.

Eddey said, "What's going on?"

Mander didn't know, and crossed toward the great
Hutt. It would normally be a transgression to approach
him, but Popara was clearly in pain now. Popara's belly
started to swell, and the great Hutt patron started to
croak like an injured frog. The Twi'leks were clearly
frightened now, and one of them pushed Mander back,
away from their master. Still the Hutt's massive form
expanded, his eyes wide with panic. His skin was stretched
taut now, like a balloon about to pop.

Reen shouted, "I'll get help," and turned back to the
doors, pulling them open. They slid easily apart, and
Mander realized what it would look like to the assembled party—Popara in obvious pain, the Twi'lek shouting in fear, and the rest of them standing right in front of
the Hutt's distended form.

"Reen, don't!" Mander said, but Eddey grabbed him
and pulled him to one side. Popara was almost ovoid in
shape now, and screaming in a low, throaty roar.

And then the flesh gave way in half a dozen places and
Popara exploded, his organs rupturing in all directions
around the room. The Twi'leks screamed, diving for

cover, and Reen was flung forward by the power of the explosion and bounced off the force field, along with the former Hutt patriarch's interior organs. Both the Pantoran and the Hutt's digestive system were moving too fast to allow the screen to let them pass.

There was silence for a moment, and Mander looked out at the assembled guests—Hutt and Quarren, Bimm and Rodian, Wookiee and Cerean. All of them looked at the gory tableau beyond the open doors in shock. It was only for a moment, but Mander felt his heart hammer from the certain knowledge of what was to come.

Then Zonnos shouted in a drunken bellow, "They killed my father! Death to the *Jeedai* and his allies!"

Mander, Reen, and Eddey were fortunate, in that the first impulse of the guests and bodyguards was to pull whatever weapons they had, concealed or otherwise, and unleash a volley at the three accused killers. Fortunate in that the energy screen held and their initial high-caliber energy shots splayed helplessly against the invisible barrier.

Mander scanned the room. There was no obvious way out, other than the lift at the far side of the chamber— and on the wrong side of the now-howling mob. Popara probably had a hidden turbolift somewhere in his office, but locating and activating it would take time. Time they did not have.

"You have a plan?" asked Eddey. His small blaster had manifested from beneath his voluminous tunic.

"Get Reen and follow me," said Mander.

Reen, her back splattered with blood, was already up. Two of the green-skinned Twi'leks were in shock, moaning over the remains of their Hutt master. The third descended on Reen in an enraged fury, head-tails lashing and sharpened nails curled to rend the Pantoran. Reen ducked inside the blow and brought her elbow up hard against the Twi'lek's chin. The handmaiden went down with a whimper.

Mander ignored the battle and ran to the back of the audience room, to the grand window that displayed the expanse of Nar Shaddaa beyond. It seemed like he was looking out at an inverted sky, Nal Hutta solid, dark, and gravid above them, the lights of the city-moon cluttered constellations below. Aircars and sign-blimps moved like comets in these overturned heavens. Mander pulled his lightsaber and thumbed the switch. The blade erupted with a satisfying hiss. The Jedi drove the blade against the glass wall.

The glass did not break, and only grudgingly melted, which gave Mander hope. He strained and forced the blade through the glass like an oarsman struggling against a flowing river. In a matter of moments, he had carved a humanoid-sized circle in the back wall.

Mander looked over his shoulder as the first blaster bolts fell among them. The Niktos, Wookiees, and Cereans were using the doorway for cover, their carbine barrels jutting into the room beyond the screen. Apparently Eddey had hidden Reen's blaster under his tunic as well, and the pair of them were returning covering fire over the cooling remains of Popara and the now-shrieking Twi'leks.

Mander kicked the molten oval of glass outward, and it disappeared into the darkness, glittering in the reflected light of the surrounding buildings. "Onto the ledge!" he shouted, and stepped out into the void himself.

The ledge was ornamental, but ornamental in a Hutt style, which meant that it was narrow but not impossible for a normal-sized humanoid to navigate. He slipped out to the right, and Reen and Eddey followed him. The winds at this altitude curled around the buildings and threatened to pluck them from the ledge and send all three of them screaming to their deaths below. He flattened against the glass wall behind him and moved toward the corner.

Behind him, the glass shuddered with blaster fire. Eddey flinched at the impacts.

"It is made of transparisteel," said the Jedi. "They'll be able to break through it, but it will take time. We have to get off this side of the building."

The shots tracked them as they reached the corner, and now a pair of Niktos had made it to the egress the Jedi had cut and were firing along the side of the building behind them. Reen, pulling up the rear, used the corner for cover and returned fire. This wall was also made of the glass, and the Wookiees were concentrating their fire ahead of their path, hoping to break the glass before the escapees got to that point. They were trapped.

"Good plan," Reen shouted over the gusts. "Now how do we get off this crazy thing?"

"Shush," said Eddey. "He's working on it."

Mander leaned back against the shuddering glass and cleared his mind. Ahead of him one of the signblimps was sagging its way slowly across the sky. He reached out, mentally, and pulled it toward them. The lighter-than-air vehicle bobbled but the droid driver revved its engines to let it clear the building.

"Size matters not," Mander muttered.

"Inertia, however, is a pain in the butt."

He shifted his attention, transferring it away from the signblimp and to the air between him and the vehicle. The air gusted away effortlessly, and pulled the blimp, with its surprised and cursing droid pilot, right up against the side of the building. There was a crinkling impact as the thin heglum gas envelope crumpled slightly.

"Jump on!" shouted Mander, but Eddey was already scrambling over the airship's diode-laced sides, his boots knocking light emitters loose and scrambling the signblimp's message. Reen took a pair of final shots and joined him.

Mander leapt and the transparisteel wall behind him shattered. Bolts laced among them, and a couple struck the signblimp, leaving jagged tears in the outer skin and puncturing some of the flotation cells as well.

The signblimp fell away from the building, losing altitude steadily.

"We're falling!" shouted Reen. Beneath them, the droid sputtered a mixture of orders and obscenities in Huttese. Behind them, the blaster fire was already dropping off.

Mander pointed to one of the gallery bridges between skyscrapers and bellowed in Huttese *"Aim for the bridge!"* He threw in a few Huttese curses as well. Whether the instructions, the curses, or the winds were the cause, the signblimp lunged to port and mated in an ungainly fashion with the span. The impact burst the bulk of the flotation cells and the bridge groaned as the entire weight settled upon it. The three escapees clambered onto the bridge and into the wide atriums of an adjoining sky bridge.

"What happened back there?" said Reen.

"Our patron, Popara the Hutt, blew up," said Mander.

"I caught that part," said the Pantoran. "How?"

"Binary Bio-Explosive, most likely," said Eddey. "One component administered by one vector, the other administered by another. Neither traceable as dangerous by themselves."

"Something in the smoke, something in the worms," said Mander, "and maybe a trigger as well to go off at a certain time or in a particular place. We'd have to search the penthouse for that."

"Unlikely they would let us do that. Zonnos has already determined we're responsible," Eddey said.

"He was quick with the accusation," said Reen. "And

he was giving you the hard eyes the entire meal. Think he was expecting it?" The implication was clear that she was asking, *Do you think he did it*?

"Perhaps," said Mander. "Or maybe Lungru or Parella or someone we don't know about."

"Or perhaps the Bomu clan is not as incompetent as we thought," Reen added. "The Hutts do not lack for enemies and schemes."

Mander thought about it. "Adding the attempt on Mika's life this morning, it is most likely a definite effort to thin the ranks of Hutts interested in where the Tempest comes from." He looked around. "Either of you know where we are?"

"No," said Eddey. "We could probably find our way back to the *New Ambition*, but it is likely that Zonnos and his Wookiees will get there first. No, make that definite."

"We just got that ship!" said Reen. "We can't abandon it!"

"It wouldn't be the first time," Eddey said. Reen scowled at the Bothan.

"We have the datapad of tapcafes selling Tempest," said Mander, producing the pad from beneath his robes. "If Popara's death is connected with the spice, we can track our suspects through it."

"And maybe find a ship to get us off-planet," added Eddey. "There should be a surplus of shady spacers on the Smuggler's Moon."

"Regardless, I'm going to need a new outfit," said Reen. "I reek of dead Huttlord."

The vendor-droid they came across was incredibly disinterested in Reen's bloodstained gear, and suitable replacements were gathered, along with hooded robes for both Eddey and Mander. The vendor-droid wasn't the only one not interested in the trio. The bulk of Nar Shaddaa's population seemed singularly unaware of Popara's sudden and explosive passing, or that there was any pursuit of his accused assassins.

"It is the nature of the Hutts," Eddey said. "They try to solve things inside the family. Let's hope it stays that way. What is our first opportunity?"

Kuzbar's Cantina was an upscale tapcafe on level 42, not far from Popara's skytower. A Rodian chanteuse warbled in the corner in Huttese, accompanied by a Bimm on a Kloon Horn. The barkeep, a member of a humanoid race that Mander could not immediately place, took a few credits from them and directed them to a particularly corpulent Sullustan named Min Gost, who had occupied a corner booth as if it were his own personal fiefdom.

"I understand you're looking for information," said the Sullustan, lacing his fingers before him on the table in an expectant pose.

"We need to travel off-planet," said Mander. "Can you arrange it?"

"Easy for me, expensive for you," said Min, his lips curling up in an amused expression.

"Set it up," said Mander. "Payment on delivery." The Sullustan shrugged.

"What do you know about Tempest?" Reen asked suddenly. Mander frowned. In his desire to get everyone away, he had forgotten why he had the list of tapcafes in the first place.

The Sullustan's eyebrows twitched. "Others have been asking about Tempest. Those others smell of military, and I have told them nothing."

"Do we smell of military?" asked Reen, and the Sullustan laughed. Mander put several Huttese truguts and a few of his remaining credits on the table. Reen smiled back and pressed, "So what do you know about Tempest?"

"I know many things about this Tempest," said Min.

"It is new. It is profitable. It is very, very hard. Tends to kill your customers. Bad for repeat business. You want some, I can find some for you."

"Do you know where it comes from?" asked Reen.

Min shrugged again. "No one knows. We had a dealer here, Minnix. Nice Trandoshan male. Did good business. No one has seen him in a while."

"You know where he got his supply?" asked Reen, and Mander made to put a few more coins from his depleted supply on the table, but the Sullustan waved him back. "If I knew, I would not be selling information. I would be selling Tempest."

"Who did this Minnix sell it to?" asked Eddey, and the fat Sullustan blinked, as if noticing the Bothan for the first time.

The Sullustan paused, rolling the flavor of his information on his tongue before letting it loose. "A select few. Mostly upscale. Popara's boy, Zonnos, was a buyer."

Reen sat upright and looked around the room. "Zonnos comes here?"

Again the Sullustan laughed. "A Huttlord's son come here? No. He sends his Wookiees. He thinks he is being subtle, but who else employs Wookiees?" He laughed again.

A squat droid with a holoprojector mounting on its bulbous head lumbered into the tapcafe, taking up a position in the center of the room. It let out a soft clanging noise to draw attention. Mander felt the hairs on the back of his head bristle as the face of Zonnos the Hutt manifested in the holobeam. Mander realized now that he could see the veins at the sides of Zonnos' head throb with anger.

"*Wundara Nar Shaadaa seetazz!*" boomed Zonnos in Huttese, a melodious female voice translating in Basic simultaneously. "Attention citizens of Nar Shaddaa! Popara Anjiliac the mighty has been assassinated, cruelly slain by these creatures!" The screen changed to pictures of Reen, Eddey, and Mander, taken in one of the turbo-lifts before the party. "I will pay one hundred thousand peggats for their arrest and/or destruction!" The holo-beam winked off and the droid turned to leave.

Mander fought the urge to scan the other patrons to see if they had noticed them. Reen flipped up the hood of her new jacket. Eddey leaned back into the deep plush of the booth. "I don't think it is being kept in the family anymore," he muttered.

Min Gost laced his chubby fingers in front of him again and smiled at the three fugitives. "So, it seems I have a question for you: How much of my silence are you willing to pay for?"

"How long do you think we have?" said Reen as they left the bar.

Mander was scanning the area outside the tapcafe for immediate threats. It was a maze of archways and bridges. He considered the remainder of his funds provided to the Sullustan, translated it into time, and divided by two. "Twenty minutes before he tells some-one we were here. If we're lucky."

They were not lucky, and the Sullustan was greedier than they thought. It turned out they had only ten. They had descended one of the larger interior ramps and were making for one of the more fragile suspension connec-tors when there was a hideous screeching of metal be-hind them, and a thunderous mechanical voice shouted out, *"Hagwa doopee!"*

Don't move! Turning, Mander saw a strange form emerge from the shadows of an archway beyond the bridge. It looked like a Hutt wrapped in metal, its semi-fluid body covered with overlapping plates. Its neck-less head was enshrouded in a dome of durasteel, with narrow windows cut for the eyes and ringed with sensors. The entity carried a stun baton in its metal-shod hands. The armored Hutt barked again, and this time a translation voder squawked in Basic.

"Flee, you cowards!" said the translator. "Make this a good sport! For you are the prey of Parella the Hunter!"

"You have *got* to be kidding me," said Reen, and opened up with her blaster. Eddey joined her. Their bolts ricocheted off the metallic hide and into the space between the buildings.

"Flee!" shouted the translator. "Do not make it too easy for me!" Parella the Iron Hutt lumbered onto the bridge. Its supporting wires hummed at the additional weight, and the bridge itself sagged slightly.

"Can we outrun it?" asked Reen, still firing.

"Possible," said Eddey, as small wheels appeared at the edges of the battlesuit. "Make that unlikely."

"I will handle this," Mander said. "You go on, find a place to hide, and wait for me." He unleashed his lightsaber. "Five minutes, then go on without me. Check the other tapcafes on the list, and if they don't pan out find a ship off this moon."

Eddey and Reen fell back, firing at the Hutt's eye slits as they did so, only to discover that the windows were as heavily reinforced as the rest of the suit. For his part, Mander strode back onto the bridge, lightsaber in hand.

"Oho, a challenge!" said the Hutt, and raised its one-handed stun baton in a salute.

Mander returned the salute and leapt forward in a sweeping overhand attack, his blade catching the stun baton. The lightsaber should have sliced through the stun baton, but instead it slid along the haft, leaving the weapon unscathed.

"Mandalorian iron," belched the voder, and brought the baton around, its surface humming with accumulated discharge. Mander somersaulted backward, landed on his feet, and launched himself at his assailant.

Mander ran forward and the Hutt swung low, hoping to chop out his legs beneath him. The Jedi jumped at the last moment, clearing the blade and pushing off from the armored Hutt's gauntlets. He landed on the helmeted head and drove his blade downward, between its eyes.

Or rather, he attempted to do so. The blade slid off the helmet as effortlessly as it did the weapon. Mander was surprised, and his surprise became literal shock as electricity raged through his body. He fell backward, holding onto his lightsaber but landing in a sprawl on the bridge, its support cables straining from the weight.

The armored Parella could have pressed the advantage, but instead let out a throaty laugh, its transvoder keeping up with it. "You cannot cut my weapon. You cannot cut my armor. Your allies have all fled. What now, little *Jeedai*?"

What now, indeed? wondered Mander. He picked himself up and saluted the Hutt once more. The Hutt returned the salute and Mander charged again, exactly as he did before. The Hutt brought up his stun baton to block, but this time Mander took the parrying blow and slashed to his right, slicing through the bridge's support cable on that side. Then he rolled to the left, and, coming up, cut through the cables on the other side.

The armored Hutt spun on its wheels to face him, raising its baton to smash him off the bridge. That was when, even through his sensors, Parella could hear the sound of the bridge's cables begin to separate, the metal peeling back as the strands gave way one at a time.

Parella the Hunter had time to let out a surprised curse as the remaining support cables separated with sharp twangs, and the bridge surface cracked apart beneath the heavy Hutt. Mander leapt for one of the hanging cables. Parella lunged forward as well, hoping to take the Jedi with him, but the Hutt's gauntlets closed on empty air and the great metallic slug fell, tumbling end over end, down into the canyon between the buildings.

Mander, hanging from one of the remaining cables, sheathed his lightsaber, then swung himself overhand toward where the stump of the bridge remained. Once he landed, he looked down, but all he saw was swirling pollutants of the lower levels.

Reen and Eddey were waiting for him around the next turn. "What happened?" said Eddey, relieved to see the Jedi alive.

"We had a falling out," said Mander, no hint of a smile on his face. "We need to be more careful. Zonnos has decided to make this more than a clan matter, and we should see other pursuers soon."

They made their way carefully now, their hoods up, through the lower areas. Now the opulence of the upper levels was far behind him, and the walls were stained with blood, oil, and other fluids. The walkways were crazed with cracks, and those inhabitants they could see watched them with suspicion from doorways and storefronts.

The Dark Melody was on level 35, and most inhabitants were aliens, brought here to Nar Shaddaa years before for one reason or another, and who upon arrival never developed the ability or the reason to leave. Attempts to secure passage off-planet at the Melody were met with derision, and when Mander asked about Tempest, they were directed to a Trandoshan corpse propped by the front door.

"I think we found Zonnos' connection," said Eddey.

"Hmmm," said Mander. "He has the pronounced dark veins of a Tempest user, but no signs of violence."

"So?" asked Reen.

"So," said Mander, "he probably didn't fall victim of the rage we've seen elsewhere." Turning to the ponytailed barkeep, he asked, "How did this one die?"

The barkeep shrugged his tattooed shoulders and said, "He was alive, then he was dead. That was it."

"What are you thinking?" Eddey said to Mander.

"If we had the chance to check out the corpse," said Mander, "I think we'd find that he was poisoned. By something he *thought* was Tempest."

"How do you figure?" asked Reen.

"No one knows how Tempest is made, or by whom," said Mander. "Let's assume that the individuals responsible are advanced biochemists, since no one seems to be able to synthesize it."

"And such a biochemist would be able to create a binary bioexplosive that could slide through a Huttlord's security," said Eddey.

"And would be able to poison our friend here," said Mander. "Someone is cleaning up his tracks. Whoever is behind this knows someone is looking for him. We have one more place on our list. Let's go."

The lights grew more infrequent, the corners and alleys darker. There was no sky above now, only a jagged ceiling made up of taller structures. It was impossible to determine if they were in any particular building, or if the towers of Nar Shaddaa had all broadened into one great moon-girding sprawl. The passages were little more than tunnels, broadening into larger courtyards bereft of plants or fountains. The people were now fewer, but Mander Zuma sensed they were everywhere as they passed, watching them, waiting for something to happen. Ahead of them was a dip in the tunnel, once perhaps part of an underpass now buried deep in the heart of the arcology that swallowed it.

It was a perfect spot for an ambush, Mander realized, just before the first blaster bolts erupted around them.

There were just two attackers, hunkered down behind some trash compactors at the far end of the tunnel, their green trumpetlike antenna visible only when they popped up and shot. Bomu Rodians, laying down quick, random bursts, not risking their safety by poking their heads too far into view.

Mander had his lightsaber out, but too slowly, and the stresscrete around them fractured and chipped. He had the blade up soon enough, though, and deflected the most accurate of the shots. Reen and Eddey had their blasters out now as well.

"Back up!" shouted Eddey. "We can try another route."

Mander started to shout that this would be impossible, that the Rodians ahead were not trying to kill them, but rather to herd them. But then the blaster fire came from behind them as the larger force of Bomu set up more withering, accurate fire and his observation was rendered moot.

Reen and Eddey both returned fire on the more-exposed pursuers, but Mander found himself torn in two directions, trying to deflect charged energy bolts from the front and rear, protecting the others while not getting in their way. Following the course of the bolts by mere feeling as opposed to careful thought, he felt his control slipping, and one bolt passed deadly close to the side of his head.

To discover what happens to Mander, Reen, and Eddey, make sure to read

STAR WARS: SCOURGE

On sale from Del Rey Books
In paperback and eBook formats
Summer 2012

THE SAGA CONTINUES

For over three decades, the *Star Wars* universe has been expanding. New drama, new adventures, and new revelations have played out in the pages of bestselling *Star Wars* novels. Now, almost forty years after the end of *Return of the Jedi*, Luke Skywalker, Princess Leia, and Han Solo are living legends, starring alongside a new generation of heroes in their endless struggle to bring peace to a beleaguered galaxy.

This is the start of Fate of the Jedi, the newest *Star Wars* saga: nine books, three authors, one spectacular epic adventure!

Read on for a brief refresher course on the current standing of the characters and worlds of the galaxy far, far away . . . or skip straight to a sample from the first book of *Star Wars: Fate of the Jedi: Outcast,* by Aaron Allston!

THE STATE OF THE GALAXY

The Clone Wars are distant history. The Galactic Civil War between the Empire and the Rebel Alliance is a fading memory. In the four decades that followed the deaths of Darth Vader and the evil Emperor, the galaxy has known only a few scant stretches of peaceful times.

The Rebel Alliance transformed from a revolutionary military force to a legitimate government—the New Republic—in a long process as it liberated worlds from the iron grip of the Empire. The Senate was restored. Luke Skywalker rebuilt the Jedi Order.

Then, the Yuuzhan Vong came. A violent species of alien invaders, they destroyed entire worlds in their quest to conquer the galaxy. The New Republic teamed with the shrinking Imperial Remnant to counter this threat, and although the alien menace was defeated, the galactic government was just one of many casualties of this brutal war.

From the fragments of the New Republic emerged the Galactic Alliance, but its attempt to enforce order on a war-weary galaxy proved difficult. Isolationists and independent-minded cultures like the Corellians did not bow down to Alliance rule. When the Galactic Alliance came under the draconian rule of a fallen Jedi, Jacen Solo, who adopted the Sith guise of Darth Caedus, this tinderbox exploded into the Second Galactic Civil War. Violence erupted between the Alliance and a Confederation of worlds wishing independence. The Jedi Order split from the Alliance, going rogue to take down Caedus, slain by his twin sister, Jaina, the Sword of the Jedi.

By the end of this latest conflict, the galactic players were once again rearranged. The Galactic Alliance is still in power, but a new Chief of State has been installed: a former Imperial, Natasi Daala. The Galactic Empire's influence has grown, as beings everywhere see and appreciate its relative stability and order compared to the shaky years of Alliance rule.

But Daala has never had great love for the Jedi, and their willingness to abandon the Galactic Alliance has given some reason to doubt their reliability or even loyalty. How exactly the Jedi will fit comfortably into this new order remains to be seen. . . .

LUKE SKYWALKER
Farmboy. Pilot. Rebel. Jedi.
Grand Master. Father.

Luke Skywalker has come a long way from the starry-eyed farmboy whose biggest concern was picking up power convertors from Tosche Station. After helping defeat the Emperor alongside his redeemed father, Skywalker carried out Yoda's dying command to pass on what he had learned.

At first, Luke's role was very similar to the one he had during the Rebellion. He continued serving as a pilot and military leader for the New Republic, but he gradually withdrew from this active service to pursue his studies in the Force. His travels across the galaxy led him to uncover fragments of Jedi knowledge that the Emperor and his agents had not wholly eradicated. Luke, though, had to improvise in his teaching methods, adopting practices that would have been considered forbidden during the time of Obi-Wan Kenobi and Anakin Skywalker. For example, there was no age limitation placed on prospective students, and the idea of romantic attachment was not taboo among this new generation of Jedi.

For many years, the idea of settling down and starting a family seemed impossible to Luke, who was much more focused on larger galactic matters. But fate has a way of laying unexpected paths before a Skywalker. He fell in love with and married Mara Jade, a former Imperial agent who was also powerful in the Force. Together, they had a son, Ben, during a time of great conflict in the galaxy—the invasion of the violent Yuuzhan Vong.

The Yuuzhan Vong War tested the Jedi Order, and ultimately forced Luke to adopt the mantle of Grand Master of the Jedi and reinstate the Jedi Council. The new Jedi Order found difficulty in fitting into the structure of the Galactic Alliance, a situation made worse when the Alliance began adopting some draconian methods of enforcing loyalty among its member worlds. Jacen Solo, Luke's nephew and former student, grew powerful in the Force and—like his grandfather Anakin Skywalker—turned to the dark side in a Faustian bid to bring order and protection to the galaxy and his loved ones. He emerged as Darth Caedus, a Sith Lord, and brought more war and heartbreak to the extended Skywalker family, including murdering Mara Jade Skywalker.

Though tragic, the death of Mara Jade brought Luke and Ben closer than they had ever been before. In the Fate of the Jedi series, father and son will depart on an important quest together that will test that bond and their formidable Jedi skills.

HAN SOLO

No one could have predicted that a Corellian smuggler would someday become a First Husband of the New Republic and the father of a new generation of Jedi. But these unlikely events came to be. As Han would say, "Never tell me the odds." After the defeat of the Empire, Han was branded as "respectable" by the rogues and pirates he had once done business with. Solo's role as a general in the Rebel Alliance meant that he became a key player in the New Republic's formative years. His numerous underworld contacts helped the New Republic in its continued battle with the shrinking Imperial presence in the galaxy. Han eventually married Princess Leia, and together they had three children—the twins, Jacen and Jaina, and their younger brother, Anakin.

Han's most recognizable traits were passed on to his children—they all exhibited a mix of his sense of humor, his mechanical aptitude, and his amazing piloting skills. But the three Solo children were known foremost as some of the most capable Jedi of their generation. It was a world that was alien to Solo—he could not touch the Force and couldn't experience this particular connection the children shared with their mother. He was nonetheless often dragged into the affairs of the Jedi, in much the same way that he ended up pulled into Leia's political involvements.

The Yuuzhan Vong War took a heavy toll on the Solo family. One of the earliest casualties of the invasion was Solo's oldest friend, his beloved Wookiee co-pilot Chewbacca. Chewie's death hit Han hard, and for a time, he turned his back on his family to exorcise his demons in some of the shadiest corners of the galaxy. Han smartly returned to the love and security that Leia and his family offered him; he would need it, for the next tragedy was the death of his sixteen-year-old son, Anakin Solo.

By war's end, Jacen and Jaina would take on principal roles in defeating the Yuuzhan Vong—this war was to their generation what the original struggle against the Empire had been to Han, Leia, and Luke. Jacen in particular proved to be irrevocably changed by his experiences in the war. During the growing conflict between independent-minded Corellians and an overreaching Galactic Alliance, Jacen succumbed to the dark side in an attempt to enforce order in the galaxy.

Jacen became Darth Caedus, an evil warlord whose actions resulted in even more destruction and betrayal. To Han, his son was no more—a casualty of the last war. The abomination who replaced him, Caedus, needed to be stopped no matter the cost. It fell to Jaina to defeat and ultimately kill her brother. His reign of terror ended, Jacen left a surprising legacy—a young daughter, Allana, born to the Hapan Queen and former Jedi Tenel Ka. To keep Allana safe, Han and Leia have now resumed the role of parents, adopting the young girl and raising her under the alias "Amelia."

LEIA ORGANA SOLO

Since her teen years, Princess Leia has been trying to make the galaxy a better place. Once a Senator from Alderaan, she later served as a leader in the Rebel Alliance. When she discovered she was Luke Skywalker's sister, she found she had to make a choice as to what her role in the changing galaxy would be. Would she pick up the lightsaber?

The needs of politics won out. Leia became one of the foremost leaders of the New Republic, eventually serving as Chief of State. Another important role she played was that of mother—she married Han Solo, and together they had three children. The twins, Jacen and Jaina Solo, and their younger brother, Anakin, all proved strong in the Force. Leia practiced her skills as a Jedi with her brother, but a galaxy of distractions kept her from reaching her full potential.

It was the turmoil of the Yuuzhan Vong War and its fallout that caused Leia to return to her Jedi studies with renewed focus. The tragic deaths of Chewbacca and her youngest son, Anakin, greatly tried the bonds of the Solo family, but they emerged stronger from that terrible crucible. Leia would rarely leave Han's side, and she became the Millennium Falcon's co-pilot, capably filling the role left void by the loss of the mighty Wookiee.

Once more, Leia had to let go of one of her children when it became apparent that Jacen had succumbed to the dark side. It was one of Leia's longest held and deepest fears—that one of her children might one day follow a dark path similar to that of her father, Darth Vader. That it fell to Jaina to kill Jacen was all the more appalling, but Jaina did her duty as a Jedi Knight.

After a lifetime of struggle to keep the galaxy from falling apart, Han and Leia have no real grasp of the concept of retirement. By all rights, they could retreat to a remote and peaceful world and live out a quiet life together, but they are once again thrust into the center of galactic conflict. A new wrinkle this time is that now, decades after their last child reached adulthood, they are once again playing the role of parents. Han and Leia have adopted the daughter that Jacen Solo left behind and are raising her as their own.

LANDO CALRISSIAN

The consummate gambler and lady's man, Calrissian is always looking for angles and opportunities. Though he stepped up to a larger calling by serving as a general in the massive space battle that saw the destruction of the second Death Star and the deaths of Darth Vader and the Emperor, Calrissian quickly returned to his entrepreneurial ways after the war. In the four decades since, he has started many businesses and made and lost a few fortunes along the way. Always looking for a challenge, he tackled the biggest one when he decided to find a wife.

After a lengthy search for a possible partner compatible in both business and romance, he discovered Tendra Risant. She was a wealthy businesswoman, and together they founded several mining ventures and other profitable enterprises. They are the co-founders of Tendrandro Arms, a weapons-development firm that was a key supplier during the Yuuzhan Vong War.

Lando is now the father of a young boy, Lando Calrissian, Jr., whom he nicknamed "Chance." Lando and Tendra currently own and operate the spice mines of Kessel and remain close friends of the Solo family.

BEN SKYWALKER

The son of Luke and Mara Jade Skywalker, young Ben was born at a time of brutal war. The vicious Yuuzhan Vong destroyed entire worlds in their crusade to conquer the galaxy, and targeted the Jedi specifically as heretics that needed to be destroyed. As the son of Luke Skywalker—grandson of Anakin Skywalker—Ben was genetically predisposed to be an immensely powerful Force user. But, as a young boy, Ben shied away from his connection to the Force. He withdrew, possibly retreating from the constant disturbances in the Force caused by the terrible destruction of the war.

Only one person seemed to be able to coax Ben from out of his shell—his cousin, Jacen Solo. Ben grew connected to Jacen, learning the ways of the Force as his apprentice. When Ben was a teenager, Jacen's explorations of the Force's strange, darkened corners, as well as the growing conflict between Galactic Alliance and independent-minded Corellians, led Jacen to the dark side.

Ben did not see it at first. He saw Jacen as being forced to take the necessary steps to enforce order in the galaxy. Jacen founded a secret police—the Galactic Alliance Guard—to deal with insurrectionists or any who would threaten the peace of the Galactic Alliance. Ben became one of its youngest members, learning effective investigation and combat techniques.

In time, Ben came to realize what Jacen was willing to

sacrifice in his obsessive pursuit of order. He even discovered the horrible truth that Jacen was a Sith Lord, and that he had murdered his mother, Mara Jade.

The loss of Mara brought Luke and Ben closer together. Ultimately, Jacen was defeated, but at great cost to the Jedi Order and its standing in the galactic government. During the Fate of the Jedi series, Luke will leave the comfortable borders of the Galactic Alliance, heading to parts unknown to find clues to whatever may have twisted Jacen Solo's fate to the dark side. Ben will accompany Luke, bringing his fresh insight, as well as a hard-earned pragmatism far beyond his teenage years.

JAINA SOLO

The daughter of Leia and Han Solo, Jaina Solo is, sadly, the last remaining Solo child. She was born a twin, with her brother Jacen. Only a few years later, they were joined by their younger brother, Anakin. All three were very strong in the Force. As a child, Jacen exhibited a compassion for animals and a natural attunement to the Force. Jaina's skills leaned toward the mechanical, for she, more than her brothers, inherited her father's talent for piloting and mechanics.

During the Yuuzhan Vong War, Jaina, Jacen, and Anakin were all pressed into frontline service, fighting against the brutal alien invaders. Jaina became an ace starfighter pilot, flying an X-wing in the legendary elite unit Rogue Squadron. This war would claim many of Jaina's closest friends, and her brother Anakin, as well. It would also force her to mature and recognize her role in the future of the Jedi Order. Luke Skywalker branded her "The Sword of the Jedi" during the ceremony that saw her elevated to Jedi Knight.

It was this role that required her to confront and defeat her brother Jacen once he had turned to the dark side. Jacen Solo, in an effort to enforce order in a rapidly fragmenting Galactic Alliance, succumbed to the dark side and emerged as the Sith Lord Darth Caedus. It was only Jaina who could confront and defeat him. She studied new deadly combat techniques from armored Mandalorian warriors, coupling them with her natural Jedi abilities and her attunement to her brother to ultimately defeat him.

For a long time, Jaina's role as a Jedi prevented her from establishing a romantic connection to anyone, though she had no shortage of would-be suitors. It was often Zekk, a fellow Jedi, or Jagged Fel, a fellow pilot, who would vie for her affections, but she could not let herself choose between them or allow herself the luxury of romance. Now, though, after having faced the hardships and threat that she has triumphed over, she recognizes how fleeting moments of peace and tenderness can be in a war-torn galaxy. She has lowered her guard to let Jag into her heart.

JAG FEL

Jagged Fel is an amazing pilot, the son of a legendary Imperial flying ace. Jag was raised in an extremely regimented environment, a militaristic upbringing surrounded by coldly methodical aliens known as the Chiss. This resulted in a very serious, disciplined, and focused young man. Opposites truly attract, for this coolly collected, even-tempered man established a strong connection to the fiery-tempered child of the fates Jaina Solo. The two shared a love of piloting and a skill behind the controls of a starfighter, and during the war against the Yuuzhan Vong, they found that their complementary approaches to problems balanced each other well.

As part of the fallout of the Second Galactic Civil War, the ruling council of the Imperial Remnant was reprimanded for its attempt to take advantage of the internal strife plaguing the Galactic Alliance. Luke Skywalker negotiated terms with the Imperial Remnant, and surprised everyone when one of his conditions of peace was the installation of Jagged Fel as head of the Imperial state. As Luke explained it, the Empire suffered from no shortage of overly ambitious shortsighted leaders, and needed someone in command who did not crave power for its own ends. Jagged Fel fit the bill perfectly.

NATASI DAALA

Natasi Daala is a former Imperial officer who is now serving as Chief of State of the Galactic Alliance. She sat out much of the Galactic Civil War, sequestered in a top-secret Imperial weapons think tank. She is one of the very few high-ranking female officers in the Galactic Empire. Some whisper that she landed her position only because of an illicit love affair with Grand Moff Tarkin, but talk like that belittles her command skills.

When the Empire was defeated at the Battle of Endor, Daala never knew of the government's fate, for no one knew of her secret installation in the Maw. No news of the Rebellion or the New Republic's victory ever reached her ears. When she emerged from the facility, in command of a task force of Star Destroyers, she attempted to continue the war against the enemies of the Emperor, even though he was long dead. She was eventually defeated, and she retired from galactic view and military life.

Daala returned decades later to stop Darth Caedus, and her forces helped in the defeat of the Sith Lord. She was installed as Chief of State of the now leaderless Galactic Alliance, as she was the only choice that all the various fragmented factions could agree upon. But the haste to find leadership resulted in the Galactic Alliance now being led by someone with strongly voiced anti-Jedi sentiments.

THE NEW JEDI ORDER

Luke Skywalker's Jedi Order is in many ways different from the previous generation of Jedi Knights that produced such legends as Obi-Wan Kenobi, Anakin Skywalker, and Mace Windu. The necessity of rebuilding the Order from scratch and the lack of records of its predecessors forced Luke to allow exceptions to long-standing Jedi traditions. In this new order, prospective candidates were allowed to undergo training regardless of their age. No longer was anyone "too old" to begin training. A Jedi Master could also have multiple apprentices at the same time—the old Master-Padawan one-on-one relationship was left in the past. Furthermore, the concept of attachment as it pertained to romantic relationships or family was no longer forbidden. Jedi were encouraged to stay connected with their families or to start families of their own.

AMONG SOME OF THE MORE NOTABLE
MEMBERS OF LUKE SKYWALKER'S JEDI ORDER

TAHIRI VEILA: She was a young girl from Tatooine who befriended Anakin Solo during their time as young Jedi students. As they grew older, a romance between the two began to blossom but was tragically cut short by Anakin's death at the hands of the Yuuzhan Vong. Ta-

hiri has never really recovered from that loss, and her instability was recently exploited by Darth Caedus, who attempted to groom her to be his apprentice. After Caedus was defeated, Tahiri's life was spared, and she has withdrawn from the Jedi in an attempt to understand her own motives and find her true destiny.

TAHIRI VEILA

CILGAHL: A gentle Mon Calamari, this Jedi Master is also a biological scientific expert and renowned healer.

TEKLI: A short, bat-faced alien Chadra-Fan, she is a Jedi healer.

CILGAHL

KYP DURRON: When he was a teenager, he was possessed by the spirit of a long-dead Sith Lord and wreaked much havoc on the galaxy. He has long since reformed and is now one of the most powerful of the current Jedi, with a reputation for recklessness that did not prevent his elevation to the rank of Master.

KYP DURRON

SABA SEBATYNE: A powerfully built, lizard-like Barabel alien, she is a natural hunter who, as a Jedi Master, also served as an instructor for Leia Organa Solo.

CORRAN HORN: A former Corellian security officer turned Jedi Knight, he is now a highly respected Jedi Master.

CORRAN HORN

KENTH HAMNER: A former colonel in the New Republic military who resigned his commission to study in the Jedi Order, he is a level-headed, extremely reliable Jedi Master.

KENTH
HAMMER

VALIN HORN: The son of Corran Horn, he was a child during the Yuuzhan Vong War, one of many sequestered from the fighting in the hidden base in the Maw. He became a Jedi Knight and served during the Second Galactic Civil War.

ZEKK: A friend of Jacen and Jaina Solo since childhood, Zekk climbed up from the lower levels of Coruscant to become a prominent Jedi Knight. He was very close to Jaina, but her focus on her role as a Jedi prevented them from exploring their strong connection any further. He vanished from sight and from the Force during the final battle against Darth Caedus, and his current whereabouts are unknown.

ZEKK

READ ON FOR AN EXCERPT FROM
STAR WARS: FATE OF THE JEDI: *OUTCAST*
BY AARON ALLSTON
PUBLISHED BY DEL REY BOOKS

Chapter One

GALACTIC ALLIANCE DIPLOMATIC SHUTTLE,
HIGH CORUSCANT ORBIT

One by one, the stars overhead began to disappear, swallowed by some enormous darkness interposing itself from above and behind the shuttle. Sharply pointed at its most forward position, broadening behind, the flood of blackness advanced, blotting out more and more of the unblinking starfield, until darkness was all there was to see.

Then, all across the length and breadth of the ominous shape, lights came on—blue and white running lights, tiny red hatch and security lights, sudden glows from within transparisteel viewports, one large rectangular whiteness limned by atmosphere shields. The lights showed the vast triangle to be the underside of an Imperial Star Destroyer, painted black, forbidding a moment ago, now comparatively cheerful in its proper running configuration. It was the *Gilad Pellaeon,* newly arrived from the Imperial Remnant, and its officers clearly knew how to put on a show.

Jaina Solo, sitting with the others in the dimly lit passenger compartment of the government VIP shuttle, watched the entire display through the overhead transparisteel canopy and laughed out loud.

The Bothan in the sumptuously padded chair next to hers gave her a curious look. His mottled red and tan fur twitched, either from suppressed irritation or embarrassment at Jaina's outburst. "What do you find so amusing?"

"Oh, both the obviousness of it and the skill with which it was performed. It's so very, *You used to think of us as dark and scary, but now we're just your stylish allies.*" Jaina lowered her voice so that her next comment would not carry to the passengers in the seats behind. "The press will love it. That image will play on the holonews broadcasts constantly. Mark my words."

"Was that little show a Jagged Fel detail?"

Jaina tilted her head, considering. "I don't know. He could have come up with it, but he usually doesn't spend his time planning displays or events. When he does, though, they're usually pretty . . . effective."

The shuttle rose toward the *Gilad Pellaeon*'s main landing bay. In moments, it was through the square atmosphere barrier shield and drifting sideways to land on the deck nearby. The landing place was clearly marked—hundreds of beings, most wearing gray Imperial uniforms or the distinctive white armor of the Imperial stormtrooper, waited in the bay, and the one circular spot where none stood was just the right size for the Galactic Alliance shuttle.

The passengers rose as the shuttle settled into place. The Bothan smoothed his tunic, a cheerful blue decorated with a golden sliver pattern suggesting claws. "Time to go to work. You won't let me get killed, will you?"

Jaina let her eyes widen. "Is that what I was supposed to be doing here?" she asked in droll tones. "I should have brought my lightsaber."

The Bothan offered a long-suffering sigh and turned toward the exit.

They descended the shuttle's boarding ramp. With no duties required of her other than to keep alert and be the Jedi face at this preliminary meeting, Jaina was able to stand back and observe. She was struck with the unreality of it all. The niece and daughter of three of the most famous enemies of the Empire during the First Galactic Civil War of a few decades earlier, she was now witness to events that might bring the Galactic Empire—or Imperial Remnant, as it was called everywhere outside its own borders—into the Galactic Alliance on a lasting basis.

And at the center of the plan was the man, flanked by Imperial officers, who now approached the Bothan. Slightly under average size, though towering well above Jaina's diminutive height, he was dark-haired, with a trim beard and mustache that gave him a rakish look, and was handsome in a way that became more pronounced when he glowered. A scar on his forehead ran up into his hairline and seemed to continue as a lock of white hair from that point. He wore expensive but subdued black civilian garments, neck-to-toe, that would be inconspicuous anywhere on Coruscant but stood out in sharp relief to the gray and white uniforms, white armor, and colorful Alliance clothes surrounding him.

He had one moment to glance at Jaina. The look probably appeared neutral to onlookers, but for her it carried just a twinkle of humor, a touch of exasperation that the two of them had to put up with all these delays. Then an Alliance functionary, notable for his blandness, made introductions: "Imperial Head of State the most honorable Jagged Fel, may I present Senator Tiurrg Drey'lye of Bothawui, head of the Senate Unification Preparations Committee."

Jagged Fel took the Senator's hand. "I'm pleased to be working with you."

"And delighted to meet *you*. Chief of State Daala sends her compliments and looks forward to meeting you when you make planetfall."

Jag nodded. "And now, I believe, protocol insists that we open a bottle or a dozen of wine and make some preliminary discussion of security, introduction protocols, and so on."

"Fortunately about the wine, and regrettably about everything else, you are correct."

At the end of two full standard hours—Jaina knew from regular, surreptitious consultations of her chrono—Jag was able to convince the Senator and his retinue to accept a tour of the *Gilad Pellaeon*. He was also able to request a private consultation with the sole representative of the Jedi Order present. Moments later, the gray-walled conference room was empty of everyone but Jag and Jaina.

Jag glanced toward the door. "Security seal, access limited to Jagged Fel and Jedi Jaina Solo, voice identification, activate." The door hissed in response as it sealed. Then Jag returned his attention to Jaina.

She let an expression of anger and accusation cross her face. "You're not fooling anyone, Fel. You're planning for an Imperial invasion of Alliance space."

Jag nodded. "I've been planning it for quite a while. Come here."

She moved to him, settled into his lap, and was suddenly but not unexpectedly caught in his embrace. They kissed urgently, hungrily.

Finally Jaina drew back and smiled at him. "This isn't going to be a routine part of your consultations with every Jedi."

"Uh, no. That would cause some trouble here and at

home. But I actually *do* have business with the Jedi that does not involve the Galactic Alliance, at least not initially."

"What sort of business?"

"Whether or not the Galactic Empire joins with the Galactic Alliance, I think there ought to be an official Jedi presence in the Empire. A second Temple, a branch, an offshoot, whatever. Providing advice and insight to the Head of State."

"And protection?"

He shrugged. "Less of an issue. I'm doing all right. Two years in this position and not dead yet."

"Emperor Palpatine went nearly twenty-five years."

"I guess that makes him my hero."

Jaina snorted. "Don't even say that in jest . . . Jag, if the Remnant doesn't join the Alliance, I'm not sure the Jedi can have a presence without Alliance approval."

"The Order still keeps its training facility for youngsters in Hapan space. And the Hapans haven't rejoined."

"You sound annoyed. The Hapans still giving you trouble?"

"Let's not talk about *that*."

"Besides, moving the school back to Alliance space is just a matter of time, logistics, and finances; there's no question that it will happen. On the other hand, it's very likely that the government would withhold approval for a Jedi branch in the Remnant, just out of spite, if the Remnant doesn't join."

"Well, there's such a thing as an *unofficial* presence. And there's such a thing as rival schools, schismatic branches, and places for former Jedi to go when they can't be at the Temple."

Jaina smiled again, but now there was suspicion in her expression. "You just want to have this so *I'll* be assigned to come to the Remnant and set it up."

"That's a motive, but not the only one. Remember, to the Moffs and to a lot of the Imperial population, the Jedi have been bogeymen since Palpatine died. At the very least, I don't want them to be inappropriately afraid of the woman I'm in love with."

Jaina was silent for a moment. "Have we talked enough politics?"

"I think so."

"Good."

HORN FAMILY QUARTERS, KALLAD'S DREAM VACATION HOSTEL, CORUSCANT

Yawning, hair tousled, clad in a blue dressing robe, Valin Horn knew that he did not look anything like an experienced Jedi Knight. He looked like an unshaven, unkempt bachelor, which he also was. But here, in these rented quarters, there would be only family to see him—at least until he had breakfast, shaved, and dressed.

The Horns did not live here, of course. His mother, Mirax, was the anchor for the immediate family. Manager of a variety of interlinked businesses—trading, interplanetary finances, gambling and recreation, and, if rumors were true, still a little smuggling here and there—she maintained her home and business address on Corellia. Corran, her husband and Valin's father, was a Jedi Master, much of his life spent on missions away from the family, but his true home was where his heart resided, wherever Mirax lived. Valin and his sister, Jysella, also Jedi, lived wherever their missions sent them, and also counted Mirax as the center of the family.

Now Mirax had rented temporary quarters on Coruscant so the family could collect on one of its rare occasions, this time for the Unification Summit, where she and Corran would separately give depositions on the relationships among the Confederation states, the Imperial Remnant, and the Galactic Alliance as they related to trade and Jedi activities. Mirax had insisted that Valin and Jysella leave their Temple quarters and stay with their parents while these events were taking place, and few forces in the galaxy could stand before her decision— Luke Skywalker certainly knew better than to try.

Moving from the refresher toward the kitchen and dining nook, Valin brushed a lock of brown hair out of his eyes and grinned. Much as he might put up a public show of protest—the independent young man who did not need parents to direct his actions or tell him where to sleep—he hardly minded. It was good to see family. And both Corran and Mirax were better cooks than the ones at the Jedi Temple.

There was no sound of conversation from the kitchen, but there was some clattering of pans, so at least one of his parents must still be on hand. As he stepped from the hallway into the dining nook, Valin saw that it was his mother, her back to him as she worked at the stove. He pulled a chair from the table and sat. "Good morning."

"A joke, so early?" Mirax did not turn to face him, but her tone was cheerful. "No morning is good. I come light-years from Corellia to be with my family, and what happens? I have to keep Jedi hours to see them. Don't you know that I'm an executive? And a lazy one?"

"I forgot." Valin took a deep breath, sampling the smells of breakfast. His mother was making hotcakes Corellian-style, nerf sausage links on the side, and caf was brewing. For a moment, Valin was transported back to his childhood, to the family breakfasts that had been somewhat more common before the Yuuzhan Vong came, before Valin and Jysella had started down the Jedi path. "Where are Dad and Sella?"

"Your father is out getting some back-door information from other Jedi Masters for his deposition." Mirax pulled a plate from a cabinet and began sliding hotcakes and links onto it. "Your sister left early and wouldn't say what she was doing, which I assume either means it's Jedi business I can't know about or that she's seeing some man she doesn't *want* me to know about."

"Or both."

"Or both." Mirax turned and moved over to put the plate down before him. She set utensils beside it.

The plate was heaped high with food, and Valin recoiled from it in mock horror. "Stang, Mom, you're feeding your son, not a squadron of Gamorreans." Then he caught sight of his mother's face and he was suddenly no longer in a joking mood.

This wasn't his mother.

Oh, the woman had Mirax's features. She had the round face that admirers had called "cute" far more often than "beautiful," much to Mirax's chagrin. She had Mirax's generous, curving lips that smiled so readily and expressively, and Mirax's bright, lively brown eyes. She had Mirax's hair, a glossy black with flecks of gray, worn shoulder-length to fit readily under a pilot's helmet, even though she piloted far less often these days. She was Mirax to every freckle and dimple.

But she was not Mirax.

The woman, whoever she was, caught sight of Valin's confusion. "Something wrong?"

"Uh, no." Stunned, Valin looked down at his plate.

He had to think—logically, correctly, and *fast*. He might be in grave danger right now, though the Force currently gave him no indication of imminent attack. The true Mirax, wherever she was, might be in serious trouble or worse. Valin tried in vain to slow his heart rate and speed up his thinking processes.

Fact: Mirax had been here but had been replaced by

an imposter. Presumably the real Mirax was gone; Valin could not sense anyone but himself and the imposter in the immediate vicinity. The imposter had remained behind for some reason that had to relate to Valin, Jysella, or Corran. It couldn't have been to capture Valin, as she could have done that with drugs or other methods while he slept, so the food was probably not drugged.

Under Not-Mirax's concerned gaze, he took a tentative bite of sausage and turned a reassuring smile he didn't feel toward her.

Fact: Creating an imposter this perfect must have taken a fortune in money, an incredible amount of research, and a volunteer willing to let her features be permanently carved into the likeness of another's. Or perhaps this was a clone, raised and trained for the purpose of simulating Mirax. Or maybe she was a droid, one of the very expensive, very rare human replica droids. Or maybe a shape-shifter. Whichever, the simulation was nearly perfect. Valin hadn't recognized the deception until . . .

Until *what*? What had tipped him off? He took another bite, not registering the sausage's taste or temperature, and maintained the face-hurting smile as he tried to recall the detail that had alerted him that this wasn't his mother.

He couldn't figure it out. It was just an instant realization, too fleeting to remember, too overwhelming to reject.

Would Corran be able to see through the deception? Would Jysella? Surely, they had to be able to. But what if they couldn't? Valin would accuse this woman and be thought insane.

Were Corran and Jysella even still at liberty? Still *alive*? At this moment, the Not-Mirax's colleagues could be spiriting the two of them away with the true Mirax. Or Corran and Jysella could be lying, bleeding, at the bottom of an access shaft, their lives draining away.

Valin couldn't think straight. The situation was too overwhelming, the mystery too deep, and the only person here who knew the answers was the one who wore the face of his mother.

He stood, sending his chair clattering backward, and fixed the false Mirax with a hard look. "Just a moment." He dashed to his room.

His lightsaber was still where he'd left it, on the nightstand beside his bed. He snatched it up and gave it a near-instantaneous examination. Battery power was still optimal; there was no sign that it had been tampered with.

He returned to the dining room with the weapon in his hand. Not-Mirax, clearly confused and beginning to look a little alarmed, stood by the stove, staring at him.

Valin ignited the lightsaber, its *snap-hiss* of activation startlingly loud, and held the point of the gleaming energy blade against the food on his plate. Hotcakes shriveled and blackened from contact with the weapon's plasma. Valin gave Not-Mirax an approving nod. "Flesh does the same thing under the same conditions, you know."

"Valin, what's *wrong*?"

"You may address me as Jedi Horn. You don't have the right to use my personal name." Valin swung the lightsaber around in a practice form, allowing the blade to come within a few centimeters of the glow rod fixture overhead, the wall, the dining table, and the woman with his mother's face. "You probably know from your research that the Jedi don't worry much about amputations."

Not-Mirax shrank back away from him, both hands on the stove edge behind her. "What?"

"We know that a severed limb can readily be replaced by a prosthetic that looks identical to the real thing. Prosthetics offer sensation and do everything flesh can.

They're ideal substitutes in every way, except for requiring maintenance. So we don't feel too badly when we have to cut the arm or leg off a very bad person. But I assure you, that very bad person remembers the pain forever."

"Valin, I'm going to call your father now." Mirax sidled toward the blue bantha-hide carrybag she had left on a side table.

Valin positioned the tip of his lightsaber directly beneath her chin. At the distance of half a centimeter, its containing force field kept her from feeling any heat from the blade, but a slight twitch on Valin's part could maim or kill her instantly. She froze.

"No, you're not. You know what you're going to do instead?"

Mirax's voice wavered. "What?"

"You're going to *tell me what you've done with my mother!*" The last several words emerged as a bellow, driven by fear and anger. Valin knew that he looked as angry as he sounded; he could feel blood reddening his face, could even see redness begin to suffuse everything in his vision.

"Boy, put the blade down." Those were not the woman's words. They came from behind. Valin spun, bringing his blade up into a defensive position.

In the doorway stood a man, middle-aged, clean-shaven, his hair graying from brown. He was of below-average height, his eyes a startling green. He wore the brown robes of a Jedi. His hands were on his belt, his own lightsaber still dangling from it.

He was Valin's father, Jedi Master Corran Horn. But he wasn't, any more than the woman behind Valin was Mirax Horn.

Valin felt a wave of despair wash over him. *Both* parents replaced. Odds were growing that the real Corran and Mirax were already dead.

Yet Valin's voice was soft when he spoke. "They may have made you a virtual double for my father. But they can't have given you his expertise with the lightsaber."

"You don't want to do what you're thinking about, son."

"When I cut you in half, that's all the proof anyone will ever need that you're not the real Corran Horn."

Valin lunged.

IN A GALAXY DIVIDED
YOU MUST CHOOSE A SIDE

CREATE YOUR OWN EPIC STORY

IN THIS HIGHLY ANTICIPATED

MULTI-PLAYER ONLINE VIDEOGAME

YOUR SAGA BEGINS AT
WWW.STARWARSTHEOLDREPUBLIC.COM